Chocolate Milk

Nathaniel Troutman

Copyright © 2001 by Nathaniel Troutman

All rights reserved. No part of this book shall be reproduced or transmitted in any form or by any means, electronic, mechanical, magnetic, photographic including photocopying, recording or by any information storage and retrieval system, without prior written permission of the publisher. No patent liability is assumed with respect to the use of the information contained herein. Although every precaution has been taken in the preparation of this book, the publisher and author assume no responsibility for errors or omissions. Neither is any liability assumed for damages resulting from the use of the information contained herein.

This is a work of fiction. Names, characters, places, and incidents either are the product of the author's imagination or are used fictitiously. Any resemblance to actual events or locales or persons, living or dead, is entirely coincidental.

ISBN 0-7414-0734-5

Published by:

INFINITY
PUBLISHING.COM

Infinity Publishing.com
519 West Lancaster Avenue
Haverford, PA 19041-1413
Info@buybooksontheweb.com
www.buybooksontheweb.com
Toll-free (877) BUY BOOK
Local Phone (610) 520-2500
Fax (610) 519-0261

Printed in the United States of America
Printed on Recycled Paper
Published August, 2001

Dedicate To
Stacey

You destroyed my life. If I'm ever to be a creative person,
I couldn't have done it without you.

Special Thanks
Jen Curran
Aggie Kelly
Michael Sevareid
David Downing
Scott Lambert

Chapter One
The Awakening

She touched my face gently with the side of her hand and said, "You are indeed as brave as I have heard."

I replied, "And you as beautiful."

"I want to make love to you. You excite my soul as no other can. Take me away from this prison my father calls a castle."

"Let us go." I grabbed her hand and kicked open the door to the hallway. Several guards glared angry stares in my direction.

They barked, "Where are you taking the princess?"

"To a place where she can be loved. Gentleman, it would be best if you stepped aside." They chuckled as they drew their swords and the slicing sound of metal ripped through the stale air. I drew mine. It was four on one. There was a moment of tense staring before one of the guards made the first strike. The others quickly followed his attack. After an explosively quick parry, I spun around and killed the first guard with a quick slash across the chest. I deflected another couple blows before I kicked a guard in the stomach. Now only two remained. They paused looking at my blade. I made the first slash. The clashing of steel echoed through the hallways. They recovered and managed to force both of their swords onto mine. I was pushed up against a wall.

I laughed and said, "So, do you think you have me?" then I spat at them. With lightening speed, I pushed them off, ducked, and spun around. I smacked one guard in the butt. He yelped like a sissy and leapt into the princess's room. I gave her a wink; she smiled, and slammed the door shut. The final guard I hit over the head with the handle of my mighty sword.

I looked at the princess and said, "No one will stop us."

"You are so brave. I love you!" She kissed me. I grabbed her hand and we ran down the hall. More guards were running to their positions. We rushed down the stairs and out into the courtyard where I grabbed a horse and jumped on. I pulled her up and she wrapped her hands around my waist. I gave the horse a kick and we were off. We flew through the gates before any of the guards had a chance to stop us. I headed straight for the forest. The guards were screaming behind us, but in front of us only the peace of freedom remained. The clean smell of the dew covering the green grass was invigorating. It wasn't long before we were into the forest. The guards would not find us now. We rode in a good ways following a path I knew. Eventually, we stopped at a grassy knoll and hopped off. I tied the horse. She was waiting when I turned around, her eyes ignited by passion. She looked deep into my eyes and kissed me. Our hearts were burning, hotter than ten thousand blowtorches.

She slowly said with her eyes fixed on mine, "You have saved my life and rescued my soul," and untied her gown. It slid slowly like cold molasses off of her amazingly hot body.

"Chad! Chad! It's time to get up." What the hell was that? Her gown was untied and it was slowly sliding off her body. She was standing there naked as the moon to the dark sky. I came over to her and gently caressed her warm smooth skin, as she started unbuttoning my shirt.

She said, "Wake the hell up, boy! You're going to be late." Shut up Dad, five more minutes, just five more minutes. Now, she was going to say how much she loved me and something like, "take me now." I ran my fingers down her naked back as she ran her hands down my chest.

"Get up now, Chad! I should make you get up to help with the cows. You've already gotten to sleep in." It's not my fault he wanted to be a farmer and get up at five in the morning to make sure the cows are ready to be milked when the truck arrives, so much for the dream, thanks to Dad's big mouth. The awesome realness I'd felt was destroyed. I couldn't make it come back. I don't know why it has to get to the good parts right before I have to wake up! Well one thing's for sure; it's gonna be a few minutes before I can go to the bathroom.

Dad

I yelled down the stairs, "I'm up!"

"Oh, thank you Sleeping Beauty for gracing us all with your royal presence," Dad sarcastically said in a high voice. "Time for school," echoed up the stairs, bouncing off the plastered walls into my room. It might as well have been a stern gavel slamming onto a stalwart oak bench. School is the twelve-year punishment for a crime I swear I didn't commit. It isn't a marvelous land of learning that's for sure. It's a place of negotiated identity, and I, Chad Hardly, negotiate like a drunken supertanker skipper; although, I maintain none of the "coolness" of a drunk person. I don't understand that whole mentality.

I rolled myself out of bed and sat on the side looking out the only window in my room. I watch a lot of stars from that window. My little eight by ten room, desperately in need of paint, is the nasty vision that always signals it's time to reenter reality. The carpet is puke green, and the walls are a chipped and cracked brown. There's a big darkish brown water stain in the left corner of the ceiling. The outside of the house is just as bad; although, Dad put up some white siding that helps a little. We're far enough from the road that the house is hard to see anyways.

As I sat on my bed, I scratched my head and thought: how can someone who can barely walk, talk, or puke in a specified hole, be popular? Obviously, intelligence has nothing to do with it. This fact puzzles me; intelligence should be the goal in school, right? Intelligence is an easy thing, just work hard and it will happen. Popularity is a world of vagueness. Is it something you learn? Is it something you're born with? Can you develop this ability? (If so, I want someone to start offering classes.) Personally, I think it's a thing that comes natural, and if you don't have the talent, well, you don't have the talent.

"I'll tell you what boy, if you miss that bus, I'll tan your hide three shades of red!" Good ole' Dad, I guess I was rambling on about school and everything. I slid my feet onto the cold floor and stood up. How should I describe Dad? Dad's a good guy, most everyone who knows him would agree with that. However, they don't live with him nor do they get the esteemed honor of being his son. From my royal position, I have a little bit different version of the mighty king. I can't stand him. He doesn't respect me. I don't want to live my life as a farmer, and I'm tired of being his personal slave. He's the drill sergeant and I'm his only recruit.

I stretched and yawned. I try not to see him as all bad. He certainly doesn't drool love all over the place, but I know he'd be there for me if I needed him, I think. At least I try to tell myself that. Dad's a real hard worker, but also demanding, overbearing, and it's his way or no way. Take the bad with the good; that's what you get with my old man. If I ever could find a girlfriend, I'd make sure to hide 'em the first time she was over. He would smudge refinement like his dirty hands on a clean dress shirt. At times I wish I could stash him away like the laundry I push under my bed when Aunt Jackie comes over. But, if there's one thing about Dad, he's there when you don't want him and hard to find when you do.

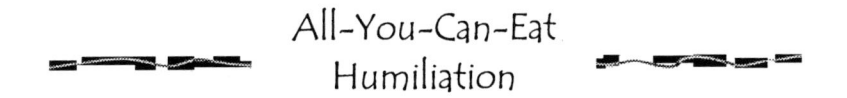

All-You-Can-Eat Humiliation

Here's a good story to explain Dad. There was this one time the whole family went out to eat for Dad's birthday. The whole family is Mom, Dad, me, and my sister Becky. It was probably six or seven years ago. We hardly ever pack the family up and venture from our hole called Canton, but for special occasions we manage to clean ourselves up a bit. You can almost believe we're normal, everyday, middle-class white people; although, Dad never seems to get all a' the dirt out from under his nails. He's white everywhere else and black under the nails. Mom always scolds him for that, I think that's how they profess their love for each other. I'm rambling again. Anyways, we reach the restaurant, Big Jake's Smorgasbord. It's in a town just north of us called Mountville.

This is the perfect restaurant for our family. It's all you can eat, gorge the food into yourself until you're ready to erupt, but, most importantly, it's BYOB. Of course there are the conventional all you can drink soda fountains, but Dad brought along plenty of Busch light, 'his beer,' as he calls it. Mom should've limited his alcohol consumption, but, 'It was his birthday!' she would later exclaim in her defense.

Becky, my twelve-year-old sister, who would've been about six or seven at the time, attacked the mighty food bar. My sister can beat up every guy in her grade, and probably most of the guys in my sophomore class. She doesn't look tough, but she is. Put a girl on a farm with my father, especially when she's 'daddy's little girl' and amazing things can happen. You can dress Becky up and she can look very lady like; however, like a true tomboy she'll either rip off or destroy those clothes. Becky can do things most girls couldn't even talk about. You won't see too many cheerleaders delivering a calf – ah, ewweee it's like slimy and gross. As Becky scared people away from the food she wanted, Dad got drunk and drunker.

I ate a couple slices of warm homemade bread, meatloaf, ham steaks, creamed corn, fried chicken, sweet potatoes, blueberry pie, tapioca pudding, and ice cream, so I could hardly walk by the end of the event. As I leaned back in my chair to allow the food to settle so there'd be more room for more food, I saw Dad.

To my dismay, he was holding a tray of potatoes and whipping handfuls of the spuds at one of the serving girls. Why he was doing this was never determined. We were too embarrassed to ask the girl (she probably wouldn't have had an answer anyhow) and good ole' Dad doesn't remember a thing. I guess that's the beauty of being drunk. In any event, the whole scene was pretty funny. We were all laughing like most everyone else in the place, except for the people who worked there. The managers were especially angry. Becky had eaten more food than me. She was laughing so hard that in one amazing bellow the volcano erupted. Becky's eyes were screaming disbelief as her mouth became a spewing fountain.

While Becky was making her own mess, Mom was trying to stop Dad. Dad, however, must've thought this was some kind of game. He started running with the pan and throwing handfuls at her. Eventually, she got him under control, but not before he had made a huge mess. It was really funny. Dad had always been the life around the house. I used to idolize him. He always made me laugh, but that was until people realized we were related to this drunken fool.

I saw angry stares and heard whispering. With a disgusting twist in my stomach, I began to realize what people were thinking about us. It was no longer funny. The restaurant was a disaster. Dad had mashed potatoes dripping off the ceiling, caked all over the serving girl, and smeared into the floor. He was mumbling and yelling incoherent words and songs as Mom dragged him over to our table. He was a fool. I felt humiliated, humiliated by my own father. That was a feeling I'd never felt before. Dad was my hero, but that night I started to see through the costume. It's like living in this awesome mansion all your life and then one day waking up in my room.

Everyone was laughing and staring at us and I couldn't get it out of my head. Y'know before, I just played and ran and had fun, but I realized what we were that night. As we walked out, I saw lots of angry workers trying to clean up the messes we'd created. We were banned from the restaurant for life. Like dumb hound dogs with our tails between our legs, we slunk back home.

Constructing Popularity

I'd like to hide Dad, but it's impossible. He runs the house. Personally, I think Dad only rules by title; Mom's the one that makes it work. You'll get a chance to meet her in a bit. Dad sure thinks he's the man of the house, so I don't have much choice. When it comes to farming he knows his stuff. Dad'd make your head spin if he got talking on the right subject. I don't think anybody knows as much about cows or the land.

You're probably wondering why I'm telling you all a' this stuff? Even though I didn't know it at the time, this was the beginning of a very important week in my life. But before you can appreciate how much things have changed, you need to know me better: my family, my few friends, what my life was like, and what I wanted my life to be like. Maybe you'll find you're a lot like me. If you are, it'll probably make you feel better to hear about my struggles. If you're not, you might be able to see what it's like for people not like yourself. Anyhow, you want the story. Well the story begins this very normal morning as I got ready for school.

What to wear? What to wear? I was wondering, as I gazed into my little closet. I must've just stood there in a stupor for ten minutes. I need to develop some system for selecting clothing. Just picking something close to me off the floor doesn't cut it. There has to be a way to make sure I won't wear the same pair of jeans twice in the same week. If the wrong kid noticed, the fallout would last for weeks.

"Jesus H Christ boy will you get your butt down here! I'm not driving you to school if you miss the bus. You're gonna walk!"

"Yes, Dad! I'll be ready, just give me a second." Dad doesn't understand the importance of this decision. Well, it's going to be the slightly darker blue jeans. I'm almost positive I wore them early last week. Now the shirt... the shirt, the shirt, man I don't have enough shirts! All right, the button down flannel. That one's one of my favorites, and one of the few that actually came straight from a store. I try to save it for special occasions. What shirt you wear is even more crucial than pants. I could really use a system for that too. I need to get moving. I'm getting close to missing the bus. I looked down and saw I had the green light to take a piss, thank God. I had to go real bad. To the bathroom!

After relieving myself, I was ready for the real challenge. This is where the heavy-duty construction takes place. Hair styling is something every high school student needs to know. Of course there isn't a course for it. We'd be learning something useful! With a comb as my hammer and spray-gel as my nails I tried to build something cool. I can never quite follow the blueprint I have in my head. When I'm finished it's always significantly different than what I was hoping to create, but such is life.

As I'm working and looking in the mirror I exclaim, "No that isn't going to work!" and sigh with disgust. "Let's try it ALL OVER again!"

In a flurry of whirling fingers my hair is returned to its normal state. I'm convinced that I'm fighting a losing battle. My hair wants to be messy, that's its nature. I should consider being a bum. It would be a lot easier to fit in. Then again, Dad wouldn't agree to that career choice. He's more preoccupied with my "making it" than I am. Being a bum would be a great option, though. Nobody would care about me, and I wouldn't have to care what anyone thinks. At school nobody cares about me, but people are sure quick to notice anything and everything that I do, say, or wear that doesn't fit the code of popularity. Yes, bums do not have to deal with this crap.

"Chad, your breakfast is a-waiting, and there is no way you are going out this door without eating something!" yells Mom up the stairs. My parents are good at screaming. Just when I think they couldn't possibly get any louder and annoying, they crank it up another notch. Mom's always on my case about eating breakfast. Now that Mom and Dad have patched up their relationship, they're the perfect one-two combo: if one can't drive you nuts the other most certainly will. Unfortunately, the rift between Dad and I just keeps getting wider. I wish it was simply nights like the one at the Smorgasbord, but that's like getting an electrical shock compared to the lightening strike that really split us a part. It's a long story.

"Well I guess that's going to be good enough for now," I say to myself, as I survey the final construction in the mirror. "I guess. Now deodorant. . . deodorant. . .deodorant. . . . AHH!! There it is!" From the sea of Mom's cosmetics I skillfully spear the speed stick. Quickly the seaweed green, slimy stuff spreads under my pits to ward off stinky smell – another social destroyer. Kids that smell bad are crucified.

"Now, quickly wash the face. Ahh Yes! You look ready to kill today!" Quick zit check. All good, for the most part. I've been lucky. I haven't struggled with zits like a lot of other people. I can only imagine what that would be like.

It really confuses me. Sure my hair isn't perfect, and my clothes aren't designer label, but I'm in shape, I have a nice smile (I think), and a relatively clear face. Why am I unable to be popular, or at least find a girlfriend? Some of these "popular" guys aren't all that attractive. Now, I'm strickly speaking from a guy's perspective. Of course I don't find them attractive. God that would really be the end of my life if people thought I was gay! Unfortunately, because there isn't a girl in my life, and there hasn't ever been, that impression is starting to become the newest joke.

If I could get a chance with a girl, I'd have one! I'm like the only guy in the sophomore class that doesn't get it, and not even do I not get *it*, I don't get anything. Plenty of guys are doing the nasty and I haven't even kissed a girl. Man, I can't even imagine what it would be like to unhook a bra. I'd be so excited after that moment, I'd be happy for weeks. What I really want is to hold a naked girl in my arms. Sorry if this is getting to graphic for ya', but it's got to be awesome. It's the ultimate gift of trust to be comfortably naked in front of someone. All the sexual stuff aside, it just comes down to acceptance. A girl who can look at me and all my stupid mistakes, awkward moments, and ups and downs and say, 'You're the best.' That's what it's about.

Deep in my insecurity is this tiny bit of confidence that's always believed I have good things to offer. I guess you have to have a little of that or you wouldn't go on living, go on forcing your way through the daily feelings of loneliness. I just can't bring out the nice guy, the polite guy, the caring guy, the athletic guy, the guy who knows honor and integrity, or the (dare I say) cool guy. When you meet me I guarantee you'll see the goofy, the awkward, and the unpopular. I just can't find anyone who can look past that impression.

"Breakfast, right breakfast," I reminded myself. I get thinking about things too much.

Like a tornado tearing through my room (except the room is already a disaster area) I blaze from one stop to the other. First, the shirt on the bed; then the jeans from the floor (I've got my boxers on); the socks from the drawer; one shoe by the closest, the other in the trashcan of all places.

I grabbed my Swiss army knife from my nightstand and put it into the leather holder. Normally I wear the leather holder on my belt, but carrying a knife to school will get you in trouble. I stuffed the knife into one of my front pockets. I always carry it. Y'know, be prepared, that's the scout motto. The knife was a Christmas gift my first year of Boyscouts. The other thing I always carry is this little waterproof case of matches. My Boyscout leader, Mr. Enders, gave us all one a couple years ago because we'd done such a good job with fundraising. I quickly grabbed that and stuffed it into the other pocket. With a knife and matches, two tiny little things, you can do just about anything. Swiss army knives have lots of cool little features. In a cyclonic fury, I roared down the stairs.

The Fam'

"Well good morning there pretty boy. It's about time you get down here. I've poured your juice and the cereal and milk are on the counter." Mom's a lifesaver, a purple one since she's wearing the nightgown that Dad bought her two Christmases ago. I have no idea why she wakes up at 6:30 to get breakfast ready for me. She doesn't have to be at work until 9. Becky doesn't go to school until 8:00 because 6th grade is still considered a part of the Elementary school. I can always count on her, no matter what. She's a big nag, but that's a different story.

Becky and Mom are spiting images of each other. Becky is just a younger and tougher version. Mom's dark blond hair has a worn frayed look to it like binder twine.

She still looks pretty, just with a little use. Becky's hair's about the same color as fresh hay, light yellow, and it has that same sheen to it. Mom always looks out for Becky. When I was younger, Becky could do no wrong. I was the one always getting blamed for her mistakes. I was always Dad's favorite, I guess, at least for a little while anyway. I can stand Mom and we can talk, but Dad and I, well we've kind of cut off diplomatic relations.

As far as appearance, I take more after Dad with my brown hair and brown eyes. I'm pretty slim and muscular. Dad's pretty strong, but he's more farming strong which is different from athlete strong. He's got a little tiny potbelly, but for the most part he's not fat. He's big. He's got broad shoulders and big arms, they just aren't cut. I don't think Dad wears anything but boots. He's got three or four pair of them from smaller hiking boots to the big shit-kickers. He normally keeps his face shaven, but when he gets lazy about it and lets his beard grow out into a wooly mess of hair, it makes him look like a convict who's been on the run for a couple weeks. It's pretty scary.

Mom asked, "I'll make you a bagel?"

"That's OK," I replied. "I don't have time."

Dad walked over to the coffeepot and poured himself a glass, probably his tenth so far this morning. He ordered, "When you get home tonight there's work that needs done in the barn. They're droppin' off a load a' chemicals and some other shit today and I'll need it moved. Then, you can feed the cows."

I forced every part of my body to remain in control. I felt like flipping the dining room table and picking up the refrigerator and throwing it at him. I growled my reply, "Yes sir." Dad gave me a second glance, but he didn't say anything. It's good he didn't, I would've exploded on him. He just orders me around. I directed my anger at the box of Corn Pops. I ripped it open and threw its contents into the bowl, and on the worn brown counter. I splashed the milk in not far behind. Mom poured me a glass of orange juice and handed it to me.

She said, "You're gonna make yourself sick," like she always does. I've heard her say that so many times she shouldn't waste her time. I can predict when it's going to come. Mom should make a tape of her favorite comments and then carry it around to play whatever line she needs. She could save a lot of effort. The only thing I'd like is the remote so I can push stop. All I hear at home are commands: do this, do that, when are you going to do this, etc. My parents are human calendars, and everything in my life is scheduled – by them.

The Freedom of Control

I finished slurping up the cereal, put the dishes in the sink, and gave Mom a kiss goodbye. I grabbed my bookbag and raced out a' the house. From our rickety porch I can always see the bus coming over the hill before it reaches my stop. Once it has crested the hill, I have about 30 seconds until it gets to my stop. It takes me about that time to run full speed down my lane to make it to the stop. The sinister screen door laughed at me as it snapped shut. The bus had already crested the hill! Mrs. Wilbough, my bus driver, isn't a waiter. You better be there when she arrives, and tough shit if you're not. The story is she's a retired marine. I've heard that she was a part of some Special Forces unit, and she was good at her job, if you get my drift. When she smiles I envision her snapping my neck with that same smile. She's a tough cookie, but I'd feel safe if terrorists ever attacked the bus. She was known to pull away from students who were only a few hundred feet from the door. You had to be at the stop, not just in view. I exploded into action. I'd better have a good time today or my Dad would be madder than a hornet.

It's times like these I appreciate that I'm a sprinter for our school track team. It's a great feeling when you call on your body and it responds. Like a fighter pilot, I slammed the throttle hard forward, lit the afterburners, and unleashed the speed. That's how I feel. The best part is I'm both the pilot and the jet. Most of the time I feel completely out of control with my life, but sprinting is the ultimate. It's the one moment I'm the best because I'm the only one in control. Speed isn't determined by popularity, or anything else. It's you and your machine, which is also you.

After a few strides, the explosions in my legs were at full bore. I envisioned myself looking at a panel of instruments monitoring my engine status. My legs were checking in at full power. I felt really good. It was time to push the safety limits. I called for more. The damn bookbag is a pain. It throws off my rhythm. Rhythm is running. There's a harmony to it. I looked at the bus and estimated how far I had to go. I can make it, I thought. The wind was whistling around my ears, so much for my hair. I was pushing 120% and my legs still felt good. It felt awesome to move that fast and to know that you were the reason for it. I made it just as the bus was slowing down. I throttled down and brought myself to a walk.

Buying Mystique

I was out of breath and panting like a dog as the bus door opened in front of me, and there was that smile. God, she could break me in a heartbeat, I thought.

"That was quite a burst of speed you put on," she said and then gave me that icy grin once again. I smiled, and started to walk up the steps. Now I'd just had a really good time out the end of my lane, so naturally it was time for something bad to happen. The few times I actually have ups are always followed by downs. You'll catch onto this trend eventually. Probably because my legs were a little numb, I slipped on the step and fell to the ground.

Mrs. Wilbough dryly remarked, "Jeez kid, I didn't know I was that gorgeous." I faked a smile and pulled myself to my feet. I walked back the aisle to the back of the bus, where I always sit. The middle school kids at the front of the bus were looking to see what happened, but no one had really noticed my blunder.

Well, here ends any happiness in my life. Once I'm around people I can't do anything right. I know how to act around my family, but school is like being in a foreign country and not knowing the language. The people I sit with on the bus are a lot like me, so we all get along, but I kept to myself today. I like school – the learning part of it. I guess that's part of what makes me weird. I do well in my classes, and I think my teachers like me. Then again, they might be trying to pacify me. It is their job to like their students, or at least pretend to. None-the-less, I feel that I fit in more with adults than I do with other students. I have my buddies, and they're great, but apart from them, it just seems that something is missing. Girlfriend, that'd be it.

As much as I struggle to fit in with the "in" guys, girls are even more of a disaster. I'm an absolute bumbling fool. I can't play the game, and the truth is I don't want to. I'm not coming out of the closet here; it's just that the game just drives me crazy because it's all about lies. It's telling girls exactly what they want to hear. The guys that are the ladies men are the ones that can make the most girls think that their lies are the truth. There are some mega-babes that date some of the nastiest trash. I mean these girls are all around knockouts: beautiful body, often athletic, involved in lots of other activities, and, to top it off, many are very smart. How can a girl, who's so smart she could go to Harvard, date a guy who would only know Harvard if it was a beer brand?

Of course, more than anything, it's about popularity, and you know how much of that I have. But popularity doesn't matter because I wouldn't know what to do around girls even if I had the popularity to get a chance. Lately, I've taken the passive approach. Let God figure it out for awhile. I'm tired of feeling like a fool and making myself look like a fool.

There is one of these mega-babes on my bus. Her name is Heather Powell. She's not like the rest of our group at the back of the bus – she's got popularity. She's a freshman and she's adorable. There is a cuteness to her face, but she also has the athletic look to her that I love. In my opinion, a girl needs to be able to whoop a little ass every now and then. Heather's got a smooth face and one awesome ass. I'm not sure which grabs my attention more. OK, honestly, it's that ass. However, there are other girls just as hot, but they're kind of prissy and wimpy, more like cheerleaders though not every cheerleader is like all about popularity, like not ever sweating, and like never having a hair out of place. I've dreamed about asking her out at least a million times, but back in the real world, she's, at best, a friend, who (for some unGodly reason) talks to me. I remember the first time I saw her.

I was in eighth grade and I had gone to watch one of the girls basketball games. At one point in the game Heather was elbowed in the mouth. Well, she didn't fall on the ground and start crying like some of the cheerleaders would. She got up and spit in the other girl's face, and then gave this girl a look that signed her execution. I watched Heather closely for the rest of the game, for basketball reasons of course. Heather had her revenge. Later in the game she pulled down a rebound and pivoted around with her elbows sticking out like sledgehammers. She cracked that girl right in the jaw. This was middle school basketball! You can also see how smart she was. She could have gotten into a fight after the girl hit her, but then she would've been thrown out. Instead she got her licks in legally. That's one awesome girl, if you ask me.

When I try to talk to her I'm a pile of goulash. Thinking about some of the encounters I've had, just general conversation on the bus, I cringe. That's the worst; when some girl actually gives me a chance, I show her I'm exactly everything she's heard. It's not that other people give me the geek reputation, I build it myself. I regularly embarrass myself at the worst times. When I watch a movie and one of the characters is about to have an embarrassing moment, I close my eyes and grit my teeth. I can never watch those moments, no matter how funny they're intended to be. I try to be Tom Cruise in every way, but my efforts always result in stupidity. My only hope is that I might get a chance out of sympathy.

I decided not to even attempt conversation with Heather today. She looked beautiful as usual, but I didn't want to have to kick myself for the rest of the day. I'd already fallen once. My mind flashed to that really bad commercial. I saw myself floundering on the bus steps whining, 'I've fallen and I can't get up.' Uhhh, I blinked my eyes to get the image out of my head. I can't help it if someone initiates talking, but I don't have to start it. I'm too uninhibited. I plow headlong, wobbling like a newborn colt, into anything. But who knows, maybe someday I'll grow into myself. I hear all the time that geeks do turn out all right. There are plenty of Hollywood stars that were geeks. It's all about how people perceive you.

Unfortunately for me, I don't have too much else besides who I really am. I should try turning myself into like a skater. Then, maybe some girls would become interested because of my dangerous image. Nahh, Dad'd kill me. I'm sure you're ready for an interruption to my whining and it's here. We've reached the school, whoopee.

Chapter Two
Learning in so Many Ways

The first minutes before school starts are total chaos.

Everyone is lounging around outside in the parking lot or in the lobby sucking every last second of freedom. When that bell rings, the smiles are left with coats and gym bags in the lockers. Like I said before, I enjoy school, to a point. You can never really love school. You have to go! There are plenty of other things I'd rather be doing besides school, though none of them are all that interesting. Sitting at home watching TV all day seems much more exciting when you're not allowed to do it. After awhile it'd be just as boring as school.

"Hey Chad," the always in a good mood Dale yelled down the hall. When he caught up to me he added, "Why couldn't you come over last night?" Dale's my best friend. We've been buddies, it seems like, since birth.

"Dad had lots of work for me to do. That shitty Ford tractor broke again." The fact is Dad always has a lot of work for me to do. Indentured servant; that's what I am.

"You're a regular farm mechanic."

"Yeah, ha ha."

"Seriously though, I've been there working with you. You come up with some ingenious ways to fix that thing."

"It be nice to hear Dad say that once and awhile. That tractor is also the reason why I couldn't get to Boyscouts on Monday. How's our Tee Pee coming?"

"It's not going anywhere 'till you finish the lashings. Nobody does 'em better than you, so nobody's do 'em but you. Mr. Enders took us on another nature walk."

"Of course I'd miss that."

"I swear he knows every tree, plant, and kind of moss God ever created. He showed the younger scouts that rock boiling thing."

"You remember the first time he showed that to us? That was the coolest most ingenious thing I'd ever seen."

"Are you going to long term camp this year?"

"Who knows," I replied in frustration. "You might as well have Dad as you best friend. He makes all the decisions."

"Man, that's a tough drag. Did you do your Huck homework? Ha Ha Ha!! Get it...Huck homework."

"Your consonance is absolutely astonishing." Dale has a propensity for making the worst jokes. He's a wanna-be-class clown. I'm a wanna-be popular guy so I guess that's why Dale and I are such good friends. Neither of us ever fits in. Dale's poor jokes are his downfall. People don't laugh with him, they laugh at him, and that isn't even the problem. People are laughing at him when he isn't trying to be funny. I wish I knew where I was screwing up.

"Yeah I finished my Huck homework." We walked down past the library to our lockers. "So, what are your plans tonight?"

"Who knows. There's so much happening around here I'm not sure what I'm going to do. Are you working for the old man again?"

"Who knows. His wish is my command." We reached my locker and I started putting my books on the shelf. Dale's a skinny guy with short black hair, lean cheeks, and a pretty big nose. His folks have got a good bit more money than mine so Dale has some better clothes. He has a bunch of baggy pants like the ones MC Hammer wears. It makes him look a lot more like the popular crowd than I do. He also wears a lot a' silk shirts and he has a bunch of nice jeans. Dale's main feature is his big smile. It's kind of goofy, but he uses that smile a lot because Dale's social designation is jokester.

As I was finishing emptying my book bag Dale said, "Guess who's coming?" I turned to look the way Dale was looking.

I turned back to Dale and dryly said, "Great! Nothing like Patrick and his personal cheering squad Vinnie to brighten the morning. I almost missed the bus but of course I didn't miss Patrick." Vinnie is a sophomore like me, but Patrick's a junior. Patrick's been the starting varsity quarterback since his freshman year. He commands the popularity game. He's judge, jury, and player. With blond hair, blue eyes, a good 225, and ripped I bet you can't guess why. More than anything, he's smooth. There's something about him that just says this guy's got the low down. He may be dumber than a load of bricks, but in the popularity world he's an A+++.

Patrick walked up behind me and said, "Hey, it's chippy Chad." Isn't it great we have English teachers? "How are you doing this beautiful morning?" Well I guess you need to know that story as well. Chippy Chad, the big boy who's voice was still cracking as a freshman. It was no big deal, just the typical story. Guy raises hand in class, speaks, and squeak. For some reason, however, I could never live it down. In my small school, events like my squeak travel quickly. It didn't take long for the popularity kings to seize the moment and make a verdict. Chippy Chad was the result of the collective intelligence. All the guys know it irritates the hell out of me. I've tried to hide it, but I can't laugh at myself. Every time I hear that name it sends a shot of anger rippling through my mind. I'm not some fool. I hate it. I'm not some fool. I don't think I'll ever be able to laugh at myself.

I might as well tell you about the other joke that everyone likes to use. It's about my last name. That one's not too hard to figure out either. Chad Hardly, as in *Hardly* ever gets it. Yeah, I know, it makes me laugh hysterically too. Patrick has a much better nickname, Patrick the Pussy Pad. I'm not even going to go into the story, but I think the freshman poetry unit needs to be permanently destroyed. If alliteration is ever taught in high school again the teachers should be shot.

I replied, "I'm doing great today." That was my typical passive response.

"Oh, you're doing great. Well, that's good. So how long are you gonna be riding the bus? You know girls just go wild for a guy on a bus."

Vinnie started to laugh hysterically, and said, "Maybe you should try running to school." He started laughing even more. Patrick smiled; I think more at Vinnie's laugh than his joke. Vinnie's popularity rides on his friendship ties to guys like Patrick. He's got coal black hair with big dark bushy eyebrows. He's not attractive, but he is attractive. It has to be his friendship ties because at a staggering 5' 6" and pretty zitty I can't imagine why a girl could actually find him attractive. But, whenever a football player is down, Vinnie will be around. He's cool in the right eyes.

Patrick said, "Y'see girls love long and yellow; you've just got the wrong idea."

"I'm not sure what you mean," (still ever so passive). The thing is, I can think of a hundred different insults to unleash on him. Back in elementary school I knew Patrick before he was the popularity king. I know a bunch of things from those days that are perfect knock down material. What would people think of the immortal Patrick if I told them about the first time he tried ice skating, the first time he drove a tractor, or the time his Dad tanned his ass in the middle of a little league game. I can think the sharpest of swords, but I can never draw them.

"Well sure Chad, Hardly ever gets it. Let me explain. Girls aren't looking for a banana or a school bus, but they like long and yellow." He started laughing. "What you really need are some colored Trojans. You do know what trojans are don't you?"

"You know condoms!" Parrots Vinnie. Both of them started laughing. By this time people were starting to notice Patrick's show. Patrick's a crazy and funny guy. You never know what he's gong to do. When Patrick starts to do something people notice, and people were beginning to notice, including girls. That's just more fuel to fire my furnace for priesthood. The girls never really participate in the ridicule, but they don't need to. They see how low my reputation is. None of them would dare risk losing their perfectly polished public personas to even hear a phone call from me.

I replied, "Yeah, I know what they are."

Patrick commented to his growing audience, "Girls like condoms. He looked over to Ashley. Ashley is part of the popularity circuit in my grade. She's more the bimbo cheerleader type like her friend Kathy. Stacy is the all around super girl: athletic, smart, and attractive. Janet isn't nearly as attractive as the others, but, like Vinnie, because she's friends with the others it makes her popular. Patrick gave Ashley a provocative raise of the eyebrow and said, "Condoms turn you on!" Everybody laughed.

She replied seductively, "Sheepskins."

Patrick replied, "M-a-a-a."

"Oh please! Patrick you've got footballs in your head."

"I can play other contact sports."

"I've heard poorly." Everybody let out a groan. That was a good comeback. I should've said it. I was still really tense wondering if my humiliation was over, or if there was more to come.

"Ouch, but you don't really know 'till you take a test drive. I've got footballs; you've got pom poms. Put them together and let's get the game on. I'm just a little lost boy with blue ball. I'm sure you could teach me how to find my way through the bush to the lost treasure." Ashley was struggling for a reply. "Ahh, nothing to say this time."

"You just don't stop."

"Coach always told me never to give up. Come on, I'm not much of a challenge. If you wanted a real challenge just try and lead Hardly here into the woods." That got a laugh from the boys. Ashley was only a distraction for a little. Now it was time to get some real laughs, from me.

Patrick turned back to me and said, "Well, what are you going to say this year? Are you going to be a man and sign up for football?" I've heard these next lines over and over. "Track is for pussys!"

A good come back popped into my head and I thought screw it, I'm going to say it. "Sorry Patrick I'm just not interested in footballs, I prefer pom poms. I'll let you guys play with the balls." I saw Dale's face. He couldn't believe it. I couldn't believe it, but I shouldn't have done it. Patrick was going to jab back and I don't have his kind of social power. There's no way I was getting out of this looking good.

"We'll let the ladies be the judge of that. Anyone want to vouch that Chippy here knows how to spread a pom pom. Oh, that's right there's no one to ask. Y'see you join football to play with the pom poms."

Ashley broke in, "And ladies you can see what too many hits to the brain does to boys who are already genetically stupid enough."

"Errr, Ummm, show me chipsteak."

"You are a sick pig!" She started hitting him with her bag and pushed him into the locker. Patrick started smiling his golden boy smile and laughed.

"I was just kidding." Ashley was laughing and smiling and so were her friends. "You're so rough with me." I was surprised girls like Stacy were laughing. She's smart and Patrick was pretty vulgar if you ask me, but I guess she knows he's just a jokester. He's a good time. Besides, even as smart as she is, she wants to be with him. Every girl wants to be with him.

Ashley said, "Let's get out of here ladies."

Stacy added (to my surprise), "Y'know they can't handle they're own hormones."

Patrick flashed a smile her way and said with some shock, "Man everybody's on my case today. See ya later ladies." They started walking down the hall. Now Patrick could return to me. "You need to join football Chippy."

"I wouldn't be any good at it." The bell was almost ready to ring so I gave Dale a look and we started moving briskly down the hall. Thank God Patrick is too dumb to be in the honors English class. I yelled back to him, "I'll leave the football up to you brute's!" There I gave him a compliment.

"Ha, Ha, Ha," he laughed. Patrick has this torturous laugh. It's higher pitched than his normal speaking voice and it sounds like he's a druggy in a way. It drives me nuts to hear that laugh. He yelled down the hall, "You wouldn't even know what tough could possibly mean." Actually I think that it has several definitions. "I think the cheerleaders are looking for some help during the fall," and he started laughing once again. His last comment got a good laugh from Vinnie and his other goons. If it wasn't about me I might've been able to laugh along; unfortunately, it's always about me. His laughter trailed off down the hallway as we moved further away.

Dale had moved on ahead of me and was waiting down the hall just behind the last locker next to Mr. Reddish's History class. When I caught up to him he said, "Wow they were in a good mood. Where did you get that come back!"

"It just came out. It's too bad Patrick always wins no matter what."

Dale replied with his usual dead humor, "I thought that you handled it well."

I wearily respond, "Thanks for the vote of confidence. I like to think I'm an essential part to Patrick's popularity status."

Dale laughed, "Yeah, you're like one of his servants, like those Egyptian slaves only you're forced to build a temple of popularity."

"Oh thanks Dale. Your support is so greatly appreciated."

"Just kidding, dude. I've gotta go I'm already going to be late. It's a good thing that Mrs. Gundy likes me. I'm late like everyday. See ya' in Chem."

"Yeah, catch you later."

Not every morning is as bad as this one turned out to be, but these kinds of days happen too often for my liking. The really bad part was that today still had a lot of time to go for an all time low. The prom is in full swing. All the popular guys from my grade have been asked. It would be nice to get asked. As Patrick's last comment suggested, rumors about my sexual preference were widely circulating. It was beginning to become the latest rage. Either make fun of my "homosexuality" or joke that I was really a girl pretending to be a guy.

Two weeks ago in gym I was stretching out my hamstrings. I am so unaware. I just don't pay attention to what others are thinking. I have no social perception. Anyway, I'm simply stretching and I decide to really loosen up my hamstrings. I'd just started track practices a few days earlier, so I was feeling pretty sore. I had decided that I'd better stretch really well, even for the generic PE volleyball game. So, I start stretching into a split. You should have been there. They made a royal ass out of me, for doing a split and I didn't even get all the way down. The thing is,

I'm flexible, but I know there are plenty of other guys who are just as flexible or even more flexible than me. How is doing a split evidence of my "feminine nature"? And besides, what the hell is wrong with having a little feminine side; y'know it's the ying and the yang, they come as a package deal. It was a frustrating experience, as most of my public humiliations are.

That's another thing. I'm not completely an out. I don't want you to get the idea that I'm a total outcast. I'm not out out like some band geek, but I'm not in in like some football stud either. It makes things worse. The outs don't like me because they think I'm in and the in's don't like me because they think I'm out. I just never feel comfortable. I'm never myself. I'm always working to create the right perception – that's who I am.

Y'see popularity isn't about who you really are or how sexy you actually look. It's the fabricated mystique that girls believe. Tom Cruise is, "so cute" because no girl would dare say he's ugly. Now, the guy isn't bad looking, but is he really the most desirable guy on the planet? Most girls would scream yes. I'd agree, but that's not because of how he looks. It's everything else about him and I'm not talking about his great personality. You can't know someone's personality through the poster you hang on the wall? What the girls know is his mystique. He's got the looks, but it's his perceived coolness (constructed by a movie studio none-the-less), prestige, money, power, and visibility. He's the biggest trophy because of the popularity he'd bring whichever girl was dating him. That's how it works.

Fools Gold Beneath the Surface

The late bell was about to ring I could sense it. I hurried through the door into 1st period English class. English is a good subject to have early in the morning. Mr. Harbarshare really encourages everyone to contribute. It gives the class a laid back atmosphere which makes it a lot of fun. Mr. Bar, as we've come to call him, is a little creepy in ways. He's what you would expect from someone completely immersed into English, sort of troll-like qualities to him. It's like he spends most of the day buried in some cave surrounded by books and the only time he sees the light is when he comes out to teach a couple classes. He has a short educated mustache, not the big and bushy farmer type, but one more delicate and refined. It's kind of like comparing fine wine to cow piss. Thinking is the Bar's main quality. It seems thinking is what he's doing 95% of the time you're around him. With his reading glasses perched low on his nose, he studies your every word.

Everyone got settled after the bell had rung. Mr. Bar put down the book he was reading and said, "Good morning class. So how about what occurred in last night's reading?" This would be the end to most of the coherent comments from Mr. Bar. He would now drift into this semiconscious state to absorb class discussion better. We figured he could store information better in this "zoning-out" state. If his glasses are facing you, you know he's addressing you, but most of the time they face down indicating he's deep into thought. During most class discussions he serves as a mediator head down (glasses not facing you) kind of murmuring to himself, almost like he's a magician speaking a secret spell into his cauldron. I told you he was a little creepy. It sure seems that way when you first have his class, but once you get to know him you'd like his class. He's a good teacher and my personal favorite. He really wants to hear what you have to say.

"Well come on folks. You all DID READ?" This was Mr. Harbarshare's favorite line. He always tries to say it real sly with the sarcasm dripping off. After the second time you heard him say that line it began to suck a whole lot. So after our communal groan as a class Jeremy got the ball rolling, but before we get into that there's just one other thing.

You might be wondering why I'm *still* telling you all of this stuff. Like I said before, you need to get to know me. Now don't worry, I'm not going to be sitting here telling you every little detail of my day like I have been. I may have all the time for that, but I'm sure you don't. It just so happens that 1st period English is something I want to talk about. You know I'm not really a confident person, but today, I think, was the first time I stood up for my views. Actually I think it's the first time that I spoke in the class at all. I'm real proud of this moment, so I need to tell you about it. You need to hear some good things about me. Anyways, as I was saying, we groaned as a class.

Mr. Harbarshare then inquired, "Chapters 13-16?"

After a few more moments of silence Jeremy said, "As I see it Huck is just a racist kid that gets his jollies out of making fun of a black guy." His comment seemed to take a few moments to settle in because it came out so bluntly. Jeremy is the only black student at my high school. It didn't surprise me he felt that way.

"Elaborate," or at least that is what I thought Mr. Harbarshare mumbled.

"Well look here. Jim and Huck are nearly killed by the steamboat. When he finally finds Jim, Jim's about ready to bust out he's so happy. So what does Huck do, he takes advantage of Jim's kindness and plays a mean joke on him. If there is any truth in this book, it shows how the white man is even as a boy. And then . . ."

Angie cut Jeremy off. "Holy shit Jer' you're soon going to need a black cape so you can go burn crosses on white people's property. Now I think everyone in this class has tried to be considerate to your viewpoint, but there are other interpretations."

Angie is our resident feminist complete with very short hair currently died black; however, the shade changes with regularity, a long tie die shirt, a pair of white polyester pants, and these eye-grabbing fire engine red boots. She also has her eyebrow pierced. No one had an eyebrow pierced, anywhere. It was pretty freaky.

Jeremy responded, "Yeah, I'm sure there are, but you white people don't want to face the facts that racism is everywhere. They're always trying to find a new spin to put on race relations. That white fool that shot Dr. King is the same kind of fool that Huck is."

"Just because Huck says nigger doesn't mean he's a racist."

"It doesn't? I don't want to hear that word, I don't want to see that word, I don't want to read that word, and I do think any white person that says it has racist intentions." The classroom was smoking now. Jeremy had jumped up and was full to the brim with fire. Jake Stance got up real fast to make sure nothing stupid happened.

"Yo, Jer' easy man she's not disrespecting."

"No I'm not Jeremy. You've got to consider where this story takes place, Mississippi. Then you have to take into account the time period which is somewhere in the 1860's." She looked for support from Mr. Bar and he nodded his head. "You're right that it's wrong to use that word *today* because it's derogatory, but Huck isn't living today."

I think you can see that Angie's a good person, no matter how much she tries to hide it with the creative costume. It's all a look for her. I think she just tries to highlight one part of her personality – she thinks differently. I think Angie's main qualities are her openness and thoughtfulness, which aren't really expressed in the way she dresses. The look gives her an identity, which is more like a character she's playing rather than who she really is. I guess that's what I need. It prevents people you don't want to know you from getting to know you and it provides a protective shell. When people put you down you know they are only insulting the character you've created for yourself. It's a solid idea, but my Dad wouldn't tolerate that kind of look, so I can't reap the benefits. Even so, there's only so far you can hide within yourself.

Jeremy had cooled down a bit. Unfortunately, Bill had to open his big dumb mouth.

He said, "Yeah and if he was in our time he'd know that only black people can call each other niggers. Not like that ain't a double standard." Bill's like an educated version of a redneck. My Dad's the full-blooded variety. He had to know that a comment like that would really rile up Jeremy.

I didn't think there was any way in the world Jake could hold Jer' back now, but Jer' just glared the most evil vile glare towards Bill. He didn't say a thing for a couple seconds. I looked over to Mr. Bar to see if he was going to help here. He looked like he was going to say something for a second but then he went back to his normal pose.

Jeremy finally replied, "Bill your back beat trash isn't worth my time." He said those words in a cool icy tone never once breaking eye contact with him. Bill wanted to piss Jer' off, but he was smart enough to know when to stop. He didn't want to get in a fight. Bill knows Jer'd whoop his ass in a heart-beat, so he shut up just like a redneck would with a big old smile and some chomping on his gum.

The Bar must've decided that it was finally time he said something. He calmly commented, "Believe it or not you are discussing a very difficult issue this novel raises, and your comments reflect various responses to it. They are all legitimate reactions many people have had. I want us, however, to focus on Huck as not being a racist. What could justify this interpretation?"

Jer' quickly replied, "Nothing."

For some reason I got the crazy idea I was going to respond to his question. I didn't even raise my hand. I simply blurted, "He said he was sorry." Well, I felt like an escaped convict with every prison search light focused on me. Caught red handed trying to contribute to class. It seemed like they were daring me to speak again; even though most of the people in the English class weren't like that.

I guess the subject is personal for me. I don't want black people to think every white person's a racist. That's a stereotype of white people and nobody likes being stereotyped, I'm a white sprinter, for Christ's sake. Plus, I relate to Huck in ways. Despite my best efforts, if a black person found out where I'm from and met my Dad, I'd be stereotyped. Besides, I know I'd say something stupid. Nobody looks beneath all my stupidity for the real me. Jer' was doing exactly that to Huck. You've gotta look past the words to the real person who's making those words. Jer's answer was more about himself than Huck. I know Huck's a fictional character, but still. It could just as easily be me. I guess all of that's what compelled me to talk.

Mr. Bar mumbled again, "Expand."

Once you start going over the waterfall you can't stop so I just let the words gush out as fast as my mind could assemble them and throw them outta the factory. I said, "Angie made some good points, but I think the very scene that angers Jeremy is the scene that redeems Huck."

Jeremy asked, "What'd you mean?" He didn't believe me at that point, but Jeremy was smart enough to want to hear more. The people in my English class are intelligent. They're not afraid of learning about something they might not agree with.

"Huck is like every other racist person, just like his Dad probably is and just like mostly everyone else around him, but those kind of actions weren't bad at that time, especially in the way we would think. That was the right way to treat blacks, almost like animals."

Jer' replied, "Great, just great."

"Wait!" I surprised myself with my conviction. "There's a lot more. That standard set's Huck up to do something really amazing. Huck feels bad about making fun of Jim. But not only that, he says he's sorry for the joke he played."

Angie broke in. "Yeah Chad's right. That wouldn't be the expected reaction back in that time. To most people back then, what Huck is doing is dead wrong. It's twice as hard for him to do what we just assume to be the right choice. Huck takes a big risk by staying with Jim, and he treats him like a person. I think we forget just how little respect white people had for blacks." Angie looked to Mr. Bar, and he shook his head.

I added, "Huck definitely sees Jim as a lot more than just a black man. He sees him as a friend, and despite everything he's been taught, he says he's sorry. The thing is, he doesn't think he's doing the right thing, like we see it. Huck knows he *shouldn't* have such a friendship, but he figures, 'I'm just a bad person, might as well not fight it.'

The Bar said, "I believe Twain was against slavery. What he did was write a story that puts Huck in a position where he feels bad for treating a black person like a friend. That's called dramatic irony. It makes the reader the judge. Twain wanted his reader to see the stupidity in such views. What kind of society makes someone feel he's doing wrong by treating another human being like a person and a friend, regardless of his color? Rather than saying this outright, Twain chose a more subtle approach. Ultimately, it's the reader that must decide if Huck's feelings of being wrong are misguided. We're going to examine this in more detail later."

With the extra manufacturing time I had some more words ready to ship. And by this time I was starting to enjoy talking in class. I said, "Huck gives Jim true freedom in the friendship he feels. That's a lot more than just not saying nig. . . y'know that word."

Jeremy was thinking about what I said. He replied, "I think I see what you mean, but it's just one moment. There better be more than this one time." I can't understand what it means to be black in the way Jeremy does, but I thought his response was very admirable. Each time that word appears in *Huckleberry Finn,* it has to bring up a whole world of frustration and struggles for him.

I said to Jeremy, "How many people can do what Huck does even today in our modern world? You can write all the laws you want and spread layer after layer of political correctness, but Huck and Jim's relationship is the dream. That's true freedom and equality."

"Yeah, ending stereotypes and seeing each other as equals."

I was on a role. The factory was working double-time and the words were stacked up waiting to come out of my mouth. I replied, "I don't think Huck is rid of stereotypes and I'm really not sure if Huck truly sees Jim as an equal, but he's come a long way. We can never get rid of stereotypes completely, and we wouldn't want to. They're good in a way. For instance, I want to be a sprinter. A lot of black athletes don't respect me. In addition, I have this poster of Michael Johnson that my Dad can't stand – I bet you can't guess why. Dad can't respect my idol, a black man, and black sprinters can't respect that a white kid could be a sprinter and be any good at it. I take all of that frustration and anger and use it to motivate me. I know that the idea of a white sprinter from the good ole' US of A would make most people laugh pretty hard. That's a stereotype. Every time people laugh I want to go lift weights, work on my start, or run sprint after sprint after sprint. I want to be the best sprinter, but, in a way, really what I want is to fight the stereotype. Well, I'd also like to knock those peoples' teeth out, but that's really not my style." The class chuckled at my remark.

I really felt great. For a moment I felt like a normal person. I seemed to rise above my nature so that my classmates were looking me eye to eye. I think they respected me for that moment. Of course, I didn't stop there. Remember all my ups come with downs.

I added, "It's like Angie's feminist look." There was a quick moment of silence and even a little groan from the class.

"My what?"

"Wait! I didn't mean that negatively."

"I hope not."

"Angie," I should've said 'just give me a couple seconds to get this foot outta my mouth,' "I just meant you probably struggle with stereotypes just like I do, just like in a different way, but I didn't mean it that way, like that."

"I think I get it." Whew! "You know, stereotypes and respect are tied close together. Respect is a powerful feeling, it's what we all want."

The Bar replied, "Excellent point. Let's finish here and break into our discussion groups and continue on these issues from there." I thought about what Angie said for the rest of the class.

That's what motivates me. Respect. No matter what someone does in life, just to be respected makes it all worth while. What I don't get is the fact that we all need it, and we all can give it, so what's the problem? Why don't we go around giving each other respect? Everyone would feel better.

I don't know what it is, but you don't see me going around and doing it all the time. Granted I think I try harder than other people, but take Vinnie for example. While I don't insult him like he does me, I sure don't go out of my way to try and make him feel good. We're all too afraid of our own insecurity; that, by making someone else feel good, they might rise higher than us. I don't know why we're like that.

So, is there any good in me? I try to be good person, but I don't know how well I'm really doing. The truth is I think I'd be just as mean as Vinnie if I had his popularity. I never thought I'd be able to say that I'm glad I'm a loser, but I'm a nicer person because of it. Then again, I still have a long way to go.

Chemical Combustion

After English class things are more difficult for me. My classmates in English are a lot nicer. My other classes don't work that way. In English it seems like we're really doing something. My other classes are either boring or chaotic. In the afternoon I met up with Dale during chemistry class. Today chemistry was especially chaotic.

Chemistry contains an interesting assortment of dangerous students. All of them have labels on their vials that warn 'Do Not Mix'. I don't know who puts students in classes, but they sure did a bad job with this one. The whole popularity crew is together: Patrick and Vinnie and Stacy, Kathy, Ashley, and Janet. The class is all about socializing. In addition there's the hellraiser of the school Johnny, or, 'here's Johnny' as Patrick likes to introduce him. He's a senior. Don't ask me how he got into sophomore chem., but somehow Patrick did too. You add a little of this student and a little of that one and before you know it even the normally stable students turn explosive. I'd probably like the class more if I wasn't on the receiving end of so many of the jokes. Today we were supposed to be working on a lab experiment measuring the density of various liquids. Mr. Larkin, our teacher, (the poor guy) could never keep control of a crew like this. Dale and I were having a conversation before the carnival began.

"How did English go?" Dale asked as he poured some clear liquid into a beaker.

"It went really well. We had a good discussion and I actually contributed to it," I replied with a haughty aire.

"That's great. I told you that you should just start talking. You just need to be more confident."

"Sure, whatever. That's easier said than done. Today was just a moment."

"You know what you need?" I turned my palms up and waited for his reply. "You need a girl."

"Ahh, come on. Here we go again."

"Ask her."

"No, I can't."

"Oh, for cryin out loud. Give it a try. The worst that could happen is a simple little word. And even if that happens you'll at least know you tried," he chuckled as he continued, "and we'll be able to swap rejection stories." I couldn't help but smile.

"You have a great attitude about it. Getting that word doesn't seem to bother you at all." I recorded the amount of solution that was in the beaker.

"There's no need to get upset about it. There's plenty more. There are billions of them all around the world. It's like strike out all you want we'll throw you more. It's better odds than winning the lottery!" He laughed some more and then continued. "But I'm exaggerating a bit. There have been some that have said yes and others that haven't, and none of the yesses have panned out. But you aren't going to go anywhere if you don't take a chance. Why don't you ask her out?"

"No way!"

"What, you don't want to spoil your good relationship?"

"Very funny," I replied dryly. "Seriously, I don't think Heather sees me as a fool, and I don't want to ruin that. In this town, when you screw up people remember it. They're looking at you, but their remembering THAT TIME WHEN you did whatever. I don't want her to look at me that way."

"So, you don't say anything to her! How does that make any sense? That's like starving but choosing not to eat your dinner because you don't want to ruin its' beautiful organization." He sarcastically emphasized beautiful organization like he was some crazy TV gourmet cook.

"All right, maybe I will. But how do I start?" Before Dale could offer his advice here's Johnny had the class' attention and we turned to see what everyone was snickering about. Mr. Larkin was the busy beaver at the board furiously writing instructions nobody was going to follow. I knew Mr. Larkin had to know something was happening. I think he was afraid to say something. I guess like in the same way that I'm afraid to say something to Heather, or any girl for that matter. Anyhow, Johnny was mixing a drink with the beakers. He was holding up some vials in front of him and I don't think they contained the liquids we were using for our lab.

He spoke in a loud whisper. "Ladies and gentlemen, what we have here is some real chemistry," a sly smile followed his pronouncement. He continued his story with the tone of a circus announcer or a salesman depending on you perspective.

"Now what should I put together for this wonderful girl," he moved over to Ashley. With an overdone erotic tone he said, "Huh? What would you like?" Everybody was snickering, trying not to break into complete laughter. Johnny's antics are always the life of chemistry class. Ashley played right along with his tone.

She replied, "I don't know big boy. Why don't you give me a surprise." Patrick saw his cue. He was a row behind her. Ashley and Johnny were in the middle of the circle that had now formed. They were the main attraction. I saw Patrick's face and I knew right away he was going to do something pretty wild. He leaned over the desk and reached for Ashley's back.

He said, "Oh, baby, I'll give you a surprise," and in one quick motion he unhooked her bra. As much as I can't stand Patrick, any guy has to appreciate the ability to unhook a bra that lightening fast. Let's just say Patrick's had enough practice. Ashley's face got red as she grabbed on to both boobs. I really don't think she was all that embarrassed. She's hot and she knows it. She wants everyone to stare at her body and ogle over the size of her boobs. You can tell by the way she dresses and acts.

Patrick continued. "Come on, lift up your shirt. Show me titties! Titties, titties, titties!" The laughing in the classroom was starting to get louder.

With a sly smile and eyes that were just saying 'lets do it' Ashley replied, "In your dreams. This pussy isn't going to be landing on your pad." The guys all reacted with ohhs and ahhs, even Dale and I had to react. She was loving every minute. It really made me sick; I guess, truthfully, jealous because I'd like to be able to toy around with girls like Patrick does. He does have some kind of special skill. It's a way he has with people. If I unhooked her bra there would've been a much different reaction.

Mr. Larkin turned from the board and said, "Excuse me folks. Keep it down and keep working."

Patrick replied, "Yes sir. We were competing to see who could calculate the density the fastest."

"Well keep focused." He turned back to the board.

After a few moments, Johnny said, "Oh ladies and gentleman you've seen the challenge here. What will happen? Come and see the grudge match later tonight: cheerleader vs. football stud, live and uncensored." He stopped playing to the class and turned directly to her, and said, "So you won't show us the jugs, well then you need to chug a little bit of beaker A," and he moved over to her. His eyes were fixed on her as he slowly strided to her like he was a fashion model walking down the runway. He was right in front of her holding the beaker out in front of her face.

Ashley replied, "Johnny, you just think you're all that." She took the beaker from him and drained its contents.

Patrick said, "I'm in love."

She replied, "God, that stuff was nasty. I hope you're not planning on being a bar tender, Johnny. What was that shit."

"Vodka and orange juice. There was about three shots of vodka in that stuff."

"Uhh, I hate vodka. I thought that's what it was."

Patrick said, "You said you put three shots of that in there." Johnny smiled and shook his head. "Well, we'll just give that a little bit of time to work its' magic. How much more do you have?"

"Enough for one more." Patrick and Johnny continued talking quietly. It looked like they were planning something. Mr. Larkin stopped writing on the board. I guess he'd built up enough confidence to confront the class. I don't think he heard any of the specifics of what was going on, but he had to know something was up.

He loudly cleared his throat. It didn't seem anybody heard him except me. Then, he said, "Excuse me, excuse me, hey people, excuse me!" Some people had now realized that he was watching, and they sort of stopped what they were doing and looked up at him. Mr. Larkin looked more uncomfortable than any of us. He fidgeted with his chalk as he said, "I don't mind if you socialize, but you've got to keep it under control."

Patrick piped up, "Don't worry Mr. Larkin we'll be more quiet. Lab day just gets us a little excited. You know, we get to do stuff and kinda play around."

Mr. Larkin smiled a bit and said, "That's good to hear. Experimentation can be a lot of fun if you make it fun."

"Oh, we make if lots of fun. I wish we could experiment in every class."

"I tell the other teachers that it's important to let the students do hands on activities."

"I just love hands on activities, Mr. Larkin," Patrick replied. One of the guys in the back corner of the room was about ready to explode with laughter. His name's Brian. Everyone was struggling to keep their composure. I was sort of torn. I didn't know whether to laugh or to feel sorry for Mr. Larkin. He didn't seem to have a clue, but he just had to know something was up. Everybody was trying to give that classic 'good student' look but cracks were forming everywhere in the facade. Laughter was sneaking out everywhere. He just had to be able to see it.

Mr. Larkin then said, "I see, Patrick." He seemed to've realized that Patrick and he weren't talking about the same kind of hands on activities. Mr. Larkin added with a weak attempt at being commanding, "I expect those lab sheets to be filled out by the end of the period. I need to run something down to the office. This class will remain under control. Thank you. I'll be right back."

I don't know what he was thinking. I guess he was running for reinforcements, but the last thing he should've done was leaving the classroom. Everybody held the illusion of being a good class a few seconds after he left but then the damn broke and conversation was rushing all over the room.

I turned to Dale and said, "I can't believe he left the room."

"Me neither. Look at Patrick." He was talking with all the cute girls. All in all about fifteen people were socializing in the center of the room. "He sure has a way with the girls."

I replied, "Yeah, that's an understatement."

"You know, Chad, that could be you."

"What?"

"Yeah it could. You've got the looks."

"Yeah right. Whatever good looking means for a guy. The characteristics are easy to point to when you're talking about a girl: nice ass, good legs, nice size boobs, and a nice face, but for us things seem to be a bit different. The hot girls are the best looking girls. But the cool guys, at least I don't think anyways, don't stand out as the best looking guys.

"You're not going homosexual on me now?" He smiled and laughed.

"No, I don't think you need to look for me to come out of that closet. It's the truth though. I know I'm in shape. I work hard for that, but, Dale, that's just not important. It's personality for girls, and I don't seem to have any of that. I'm just a fool around girls. The other big factor is popularity. It's the two Ps: personality and popularity. Popularity is formed by your personality, so I'm losing there. It's also shaped by the clothes you wear (another negative for me because I can't afford all the cool stuff), and the car you drive (I ride the bus), and how much money you have (like I said, none)."

"Your whole problem is confidence. You knock yourself out before you even start. Looks do matter pal and you've got the chance. I don't have that but I've got a steady girl, even if I don't think it's going to work out. You've got to go give it a try. It's hard for a girl to say no to a simple date. It takes a lot of guts to do that. So, you're bound to get the chance for her to see your personality. But, you've got to try."

"You make it sound all too simple." Just then our conversation was interrupted by Johnny who had climbed on top of one of the tables.

Patrick said, "Here's Johnny," and pointed to him.

Johnny announced, "So who will be trying the second chemistry creation. Who will begin the offers? Let me see a hand. Who will give it a try?"

Patrick smiled and said, "How about Chippy!" All I could think was oh shit. Patrick slid down the table to where Dale and I had been talking at our seats by the door. "Come on speedy. This drink will really give you an extra boost tonight at practice." Everybody laughed "You'll be burning up the track, VEROOOOM!!" He acted like he was a missile.

"Sorry, Patrick, but I don't drink."

"You don't drink! Boy, we need to get you on the football team."

Ashley yelled, "He wouldn't want to drink any of the crap that Johnny makes."

Johnny pretended to be shocked as he said, "What, you no like my drink? Ahh, I am destroyed. I am dying. I have been crushed," he gradually fell melodramatically to the ground and was now lying on the floor.

"Don't worry, Johnny," said Patrick, "I'm a drinker and I just love anything you make me." He grabbed the beaker and drained it. A bunch of the guys were hooting and hollering and most of the girls were laughing and some were clapping.

I turned to Dale and said, "I really hate the way he has to make an ass out of me so the whole class can get their jollies from me. They don't know why I don't drink."

"Chad, you take it all too serious. Don't take everything so personal. They're just joking around trying to have some fun."

"Well who were they laughing at then?"

"Patrick."

"No they weren't. They were laughing at me and Patrick was reaping the benefits."

"Look, I know he is on your case a lot, and a lot of the time he's a real dick, but you need to be able to laugh at yourself a little. It's all confidence. Nobody likes to get laughed at, but if you're confident about who you are as a person you can sort of laugh a long a bit. There's a limit for everybody, but your limit is before anybody even starts. You need a girlfriend. They're the best boost of confidence."

"You're really persistent. Well, I'll agree with one thing, I really want a girlfriend, but I've pretty much decided that I won't have a chance until college. In college I'll be able to start fresh with a clean reputation. I'm telling you it's all the two Ps. This school is too small. Everyone knows my reputation. No girl is going to want to weather the storm that I go through."

"Ahh, give it a try, man," he replied like he was Captain Kirk. The doorknob was heard and everyone instantly became 'good students'.

Mr. Larkin walked in and said, "You've got about ten minutes left so you should start finishing things up. Leave your papers on my desk."

Usually Dale and I finish our work for lab class, but today even we had hardly done a thing. Mr. Larkin again tried to blend with the black chalkboard and the whispering started up. The Pussy Pad was back trying to see those boobs again.

"Ahh, come on," he begged. "Baby, sweetheart, your gorgeous. You need to let some of that inner beauty out."

"You are such a dog. Just a big ol' hound dog howling at the moon." Then she got a look in her eye. I didn't think much of it at the time, but after what happened that look was the sign of a very remarkable occurrence. She was facing the front of the room standing straight in front of Patrick in the middle of the circle that had formed around the main event. She looked him right in the eyes and said, "Well, hound dog I want to hear you howl," and with that she lifted up her shirt and bra. Holy cow I think every guys' jaw dropped in the class. Penthouse and Playboy will never compete with seeing the real thing live.

Dale just gasped an inquisitive, "Oh my." Patrick kept up his part of the bargain. He started howling like a hound dog and he even started kicking his feet. Unfortunately, Mr. Larkin couldn't help but turn around. It's not everyday that someone is howling in your classroom, and it's not everyday that you turn around to see to a set of boobs hanging out.

I swear, for a second, Mr. Larkin just wanted to stare at them. You know this makes a great point as to why we should have a female president, especially if she's hot. I mean here's Ashley, who has practically no brains. She simply lifts her shirt and every guy in the room is frozen. Dale and I are pretty smart guys, but I know for at least five seconds I don't have any idea what I was doing or thinking;

all I saw were boobs. What a tactical advantage that would be at a negotiation. I imagine that guys are all like this around the world. Women just don't seem to be affected by these things. Well, maybe they're affected but they're much more in control. If a negotiation wasn't going well all a girl'd need to do is say, "Sign this and I'll let you play with these," and lift up her shirt. Instantly guys would be running for a pen just like Patrick was howling and now rolling on the floor. It would really work. All of those politicians are old guys. They're really hard up for stuff like that. They'd beg even more than Patrick would. Anyways, I was just kidding, but it was amazing how every guy was instantly stunned like that.

Mr. Larkin managed to roll back his tongue inside his mouth and tried to gain control of his class. He asked, "What on earth is occurring in my class?" I think the shock of the whole event gave him an infusion of confidence. I had never seen him that angry. Ashley quickly put her shirt down and seemed to be trying to hide behind the inch thick desk. I just closed my eyes. I can't watch people get caught doing embarrassing things. I wanted to watch what Mr. Larkin was going to do, but at the same time I didn't. I grimaced at Ashley's impending humiliation.

Mr. Larkin slowly walked towards Ashley and Patrick as the circle of students that had formed broke up and everyone took their seats. Mr. Larkin bellowed, "I don't know what you people think this class is, but it is certainly not Hooters bar and grill!" A couple people couldn't help but snicker. That made me grimace more because I knew they had just drawn attention to themselves. "Don't you dare laugh. I've tried to let you have a good time in this class but ... I simply can't believe .... What would posses you .... Both of you to the office! Let you explain it there. I'm sure Dr. Kauffman will be impressed with you. Get going!"

Thank God the bell rang a few minutes later. The tension in that room was pretty thick. I would've never thought that Mr. Larkin had it in him. We always walked all over him, but as people left the room no one let out a peep. Dale and I put our half done papers on the table, and started to leave, but Mr. Larkin noticed us.

"Not even you two finished this assignment. I can't believe it. Unbelievable." He was taking this whole thing really hard. It made me feel lousy. I'd abused someone's trust and respect. For Patrick that didn't matter, but that's all I had. To waste that was about the worst thing I could ever do. I hoped that I could repair things with Mr. Larkin.

Dale and I didn't say anything to him. As he turned away from us, we made our way out of the room.

Empathy

Once we were in the comfort of the crowded hallway Dale said, "Wow, he's really taking this pretty tough."

"I'll say. It makes me feel like crap. Tomorrow I'm going to apologize to him. You know teaching is everything to him. When he has a bad day teaching it's like his whole life is horrible. He gets down on himself, but it's us not him. Today certainly didn't boost his confidence."

"Yeah, but did you see them," Dale's face lit up with excitement.

"That was pretty awesome."

"Wait till you get to unhook that bra yourself and stare at them at close range."

"Well that'll cost me fifty bucks."

"Oh shut up. Tonight, ask Heather to go on a date with you this Friday or Saturday. You can do the time tested, fully proven, dinner and a movie. It'll be really nice." Dale was really trying to sell the idea.

I told him, "All right, maybe I will."

"You will, just keep telling yourself that. Chad, the force is with you. Face her you must. Confront you fears. Only then can you be a Jedi ladies man. Chad, you are your only hope," his voice melodramatically faded as he pretended to die away.

"OK oh wise one, I'll give it a shot." I sarcastically replied. I said it more to get Dale off my back. "I've got to go, I'm going to be late."

"See ya later. Let me know how things go."

I thought about what Dale had said as I walked down the hall to my next class. He was right, as usual. Dale has a real good head on his shoulders, but, more importantly, he's a heck of a nice guy. I can tell him anything and he's always understanding. He's a true friend. If people knew the way I worry about things. Other guys wouldn't be so understanding. They'd have a hell of a good laugh. Dale would never do that.

Am I really that different from everybody else? I don't think so, I sure hope I'm not. I think everybody has the same fear of rejection, and longing for respect that I do. It seems hard to believe that at times even Patrick must be feeling the same things I am. Why do people need to make fun of me for things they also struggle with? Human nature is all about ego, not empathy. Unfortunately, I'm not one to call the kettle black. I do the same stuff the few chances I get. It makes you feel better. I'm actually worse. People like Patrick don't realize just how hurtful they are. They have an excuse, but I know what it's like. I've been on the other side plenty of times. It's really hard to say no to a good joke that makes you the center of the laughs. However, Dale would never do that to me and I would never do that to him, ever. There is complete trust between us. When it comes to women, I trust Dale's opinion a great deal. It was time to ask her.

Chapter Three
H-Hour

I thought about asking Heather out on a date through the last three periods of the day. It was driving me nuts, but the more I thought about it the more I realized I needed to do it. I wasn't sure about Dale's belief that she would say yes because of the pressure of having to turn someone down, but it didn't matter. I had to show myself that I could do it. I mean, I'm how old and I haven't even gone on a real date. It was time to start practicing. She'd say no, but that wasn't the point. Heather would be real nice about the whole thing. She was always nice to me.

The end of the school day seemed to come all too fast for my confidence. The final hollow buzz sounded and signaled that it was time. As students poured into the hallways, I made my way to my locker. I was trying to figure out how to say everything. Dale's right, I don't have a whole lot of practice doing this kind of thing. The opening line was the worst. There was: "Hey Heather, what's'up?" but that was too generic. Then I thought, how about, "Hi Heather, how was your day." That sounded too much like a mother. I could try, "Hey Heather, what've you been up to?" but that sounded like we were at a class reunion or something. I decided that generic would be better. So, I said to myself, first line is, "Hey Heather," no it would be better if I said, "Hi Heather, what's up?" OK, first line down. I really wished I had something to write this all down on. It was going to be tricky tactfully changing the conversation from normal talk to something more along the lines of going on a date. I couldn't just come out of nowhere and ask her out.

I finished at my locker and started to make my way to the bus. It's a good thing that Heather and I talk pretty regularly on the bus ride home because I had no idea how I was going to switch the conversation from, "So how about those Bulls," to, "Would you like to go on a date with me this Friday?" As this was running through my head, I was fighting my way up to the end of the hallway. I felt like a fish going up stream. I'm just about the only one I know that's sixteen but still rides the bus. Well, that's not true, but it feels that way. It seems everyone else is driving; at least anyone that's important. After fighting against the current, I finally made it to the doors and out to the bus. There wasn't any more thinking to worry about.

I hopped on and made my way back through the aisle. On the bus I'm something of a celebrity in a way. At the very least I certainly have seniority. There's a lot of middle school kids, some freshman, but only a few sophomores or juniors. No seniors ride the bus, but I'm sure given a couple more years I'll have the chance to change that trend. Those who are my age are just like me in a lot of ways. In a way that's a good thing. If I'd been on a bus with a bunch of guys like Patrick, there's no way I'd be able to ask Heather on a date. They'd have a field day for months making fun of how nervous I was and how much I looked like a little middle school kid trying for a first kiss. By the way, I've never done that either. When guys like Patrick were getting their first kisses in fifth grade, I was dreaming about it and that's how it's been ever since. Guys like Patrick keep moving ahead and I keep dreaming. It was time for me to start living.

Heather hadn't gotten on the bus yet, but I took my usual seat a couple from the back. Normally, she would sit in the seat right in front of me, sometimes across the aisle, and once in a long while just a seat or two away. When she sits directly in front or across from me, it's a good sign that she's in the mood to talk either privately with me or as a group with everyone else who sits in the back. When she sits a few seats away, she wants to be alone. I was praying that she wasn't going to be sitting a few seats away and I was determined that today wasn't going to be a group discussion day.

There are about five of us that usually shoot the bull. Heather's the youngest of the five. Heather's really unique. She has everything that puts her into popular society, but you wouldn't know it from being around her. She doesn't show a lot of attitude. In fact, she acts like she doesn't even realize, or care about, her popularity. A part from Heather, the rest of us all have something that puts us on the fringes of popular society (the degrading problem of having to ride the bus even though we're old enough to drive is something we all share).

There's Randy who I know from track. He runs long distance, so he's a pretty lanky guy. Randy has a deep voice that seems to plod along when he talks. It really sets him a part. I guess it sort of sounds like a geeky dumb hillbilly; although, Randy is a lot more than that, but that's what I think someone's snap judgement of Randy would be. The first time he ever said a word popular society immediately said, "this guy isn't going to be one of us." Randy reminds me a lot of myself. He has his quirks, like I do (although I wish I knew what mine were so I could change them), and he also doesn't have much of a love life. We talk about this a lot. Plus he's often on the end of someone else's joke. He's a very good person to talk with because you know that he isn't going to humiliate your soul for a few popularity points. I feel I can talk about just about anything with Randy. I never really thought about it, but I guess we're pretty good friends, almost as close as I am with Dale.

Next there's Carolyne, who usually sits in the far back. She's another story: very quiet and very weird. She's usually wearing black or some shade of black that compliments her cold black hair and dark brooding eyes. She's thin as a twig and looks about as breakable. The whole picture makes me think of her as a little spider. Her clothes often have a gypsy quality to them.

You know I just did exactly what people always do to me. I just described Carolyne as weird. This is just the kind of thing that really worries me. It wouldn't be hard for me to imagine myself joking about how unusual Carolyne is to a bunch of my cool football buddies so I could get some laughs and boost my confidence. In fact, I know that I've joked about her to Dale. Like I said before, everyone wants respect. There is no greater feeling than knowing that the people around you like you and think you're cool. One of the easy ways to get that feeling is to use other people as building materials.

It really worries me that I understand this, but have a hard time putting it to good use. I guess my redeeming quality is that there's no way I could ever make fun of someone when he or she is right there. Maybe it's a lack of guts, but I'm glad for it. I can think of a whole bunch of things I could say about Carolyne but I'd never say any of it while she was around. I guess, at the very least, I've learned not to be that mean. However, I worry about my character when my redeeming quality is that I'm unable to make fun of Carolyne to her face, but I'm still perfectly capable of doing it when she isn't around. That doesn't sound like what I'd call a good person. She wants to be understood just as much as I want to be understood.

Well, I'm in control right now and I take that back. Carolyne isn't weird. She looks weird, as for how she is, I really don't know. I've never gotten to know her to make any kind of judgement. I should probably get to know her a little better. I know I'd be surprised. She could be a lot like Angie; an exterior created to hide the person inside. Even though Carolyne sits in the back, she usually doesn't join in the conversations.

I've got to lessen some of this commentary so you can get to the story. I'm sure you can't wait to see what happens between Heather and me. Don't worry. You won't be disappointed. It's one hell of a story. So let's keep going. Last but not least is Louis. He could fix any part of your car in a heartbeat. If you could have a relationship with a car, Louie would be quite a player. He understands them inside and out. Patrick does it with pussy; Louie does it with cars. However, a good grease monkeys isn't going to qualify to date any cheerleaders. Louie does have a girlfriend and she looks like she would be pretty comfortable working on cars as well. They're a good match. Louie's a lot of fun to be around. He's happy with his girlfriend and he's glad to be doing what he wants to do. He's a big guy: about 6' 2" and around 250. He'd be a good guy for the football team if he'd have the desire. He's got long black curly hair that makes him look like some 80's punk rocker. He always wears jeans, even when it gets pretty warm, and he has the largest collection of NASCAR racing shirts that exists because I think those are the only tee shirts he wears. He also likes to wear this old beat up Marlboro hat. The red in the hat isn't just faded; it's been worn off. I'd say that hat has spent many a day underneath a car.

So, that's the crew. Randy's behind me and Louie is another seat back from Randy, which is the last seat at the back of the bus. Carolyne is across from him. The bus is just about full now, but no Heather as of yet. It's kind of a weird feeling I had thinking about her arrival. It would be nice if she didn't show up because then I could chicken out, but, on the other hand, I was sort of nervous about her not showing up. I felt I was really ready to do this so I didn't want to waste the build up confidence.

As everyone was getting situated, Heather stepped through the door. So much for the indecisive feelings, I was definitely ready to chicken out. She started to make her way back the aisle. She looked amazing. She had on a red shirt that was shiny and hung about at her belly button with a pair of white shorts cut just high enough that you'd realize they were cut just a bit high. Her black hair was pulled back in some clippy thing (I don't know how girls do their hair), but it looked nice. I was anxiously waiting to see where she would sit. As she came closer to the back of the bus, I was trying to find something else to occupy my attention besides her. I didn't want to seem like I was just waiting for her to arrive, even though that's exactly what I was doing. She sat in the seat in front of me, which was a perfect position.

As she put her book bag down in the seat, the nervousness kicked in with a jolt of adrenaline. I don't know why I was so nervous. She was a nice person. Even if she said no, she would be real nice about it, which is about all I could ask for. As she was getting situated, the bus started to pull out. Now, under the mask of engine noise, I knew it was time to have our conversation. I pulled my line out of my memory and was ready to go.

"Hey Heather, how's it, I mean, ah what's up?" Just great, really great, I thought to myself. I stumbled right outta the starting gate.

"Not too much. Just school." This was as bad as I had envisioned. She didn't follow up with a question. Now, I had to try to find something to talk about.

"So, is Mrs. Barkley's class everything that I told you about, or has she gotten more laid back?" Lame-o, just very lame, I thought. My mind was not coming up with anything original.

She laughed a little, rolled her eyes, and replied, "No, I'm afraid that she's still her crazy self. I just die when she says, 'listen up,' in that announcer voice." Well, I guess Heather hadn't noticed how pathetic my topic for discussion was. It's no wonder people think I'm such a geek. When I need something to talk about, my mind flashes to learning, and I don't talk about the students. I talk about the teachers. Man, that's bad.

I replied, "I think that's an experience that everybody gets to have if you go through the ninth grade." The trick was now trying to turn the conversation more towards going out on a date. Plus, trying to turn the conversation to something a bit more hip.

She asked, "So how's track going?"

I love talking about track so this was an easy question. "I haven't lost yet. I should have a shot at State's this year. I've been running good. The team's pretty good, as well, but we're young. I'm hoping that maybe if we won the league people would respect us more."

"I'll have to try to see you run sometime." Wow, that would be so awesome, I thought. She added, "You're a sprinter, right?"

"Yeah. I like to run, fast. We have a meet tomorrow, but it's away. The last couple of weeks we've had a lot of rainouts, so the end of the season will be pretty full." There was so much I wanted to tell her about running. What it felt like to run, my father and the poster, how I got interested, all sorts of things, but our relationship was too informal to talk that personal with her. I didn't know how she'd react.

I tried to delicately move the conversation toward the big question. "What do you do with your free time now that basketball is over?"

"Ahh," she replied and laughed, "more basketball. The off-season is more practice, but that's what you have to do to be a good player." I had no doubt that she would be; she was pretty good already. "Then I do homework and chores. My parents are pretty strict. They don't let me run around with my friends or hangout with people after school. It's straight home, do homework and chores, go to practice, and then straight home again. It gets really old."

It was a perfect time to ask, but I balked. The moment of truth was there and I just couldn't even wheeze the tiniest drop of confidence out of my mouth. Instead I said, "Yeah, I know what you mean. Here I am on the bus, and I can drive." Time was soon going to run out. Heather had to ride the bus for awhile, but I get off much earlier. The window was still open, but I couldn't get myself to jump into the burning building.

For some reason I did ask, "Who's your favorite movie star?" What a completely random question, I thought to myself the moment after the words came from my mouth.

"I don't know exactly. I guess it would be Tom Cruise."

I replied with a deep voice, "Tom Cruise?" It made her laugh, which made me feel really good. This conversation was going all right.

"Ohh stop it. Yes, he's sexy, but I like his acting."

"Now, let me get this straight. I'm supposed to believe the reason you like Tom Cruise as your favorite movie star is because of his acting. Would you believe me if I said the reason I like Cindy Crawford is because of her acting?"

She replied laughing, "You're comparing two completely different levels of acting talent."

"Regardless of talent. When you think of either one the first thing that comes to mind is,"

She cut me off by saying, "For a guy it's boobs for sure."

"Moi?"

She laughed again. "Oui, Tu. Girls have a bit more sophistication. That's why my second favorite actor is Robin Williams. It's because of talent."

"Sophisticated, ehh? So why does a guy like Patrick have girls crawling all over him?"

"That's a good point, but I'm not crawling all over him. All he wants is a trophy. Girls are still more sophisticated, Patrick is proof.

I continued in a very snooty tone, "I do believe that I have a fair bit of sophistication." Returning to my normal voice I said, "You will be happy to know that Cindy Crawford is not my favorite actress." I briefly looked out the window and realized where we were. I had basically no time. I had to ask now, right now. My mind was whirling as I tried to bring my movie star conversation to a close and quickly switch to asking her out, all while maintaining the appearance that I wasn't rushing anything. Yeah right, huh? Not gonna do it, at this juncture.

"Well, who is your favorite actress?" she asked, which got me out of my mind and back on the conversation.

"Oh, I don't know to tell you the truth, but it's not her, maybe Linda Hamilton." The bus was slowing down for my stop.

"Sure it isn't. Well, here's your stop. I guess I'll see you tomorrow morning."

I stood up and got my bag. I had to ask now. Right now! Now! Right Now! I screamed to myself. There's no way I could be that lucky ever again, having a conversation like I'd just had. I'd even started it like a real geek and it worked. I had to take advantage of the moment. The bus was stopped and Mrs. Wilbough was giving an icy stare back the aisle. So much for trying to be subtle. Every person in the bus was looking back at me as I hesitated with my stuff.

I said to her, "Heather," it was really going to come out, "I really wanted to ask you something. Ahh, you know we can talk pretty good together and you said it's a real drag that you can't get out of the house, so if you're not doing anything and your parents will let you. . ."

A tiny smile curled the corner of her mouth, "Chad, are you asking me out?" Oh thank you God, I thought. I don't know how long it would've taken me to finally get to the point.

Mrs. Wilbough bellowed, "Are you plannin' on gettin' off this bus?"

I replied, "Yes, ahh, to both of you. Just think about it, Heather. I'll talk to you tomorrow. I gotta go. See ya." It looked to me like she was stunned. I fumbled with my stuff down the aisle to the waiting glare of Mrs. Wilbough.

Stunned couldn't be good I thought, but what I said was said and done.

Mrs. Willbough mumbled to me as I was leaving, "Oh, you kids and your love make me laugh." I faked a smile and jumped off the bus. She cackled and slammed the door behind me.

Chapter Four
The Dams of Our Lives

I didn't want to turn and look back at the bus and Heather. I had to put the embarrassment behind me. I grabbed the mail from the mailbox at the end of the lane and started the long walk back to the house. There were a million different interpretations of what had just happened; some good, some bad, some unsure, but all in all I was at least happy that I took a chance. Dale was right. Even as humiliated as I was, I felt good I'd taken the chance. After the bus was out of sight I jumped up in the air, threw a punch at the sky and screamed a bit. It was a rush to know I had done it.

As I strolled back the lane, I noticed how beautiful everything was becoming. Green always made our junky old house look a lot nicer. It made it seem like we had designed our house to have a rustic look so it would blend better with the natural surroundings. When everything was dead, the house looked as bare as the empty trees, but the green made you want to keep your window open and let the breeze wash your face clean of any worries. I enjoyed the brisk spring day back to the house.

When I reached the house, I walked up the front porch. I could hear Mom doing something in the kitchen. I opened the old screen door and let it screech and then slam shut behind me. Dad and I could easily fix that door. A little WD-40 would do the trick, but it's our version of a doorbell.

When the door screeches and slams it signals to everybody that someone has arrived. We have a pretty open door policy about security. Responding to the ding-dong, Mom turned and smiled.

"Howdy, sweetheart," she said. Mom's voice is difficult to describe, but I'll try. She's a real sweet person and that comes out in her voice, but it's always mixed with a toughness that's a part of living with a farmer in such a tough old house. As tough as she is, Mom's pretty emotional; especially when compared to Dad. He's as emotional as a rock. Everyday (well maybe not quite everyday, but you get the idea) just about everyday Mom truly seems happy to see me come in the door.

I always see Mom in control, even though she just shuffles papers in an office for half the day. The way I see it she could be a president, a general, or a big wig in some corporation. She's tough enough to run the show but she's got a big enough heart to make sure she's doing the right thing. She keeps Dad on the straight and narrow. He still runs the show, but Mom's influence is always there, so Dad just thinks he's making decisions on his own. Mom's got that Linda Hamilton thing from *Terminator 2*. She's pretty thin and wirery, but her size only makes her strength come at more of a surprise.

After the hug Mom walked back into the kitchen and asked, "Do you want anything to eat?"

I replied, "Yeah, I guess a little something would be good. Not too much, though, I've got to run in forty-five minutes."

"How's track going?"

"Ahh, pretty good. My biggest meets are yet to come especially because of all the rain we've had, so it's tough to say. I should make districts again this year, but I want to get into States. I need to get a new pair of running shoes this weekend. The ones I have are just about shot."

"Jeez Chad, we just got them for you at Christmas time. I don't know if your Dad's gonna let you buy em'. We might not have the money even if he would."

"Well, if Dad'd let me get a job then maybe I could buy them myself, but he wants me available to work for free at a moment's notice. He has a slave not a son."

"Your father ain't a young man." She paused for a moment and then the tone of her voice changed. "Chad, I've been wantin' to talk to you about you and your father. The two of you have been have'in at it for the past two years and it's just getting worse."

"He doesn't understand anything. All he does is moan about all'a the things I don't do and all'a the things I don't know how to do. I don't want to be a farmer."

"Whoa, whoa, whoa! That's what I'm talking about. You can't say a decent thing about him. You can't even talk about 'em without getting all bent outta shape." She handed me a baloney sandwich she'd finished making. "Your father is a good man and,"

"Well, as soon as he realizes I'm a good kid than maybe we can start getting along. He just thinks I'm stupid. Stupid for wanting to be a sprinter. Stupid for wanting to go to college," I imitated Dad's slow tractor like talk (his words just keep ploddin' along), "Hell, all you learn there is sex and drugs. You ain't gotta pay a couple grand to find that out.'

Mom's right, Dad does get me fired up. Just the thought of him brings up a thousand arguments I'd had with him. Mom broke off my ranting by raising her voice a little.

"Chad, will you cool it and listen! Your father wants you to respect him as much as you want him to respect you. You deliberately try to irritate the be'jesus outta each other. Like your poster.

"Mom, that's my dream. I don't care if he's black; he's the best sprinter in the world. I've read a biography on him. He's got an amazing story, and he's the best. Someday I want my picture to be hanging on a wall in a black kid's house because I'm the best sprinter in the world."

"Chad, you know how your father is about black people."

I shook my head in disgust. "Like that's an excuse."

"Can't you just take it down and put it in your locker at school, or something."

"No!"

"You do it just to irritate him."

"He needs to be irritated by it. First, because it's my life and he'd better learn to deal with it. Second, because it's down right racism. Why he's such a racist?"

"Most of it's because of you, not the color of the guy. All that poster does is remind your father how little you respect him. But fine, you do whatever you want, but nothin's gonna get better until one of you gives some ground. He has tried to make things better, but you're so damn bullheaded you don't even notice. You're both just such big men that neither of you will sit down and talk."

"Yeah right." Mom went over to finish doing the dishes and I started to eat my sandwich. Something Mom had said really had hit me: 'your father wants you to respect him as much as you want him to respect you.' I'd never thought of my father needing anything from me but work. In fact, I often felt that he didn't have any feelings for me at all, except that I disgrace him. I asked Mom, "What has he tried to do to make things better?"

"You see, that's what's funny. You don't even notice. What did you get for Christmas?" I thought about what my gifts were.

"I got a pair of track shoes and a CD."

"Track shoes, huh? Well, which one of us, me or your father, knows anything about buying track shoes? But that didn't matter because your father really wanted to make you happy, and he knew that track was something you love. So, we went to the mall; your Dad was in the mall, at a Footlocker, talking about track shoes, and we bought 'em. The guy at the store told us they were the best. So after all a' your father's effort to understand you, how'd you react?"

I hadn't realized that things had been like that. I was happy with the gift at Christmas time, but Dad's gotten me so mad that even when he does nice things it just pisses me off even more. I want more than that. Those things seemed so hollow. So, I'd been sort of reserved when I saw the shoes. What was really bad was what happened a few weeks ago. The track season had just started, but I had been running a lot between Christmas and the start of the season. The shoes were working out fine, but I didn't let Dad know that. The one night Dad and I were having a very heated argument and I know I said something about those shoes.

We'd been going at it for awhile. Dad had been giving me hell about not respecting the family and his work. I was sick of hearing him yell at me. I thought back through the argument to remember just what I'd said about the track shoes.

A good ways into the argument, Dad had yelled in his slow lanky talk, "You'd better learn to give a little more respect to your Mamma and I. We put you on this earth, and helped you survive it. It sure hasn't been easy for us, but we worked hard. All you want to do is bitch and moan about everything."

I responded, "And all you want to do is order me around like I'm some slave or something."

"I ask you to do a little work around the house. I can't do all of this farm'en on my own, and if this family's gonna stay afloat, I need your help."

"That's fine, but do you ever ask for my help? No, you demand it. You don't respect me, just like you don't respect anything I want to do: college or track. Lord knows you give me hell all the time about that poster."

"So how am I supposed to feel when my own boy gives more respect to a poster than to his own father? Besides, I've got a whole lot a' reasons for not liking them. You ain't been through what I have."

"Whatever, you've got it the wrong way around. You're the one that needs to respect me, then I'll respect you."

"I may not be college edjucated, but I ain't dumb neither and you know it. I ain't nothin' that you should be ashamed of."

"You act like you know a lot about everything. You don't know anything about track."

"Well, what'd you like me to do?"

"Just back off and let me live my life." I could've just let it at that, but I added, "And don't buy me anymore track shoes. They're wearing out fast. They're nothin' but junk. Everybody knows they're junk." I tore up the stairs to my room and threw the shoes back down the stairs in frustration. That hadn't been the best way to say thank you that's for sure.

I responded, "I was upset and things were said."

"That's fine but I know that hurt him. You should have seen how proud he was of himself when he bought those shoes. All he really wanted to see was you smile at something he'd done for you. That's not too much to ask now is it? At one time you and your Daddy had a good time together. He was so excited to finally get to see you happy, like it used to be, with something he'd done, and how did you repay him? You barely said thank you Christmas morning and then you said they're junk right to his face."

"I didn't know they were that important to him."

"That's right you didn't. Just like you don't realize how much he needs you. He's been trying to bend and you don't even notice. Chad, this family depends on those crops out in those fields and that livestock in that barn. Your Daddy depends on his family to love him and to respect him for the hard work he does. He don't get a whole lotta rewards. We barely make any money and he works real hard. It frustrates him to the ends of this earth that he don't have more money to give to his family. But, just like those crops depend on the dirt, sun, and rain to nourish them, your father depends on you, me, and Becky to nourish him. I'll tell you what, if we ever did get some money he'd make sure you kids came first. He'd give you the world just so he could have his son back. That's how important you are to him. You're his only son, and his oldest child. You mean a lot to him."

"It's not that I don't believe all that you're saying, but I don't see what you're saying in the way he is."

"I'm tellin' you that's how it is."

"Well, I don't see it. It's hard to believe it's true when you're saying it for him. I'd have a hard time believing it if he said it."

"He's just not one to open up like that, but it's not that he doesn't express it. He says those things in more subtle ways. Believe me I know; I've loved him for almost twenty years. I've learned to read him."

"I'm sorry about the shoes. I didn't know." I believed Mom, but the idea that my Dad needed me to make him happy didn't fit for me. Nothing in the world seemed to faze Dad. He seemed too strong to need the emotional things in life, I guess. Maybe Mom was right, but I wasn't convinced just yet. I had finished my sandwich.

Mom asked, "Whatever happened between you two?" Mom looked like she was ready to begin the second round, so I decided to make my exit.

I said, "I need to get going. Randy'll be here soon."

"You've got at least a half hour yet."

"We're going in a little early and I like to meet him at the end of the lane. I need to get going." I gave Mom a kiss and bounded up the stairs to get my stuff from the room. I put everything in my bag and headed back down. I said, "See ya."

Instead of simply saying goodbye, Mom surprised me with, "It's all from that night, isn't it?" A part of me froze. I couldn't look at Mom. "That's what it is, isn't it?"

I was looking out the door as I said, "I don't want to talk about it."

"Then I'm right?"

"I don't want to talk about it! I let you down and Dad let me down."

"Chad, you didn't let me down! Don't think like that. Look, I wish it never happened, but I can't make it go away. Everything's healed, that'll heal on its own. You've got to put those memories and emotions away. I've tried to explain to you." The thought of everything about that night brought the emotions in me exploding through the dams I'd built.

"Yeah, you did and he didn't. Gotta go." I started walking out the door.

Mom followed and said louder, "You didn't let me down! Chad!"

I wasn't turning around. She stayed on the porch and let me go. As I turned to go out the lane, I heard her reluctantly say, "See ya."

How *Do* you play the Game of Life?

I don't like to think about that event at all. I was such a goof and it reminds me of the goof that's still inside. Moving away from the house kind of helped me restrain the rushing emotions that had broken through. The walk out to the end of the lane finished the sealing job and the dams were back to full strength. I was still a little bit worked up from my conversation with Mom, but now that I was away from the house, I thought back to Heather. It was such a relief to put my mind on less stressful things. Well, not less stressful, but definitely more enjoyable.

I tried to remember exactly what expression she had on her face when I had asked her the big question. I could remember it pretty well, but interpreting that expression was a near impossibility, as long as I tried to remain objective. There are a number of different ways to analyze her expression to determine what she was thinking. For instance she could be thinking, one: surprise, either good surprise (she's glad I asked her) or bad surprise (whoa, I've been sending him the wrong signals). Two: shock, which is kinda like bad surprise, (oh my reputation, he's going to humiliate me). Three: concern (boy, I'm going to have a hard time letting him down easy on this). These interpretations are all plausible, but I couldn't figure which was more likely. It all depended on my frame of mind.

If I was confident about how things went and confident in my sexual suave self, which is a definite negative, good surprise would be my interpretation. Since I'm pretty pathetic when it comes to the whole dating thing, I was leaning more towards bad surprise or shock, maybe even concern. I was still hoping for good surprise, but that was the kind of thing that happens in my dreams not in real life. The objective truth of the matter is that any of the interpretations could be true. Once I get myself involved, that's when one becomes more likely than the others.

Now, a guy like Patrick would have a very different reaction. In fact, he'd probably be able to come up with a couple different interpretations I hadn't even considered. Like, lust (Oh, I want him so bad) or ectasy (Yes, yes, he asked me), and probably a couple others I'll have to censor for decency.

I guess the same problem of interpretation with Heather applies to my Dad and me. If you get a bunch of Dad's buddies they'd all agree he was doing the right thing with me. He's only expecting a little return on all he's done for me, they'd say. They certainly wouldn't see Dad as the mean oppressive pain in the ass that I do. The fact is, I could just as easily find a bunch of people I know who could support my interpretation. Randy would definitely understand, and so would Dale, but, even though they're both good friends, they're no different than Dad's buddies. Randy and Dale share my perspective on the situation just as Dad and his buddies share another perspective. Now this is all great and everything, but who's got the right perspective?

I'd say I do, but Dad'd say the same thing. I really feel that my side holds a lot of weight, but I can acknowledge that Dad does have a few decent points. Wow, I can't believe I just thought that. Frankly, I don't know who's right. I just want some respect and I don't get that anywhere else. It'd be nice if my own Dad could help me out.

Life's too complicated to try to reason your way to a yes or no / true or false answer. As much as I believe I've got a very valid argument and Dad's got his head full of rocks, it's not that simple (Dad does have his head full of rocks). The truth is something that each of us creates for ourselves. Because we're so full of differences, the truth for each person must be different. Two people will never think the same way. Truth is a dream that we try to make believe into reality.

Mom had gotten me thinking more about what the truth was for Dad, not just myself. I only wanted to be angry with him because he wasn't understanding my side. I didn't want to think about the actual argument in an open and logical way. Dad never tries to understand or appreciate any of the things I wanted to do, so I fought back. I never really thought Dad needed my understanding and appreciation. Dad's Dad; he always seems to be above those kind of needs. Maybe he felt that I started the whole thing, and he, like me, was fighting back. Everything becomes a lot more complicated when you try to put yourself in someone else's shoes. It's a lot easier to just make your judgements and not worry about the rest.

Maybe?

BEEP! BEEP!

"Holy shit!" I yelled, nearly jumping into the tree by the side of the lane.

Randy started laughing hysterically in his low deep voice. He said, "I got you good. Huh, huh, jeez you nearly jumped out of your clothes, huh huh."

"If I was a cat I would be clinging to the highest branch on that tree." I grabbed my stuff and got into Randy's beat-up Ford. When I say beat-up I mean this thing has been through it all. There're more dents than smooth spots. The interior reeks of cigarettes. Even with both windows down going about seventy, you can't hide from that odor. There's no carpeting on the inside. This truck is from the olden days when all you got were four wheels and an engine. Despite the worn look, it's a great truck because it's tough. Randy's dad definitely got his money out of this baby.

We pulled out with a loud roar and grinding of gears. Randy was still laughing. I said, "Look, man, it's over. It wasn't that funny."

"Oh yes it was," and he broke down laughing again. He could hardly drive.

I sarcastically said, "Would you like me to grab the wheel so you can get all of your laughing out?"

He calmed himself down and replied, "No, I'm all right. It's just you just had to'f seen your face." He was struggling to keep himself from laughing some more. Finally he let out a big sigh and shook his head. "You sure looked deep in thought."

"Yeah I was."

"What were you thinking about?"

"Oh, Dad and I. You know how things are. Mom said some things that got me thinking. I don't know why I've got to be the rational one. I don't think Dad worries about it."

"I thought you might be thinking about something else."

"Yeah," I chuckled to myself. "I started off thinking about her. How bad did I look?"

"Holy shit cow! Man, I couldn't believe you did that."

"Dale put me up to it. He's been on my case, keeps saying that I need to take chances if I really want to get anywhere. I just hope I didn't scare away a really nice person to talk with."

"Shoot, I don't think you did. Man, I think you landed yourself a date. Now, I mean I ain't too good with the womenfolk, but I think she's going to give you the ole' green light, the okey dokey, the ole' yes sir ree no I don't mean maybe – let's do it – di do di do do do. Uh-ch-ah-ah-ch-ah-ah. . . ah-ah. Uh-ch-ah-ah-ch-ah-ah. . . ah-ah."

"Please, don't rap for me. You really think she wants to go?"

"Like I said I ain't the best judge but I think she thought you were cute being so nervous and the way everything went down."

"Oh, just great. I'm cute. It didn't happen even remotely like I planned."

"Well I think that's what surprised her so much. You were just doing from your heart cause you didn't have time to think things out. Wish I had the guts to do it."

"Randy, if I get a date outta this, anybody can get a date." Even with Randy's reassurance, I still didn't want to believe it until I knew for certain. I didn't want to get my hopes crushed, but it was something to think about. When I was stumbling up that aisle I felt like everyone was just laughing their butts off. Here's this sophomore who's acting like some fifth grader giving a girl a chocolate heart as a valentine's day gift – cute. Great, that's just how I wanted to be perceived. I'm sure in the hands of the football gods it would do wonders for my popularity. The image of me being silly "cute" made me cringe at my embarrassment. I wanted to close my eyes and try to erase the whole thing from my memory. However, as bad as it was, the big but was a yes. Dale always had a way of being right about girls. He seemed to always offer the right advice. A yes would make things a lot better. I may have been a fool, but if I got a yes it wouldn't matter. A yes, what a dream!

Everything works right in my dreams. I know what to say. The girls are impressed with me instead of afraid of me. They laugh at my jokes and love my honesty and devotion, but I can't live in those dreams. Sometimes I've thought about how great it would be to die, that maybe I could live in those dreams for once. Nothing in life compares to dreams, and how could it. Dreams are perfect. I've always wanted my dreams to leak into reality, but till now none ever came close. To think they could was none-sense thinking that only set me up to be harshly crushed. After what Randy had said, however, I was having a hard time containing my hope that this one time a dream could come to life.

I said, "Now let me get this straight, your objective opinion, you really think she'll say yes?"

"Yes!" and he started to laugh again. "Why's that so hard to believe. You've got the stuff and you're smart."

"So, it has to be my horrible popularity, and my terrible personality that created it, which keep me out."

"Or maybe just a bad attitude. I really think it's going to work with Heather."

"I guess." As I replied, we had caught up to a monster Lincoln towncar. I muttered, "Great, it's the Sunday cruiser on a Wednesday."

"I guess we're going to be a little late."

"Yeah, I guess. You know there should be a law against this. The grandpappies don't care that people have things to do. The old foggie is probably thinking, 'why's everybody in such a rush, always hurrying around. Somebody's gonna get hurt.'

"I swear, when I get old I'm not gonna drive like that."

"I swear with you. Do you think you can pass him?"

"I don't know, man. This truck isn't the newest thing in the world."

"After the turn by Shady's Church you can get him. We'll just have to hope there's not a lot of traffic. Do you think we have any luck?"

"Sure, we do."

"Well, if Heather's going to say yes, I'm all out."

"I never used none so I should have enough for the both of us."

It took a few seconds to reach the bend in the road. As Randy completed the turn, we both looked to see if it was clear.

I laughed and said, "Ha, we do have some luck." Randy dropped it down with a loud grind and a painful roar came from the engine. It wasn't too hard of a pass. The old fart was going that slow. Randy probably didn't even need to drop it down, but he's a little nervous driving his Dad's truck.

I pretended to yell out the window as we speeded past, "Why don't you live a little and go the speed limit." Randy shifted up and we pulled back into our own lane. I said, "Look at him shaking his head. He's probably saying we're a bunch of nuts."

"I don't know, if this truck would've blown up I would've felt like a nut, and when I got home I would've been a crushed nut."

"Ahh, we had it easy. The old folks are so worried about dying that they aren't living anymore."

"I swear I ain't gonna be like that. I'm goin' out with a bang. Y'know?"

"That's the way to do it, whether you're a hundred or forty. You never know when your time's up, so why worry about it."

Things to Do
And a Night to Forget Them

Track practice was especially fun; normally, that's not the case. I live for competition, but believing I was going to get a yes had me excited about everything. Running sprints was effortless. After two hours of exhausting work, we finished up and Randy and I were back in the truck on the way home. We were both beat so we didn't say a whole lot. I thanked him for the ride when he dropped me off at the end of the lane. Usually he'd drive back and drop me off at my door, but I told him I'd walk back. I wanted to think a little and enjoy the evening that was beginning to break with a mighty roar of color.

Tonight was exceptionally clear. The horizon looked like a volcano had thrown fiery baseballs across the sky. This wall of red thinned high into the sky as it collided with the first few stars that had come out to watch the spectacle. A night like that makes you think about life. How effortlessly nature creates sights with such power and beauty. When I look at the stars, I wonder where I'm supposed to fit. What is destiny?

I wish other students would be serious enough to want to think about these issues. We argue about who's the coolest, which sports team's the best, and who's going with who to the prom. What a waste of time compared to a sunset, compared to the wondrous things that I seem to rarely notice. A simple date is really puny in comparison. What I don't understand is why I can think that but not feel it. I can tell myself it's puny, but it feels so monumental.

When I look at a sunset, or any magical event in nature, I see all the wonder that is just begging to be understood. Every person has a sense of exploration, but this is gone in my parents. It's about surviving for them. I think growing up makes people focus on the most uninspiring things. I don't want to give up my dreams and become so hardened that I no longer notice, but I can feel it happening. I need nights like tonight to remind me to look around. As horrible as things seem for me sometimes, I still can wonder at the beauty of nature and I still have my dreams. I don't know how I could survive without them. Regardless of what happens with Heather, or any other girl, I will always have those two things. I will never give them up.

When I look up at those magnificent stars glowing like the cracks in a blanket, I see the possibility of my own life. Someone told me once that when you live in a big city you can't see the stars at night. That's such a symbol for the world we've constructed. We're so consumed in our own all-unimportant daily construction of personal wealth we've built places that block out the stars. We think we know so much. I think of the differences that are out there and I laugh at the differences we concern ourselves with. If I could run the show, the goal of government would be exploration and learning. NASA would probably have the biggest budget, and if you've ever seen a picture of this planet from the moon you'd understand why.

Chapter Five
H-Hour +05:00 Hrs.
Security Has Been Compromised!

It felt good to think about things so much bigger than finding a girlfriend. It's like jumping into a lake on a scorching hot day. I wish I had the time and forethought to watch a sunset everyday. I reached the house. All of my great thoughts came to an end because Dad's truck was in the driveway. I was just about to begin a war bickering over stupid unimportant things. Time to put the big picture way back in a gallery again. Like I said, I wish I could live life the way it was meant.

I walked up onto the porch and dropped my running shoes off outside to let the fresh air get at them. I pulled the screen door open with that loud screech and walked in. The door slammed behind me. Dad was at the table with a cup of coffee and Mom was at the sink doing dishes. Dad can drink coffee at any time of the day. He probably drinks several pots of it on his own, and then he can still fall asleep the absolute second nine O'clock hits. Since it was about seven now, I knew he wouldn't be able to give me hell for too long. Dad had on his trusty old John Deer hat that was slightly off center. I have no idea why he can't put his hat on straight. He gives me hell for wearing mine backwards, but I think wearing it crooked is a whole lot dumber.

The hat is dirty, greasy, worn, and beat-up. You name it because that hat has been through it. On deer hunts, out fishing, four-wheeling, farming, fixing the tractor, changing the oil, even coming to see my track meets. Dad lives in that hat. It embodies his whole world. His jeans were a little dirty with a bunch of patches on them where Mom had fixed the holes. His white socks were mostly brown now.

He didn't move when I came in. It seemed to me that Mom and Dad were probably discussing me until that me person just walked through the door. I dropped my track bag next to one of the seats at the table and walked over to the sink to get a drink.

Dad asked, "So, how was practice?" Now I guess I'm supposed to assume that remark is Dad's attempt at being understanding. Mom says he's trying. However, the only reason I assume that is because he didn't rip me apart. All my feelings of relaxation that had come from the walk were now gone. In fact, they were gone as soon as I entered the house. Dad's remark seemed like getting a BB gun when you wanted a 12 gauge.

I replied nonchalantly, "It went pretty well. You know, practice is practice."

I think Mom detected that it was a bit chilly, so she tried to lighten things up. "You're probably going to make districts this year, aren't you Chad?"

"Yeah, I should, as long as I keep working hard."

Dad said, after he took a sip of coffee, "That's good."

Things started to get ugly when Mom said, "There was a phone call for you while you were at practice. The call came just a little while after you left. A girl named Heather."

Every part of my body was screaming 'SON OF A BITCH! NOW THE SHIT'S REALLY HITTING THE FAN!' I had absolutely no desire for my parents to know about my love life. I give them the least amount of information. So far that hadn't been a problem because I didn't have any. This was a disaster about to happen. I was just waiting for Mom to get some little smile on her face as if to say, 'Oh my little boy's going on his first date.' That was gonna make me puke.

I tried to down play the whole situation. "Oh she called." How in the hell did she get my number?

"Yeah, she seems like a real nice girl." I swear my parents have no tact. What Mom was really saying was, 'It's about time that you start dating girls so your father can put to rest that his son isn't also a homo as well as a nigger lover.'

I cut Mom off and said, "Mom, just stop, OK. I'll handle my own affairs."

"Oh look at this. Our boy doesn't want his parents is his love life." Yeah she knew I didn't want her there.

Dad laughed and then asked, "So, is she pretty?"

"Yes she's very pretty which is why this is nothing. I don't even know if I'll be able to even get a date out of her."

Dad replied, "Well, now I do believe you'll be able to do that."

I shot of terror went up my spine: they knew more than I did about my own date. They were right in the middle of all the juicy details, but even worse, it seemed like they were a couple steps ahead of me. I pretended to be dumb and asked, "Why do you say that?"

"Tell him, Honey."

"She called to say that she'd love to go out with you on Friday." This was supposed to be the most exciting news I'd ever heard, but coming through a second party, which happened to be my parents, was sort of like getting cafeteria food at an expensive restaurant. This was feeling more horrible by the minute.

Dad asked, "Where you gonna go? Them lady folk like to be treated real nice." He smiled and winked at Mom who just shook her head. It made me sick. I can't understand how Dad can be so nice to Mom. The contrast made that cafeteria food in my stomach turn rancid. Now my parents were going to help me plan my date! Oh, boy. Why not go bowling, honey? You can bring her over and teach her how to use the shit spreader. That'll be fun.

There was no way to avoid them. I replied, "I think we'll go out to eat and maybe to a movie. I don't know, I didn't plan all of this out. It was sort of spur of the moment." I did not want to sit here discussing dating ideas with two people who were my age, ages ago.

"Going out to eat is nice," Mom replied.

Dad added, "Well, I hope you have a good time. Saturday and Sunday I need you here on the farm. I'm going to need help getting the plowing done. If the machines stay together I want to turn the fields up and disc all of it this weekend. The weather looks like it should be good, at least through Sunday. It's time to get goin'. I've still got to get down to Jim Williams' house and over to the Shadel's yet, and then we might even start planting next weekend." There was no way the machines were going to hold together. When we worked in the fields we spent more time working on the machines than we did actually farming. Dad had too much land to work with for such old and unreliable equipment.

I replied, "We have a campout this weekend with the Boyscouts. We're going over to the woods behind Mr. Enders' house again. I haven't gone to a weekend campout in like forever. Can't it wait until next weekend?"

"The weather's good this weekend. I'm not takin' a chance waitin' any longer. It seems like it rains every day. I can't chance the opportunity of clear weather. You'll have to stay home." Yeah what a surprise, I thought. This was the story of my life. I can't have a life because I have to ask Dad for permission. God may give you life, but after that he's sort of phased out of the process.

Dad easily realized that I wasn't too happy. "Don't give me that pissed off look. If we want to eat than I need help. Lord knows that tractor's going to break again and I'll need help fixing it." It was always a fun time when the tractor broke. Dad would get madder and madder and his frustration always landed on me. We'd both end up screaming at each other.

I muttered, "Great." That comment was just enough to break Dad's good humor. He exploded.

"I tell you what, boy. You need to get some Goddamn respect. Your Mom and I work pretty hard around here."

"What's wrong with Becky?"

"There ain't nothing wrong with your sister, 'cept she ain't never helped with the plowing before and I don't have the time to teach her this year."

Mom said, "Don't bring your sister into this Chad. She works hard too and she definitely helps around the house." The way I saw it Becky had it great. She had a social life because she was allowed to go and do things. Dad never pulled the high road on her. Yeah, she had her chores, but her chores were flexible. Mine were immediate and prescheduled by Dad, and he always took my weekends.

I said, "Well, I need to get down to Deluice on Sunday. I need a new pair of track shoes."

Dad yelled, "What! And just what in the hell do you need new shoes for? The ones you got are brand new."

I was pretty worked up, so I sharply replied, "Well, maybe you should've bought good ones, then I wouldn't need another pair."

Mom replied, "Chad!" The shock on her face reminded me about the talk we'd had. Even as mad as I was, I felt bad. Dad pushed his coffee away from him and rubbed his wrist across his forehead as he lifted his hat and then placed back onto his head, crooked of course. "I bought the ones the guy said were the best."

"Well I need a new pair." Mom was giving me a look that said, 'come on, apologize.' "You probably got the good one's. I've been doing a lot of running. I wore them out, but no matter what, I need a new pair."

"And who's payin for that?"

"Well, I sure can't. I never have time for a job."

"Yeah, I'm payin' for 'em. It wouldn't be such a big deal if you weren't such a pain in the ass to try and get to do any work around here."

"You wouldn't have to pay for them if you'd just let me have some time so I can get a job."

Dad pulled his cup back in front of him and poured himself another. "You just don't get it. Your mother and I bust our butts' everyday for you and Becky and you can't even muster an ounce of thanks. All you can do is complain about what you don't have. Well, buddy, get used to it cause no matter what you do have there'll always be somethin' you don't. Like if you've got a Chevy you'll want a Ford," a big shitty grin cracked his face. "Just imagine how bad you'd feel drivin' one of those hunday thing'ies." Mom was smiling and Dad was starting to laugh. I didn't want to smile for one second. I hate when Dad makes a joke when I'm trying to be serious. It's Dad's way of getting the last word. How am I supposed to make any point after he does that? I tried not to smile but it wasn't easy. Then Dad said poorly imitating a Japanese Kung Fu movie, "AHHH Hundayeeeeee," and he did a couple of chops with his hand.

I said, "It's a good thing you're a farmer."

Dad replied, "What, I not scare you?"

"How do you explain this one oh wise master. If people who buy 'hundays' envy every other car owner, then how should I feel, I've got my bicycle?"

"Ahh, I see my son. Hmm, much to learn, much to learn. Y'see my son before learn fly, learn walk. Before crusin' learn peddlin'."

I couldn't help but smile. It was over. My attempt to make any point had passed. This is what frustrates me. No real agreement was ever really made because there was no real discussion, but you better believe he expected me up bright and early on Saturday morning to start working. So even though I was laughing, it was a forced laugh that irritated me as it came out. Dad always uses jokes to break the tension in discussions. He's funny, but we never agree on anything. He cuts the tension before we've pulled the truck out of the mud, if you catch my drift.

I replied, "Thank you oh wise one."

Becky yelled down from upstairs, "What's going on down there?"

Mom yelled back, "Your father, that's what's going on." Mom was having a good laugh. I think it's Dad's joking ability that Mom really likes. He's always been able to make her laugh, even when he's also been able to make her cry.

Dad was trying to move stealthily over to Mom. He said, "You must be the Princess I am to find, hee ya."

I said, "This is sick, I'm getting a shower."

Mom replied, "What's sick?" Dad was already wrapping his big burly arms around her as she laughed like crazy. As tough as Mom is, she really needs those kind of moments with Dad. It's Dad's softer side that just thrills her. That's what came back and that's the West Virginia chrome that fixed everything up between them. But, I needed and wanted more than a crappy tape job. Dad and I needed to seriously talk about a lot of things.

I was just about to climb the stairs when Dad barked, "Not before you do what I told you to do this morning." I didn't reply. "You could'a did it right after school."

"He was talking with me, Erik."

"Get going." I gritted my teeth hard and went up the stairs.

I yelled, "I'm getting pants," because I know he was going to say something. I grabbed an old pair of work pants from my room and put my knife and match container in the pockets. Then I came back downstairs. I didn't look at either of them. I slammed on my boots and smashed the door on my way out. What a bunch of shit. Moving 50 pound bags of fertilizer and chemicals, what a blast. Almost as much fun as throwing hay bales in the summertime or shoveling shit outta the stalls.

I walked in the barn and flipped on the light. The lights I'd wired, none-the-less. That was another job Dad had me help with. The cows immediately looked nonchalantly my way. I couldn't contain my frustration any longer.

"Son of a bitch bunch of fucking bull shit." I grabbed an empty bucket and threw it down the barn. It rattled with a loud clang. The cows looked at the bucket and then back at me. I flipped open my pocketknife and cut the banding and plastic away from the big packs of chemicals, fertilizer, and God knows whatever else was in the pile. I considered pulling out my matches and seeing what I could do with those. Whoops, barn burnt down. The cows continued to watch me. "Yeah this is pretty fuckin funny isn't." They didn't offer a reply. I yanked one sack on my shoulder and flipped another onto my other. The anger welled inside of me and then exploded. I ran the length of the barn as fast as I could growling all the way and threw them hard against the back way. "Fuck'en bull shit!" I picked one up again and threw it against the wall and then kicked it. I could feel the anger still seething inside of me, as I put my hands on my hips and turned around. All the cows were watching.

Then one of them called, "Mooo." For some reason that cow's moo started to crack me up. I must admit I've always loved animals. They're so simple and pure with their emotions. They just like you or they don't. There's no head games. I cracked a smile and walked over to her.

"Now to most people the sound you just made was just a cow mooing, but Jimmy Dean I know that Moooo means, 'I'm hungry God damn it, so feed my ass.' We named her Jimmy Dean because this cow had the amazing ability to get dirtier than a pig. She could get herself looken' like a mess.

I mean just like a pig, so hence we figured she wasn't happy with her life as a cow and she really wanted to end up in a Jimmy Dean sausage roll. "Well, I wish all girls were as easy to talk to as you, baby." I rubbed her nose. As I walked down the row going back to the pile of stuff I had to move, the cows took turns nudging me with their noses and mooing. "Y'see what you started. I wonder if I refused to feed Heather, would she be as affectionate as you ladies?"

It took me about half an hour to finish carrying the sacks of shit to the other end of the barn. The cows watched the whole time. Now it was time to feed them. At least I get to tell you about one of my inventions. We used to just carry the feed in buckets and dump them into the trough, but there are a lot of cows. That meant a lot of trips back and forth from the feed bin carrying heavy buckets. So, I created a pulley system that I built and hung from the ceiling.

Dad wasn't in favor of the idea because he figured it wouldn't work, but he was pretty impressed when it did. We had been working with pulleys for a month or two at scout meetings. Mr. Enders had each of the patrols create some kind of useful device using a pulley. I came up with the idea of using it in the barn. After I talked Dad into it, Dale and I built it and hooked it up. It works real well and it's been working real well for over a year. The best way is to have two people. One at the feed bin filling the buckets and one at the other end dumping them. I got to do both jobs.

I filled a bucket with feed and locked it into place on the transport rope. Then, I released a clamp, which allowed a weight to fall. I'd properly balanced the weight so its rate of decent wouldn't pull the bucket too fast. The weight could be stopped with a lever so you could hold the bucket anywhere along the line. I let it go all the way to the end as I started walking down that way. It cracked to a stop as the weight hit the ground. I unhooked the bucket and poured it into the trough. Now I was the cows' best friend. They just watched with those empty eyes, until it was their turn. In their own way they said thank you. It took another half an hour to an hour to do all the feeding. All the exercise burnt off some of my frustration. I didn't do anything extra like picking up the plastic shrink rap and ties. I did precisely what I was ordered too. I clomped back to the house to find Dad was out; his hour had struck. I flipped off my shoes and went up stairs for a shower.

My Dreams

The shower felt real good. I did some schoolwork and listened to some music before I hit the sack. That night I dreamed about my dream. I thought about where my life would be in the next four years. The day when I would get my scholarship for track and leave this town for the real world. It was hard to truly believe that one day I could be a part of the real world; that people would see me as just one of them, or even admire me. The day when I'd be the one on the poster hanging in some kid's house instead of Michael Johnson hanging in my room. I wanted all of that to come true so bad that believing it could come true seemed as impossible to grasp as a shadow. Me being that. I wondered how many people thought I was out of my mind. My parents didn't believe it. It's just a stage he'll grow out of, that's probably what they thought.

People think they can see something special when it's around them and I don't qualify. I think being special is a bunch of crap. I have to believe that if I want to have any chance at my dream. I'm not special; I know that. But for some reason, despite all of my doubts, I believe in my dream. Maybe that's what's special, but for me, it's not about specialness, or feeling that I've had this calling all of my life. It's about working for what I want and making it happen. Specialness isn't a gift like everybody else thinks. I think it's a reward for trying to achieve your dream each and everyday of your life. If you don't have a dream or you don't try, you'll never be special. Life's not a total loss. There are always a lot of fun things you can do, but most people just bob up and down in the ocean of life. I want to get up on my surfboard and ride the half pipe. I may get crushed, but as long as I can get back up, I'll keep trying. When it's all said and done, I might have risked it all and have nothing to show for it, but that's just about what I have now so what's the difference? Besides, I should just be lucky enough that I can even consider such dreams. Most people in the world are just trying to stay alive.

I think, more than anything, what I want is to be able to come back home and have my classmates say, 'You know, I never thought that Chad would've – blank – but there was something about him.' That's what I want them to say, and that's what I dreamed about that night.

That, and Heather. Like a backup actress she stepped into my dreams. Not that she hadn't been in there before, but now she was the leading role in every dream I had. I dreamt about what are date would be like, provided we had one. My relationship with Heather was perfect in my dreams but the reality of the yes I had apparently gotten was so much more intense, more intense than I ever realized it could be– like those fireballs in the sky. The euphoria I felt from such a simple word made me dream dreams more exciting and real than they ever were before. However, even though I enjoyed them, I couldn't create that awesome energy that came from that moment when Randy told me he thought she was going to say yes. My dreams were great, but I found myself, for the first time, wanting real life.

Then again, when my parents screamed me out of my sleep the next morning as usual and I opened my eyes to my room, I wasn't so sure anymore. Reality greeted me like usual, with a laugh and a slap across the face.

Chapter Six
The Things a Girl can Do

I got ready in my usual fashion, ate a quick breakfast, and made my way out the lane. I made sure I didn't forget my track uniform. I have a habit of doing things like that. Like usual, I also made sure I had my Swiss army knife and matches. I wasn't sure if I should be confident or worried as I waited for the bus, but I was definitely worried. I attempted a smile for Mrs. Willabough when she arrived. She returned a cool arctic grin. It seemed like it took me hours to reach my seat. It was like I was walking through knee-deep mud. Heather was reading something. I sat down and our eyes met. We both smiled and looked away. Was she waiting for me? I think we both wanted to break the ice, but neither of us seemed able to get it going. Being the guy, I felt obligated to ask the question that would get the no or the yes that I needed to confirm. I fidgeted with my bag for a little. I said to myself, OK on three then I'll start to talk: one, two, three.

I blurted out, "Hey Heather, how ya doin'?" That was safe enough.

She replied, "Pretty good, I still have some homework to finish up."

"Like what?" I said to keep the conversation going.

She replied, "We have to read this section and search for evidence . . ." She continued talking and I continued to look like I was listening, but my mind wanted to get to the good stuff.

When she finished talking about her work I said, "Ah, about yesterday,"

"Yeah, yesterday."

"I guess I surprised you."

"Yeah, surprised."

"I sort of surprised myself with the whole thing."

"So, you didn't mean what you asked about?"

"No, no, no I mean I didn't think I was going to get it out. Ahh the truth is I thought I just ruin a nice friendship, or just having a nice girl that I could talk to. So did I do that?"

A smile curled on her face. She seemed flattered. "No, of course you didn't."

"So, does that mean you want to, you know. . ."

"That would be great," she laughed and smiled some more. Wow, I didn't get a no or a yes, I got a 'that would be great.' I felt like I was going to explode. Dale was going to go nuts. She added, "Didn't you get my message?"

"Yeah, but I just wanted to make sure. My Dad can be a real jokester. How did you get my number?"

"I have my sources."

"And that would be?"

"I have my sources."

"I see."

"So, what did you have in mind?" It was still sinking in for me. This was really for real. I mean really. What did I have in mind? Well, that wasn't an easy question. I'd been thinking about that non-stop.

- 85 -

I replied, "Well, I was thinking dinner and a movie. It'll have to be Friday night, tomorrow night, because my Dad wants me working on the farm all day Saturday, major bummer, but the old fart isn't going to budge. So, I really hope that's cool for you. I understand it's short notice and everything. Ahh, what d'you like to eat? Whoops, I mean how's Friday?"

"Chad, it will be fine. I'll have to clear it with the authorities, if you know what I mean, but they'll deal with it. For the second question, it doesn't matter." I looked confused. She continued gently laughing again, "About where we eat."

"Great, that's great." I tried to keep my composure, but inside I was doing the dance of joy. Here was another moment. Now I was the one laughing. For some reason all my frustration with everything was just gone. We were going to go out on a date. Ya'know, a real dream. I said, "How about an Outback Steakhouse and then we'll just pick a movie from there." That'll just about clean me out of money I was thinking, but so what! I still had some money from Easter somewhere in my room. I always get a little something on holidays from Grandparents and the like.

She replied, "That's sounds like fun." The bus had reached the school and everyone was getting their stuff together. Heather was fumbling with her jacket, school bag, and the homework she'd been working on. I decided to keep going with the assertive thing.

I said, "Can I help you with your stuff?"

"No, no I should be fine."

"Ahh, come on humor a gentlemen. "Me lady it t'would be my pleasure to escort thee unto thy locker whilst assisting with thy bags." She paused and looked at me with a sort of happy defeat on her face and then she held her bag out. I grabbed it with a smile and helped her put on her jacket. We were the last ones on the bus. As we started walking down the aisle, I caught a glimpse of Randy standing outside the main door. He smiled and gave me a wink and a thumbs up sign before he went in to the school. Just to walk with Heather made me feel like I was someone special. I felt so high inside that I knew at that moment what a kite feels like. Heather was the wonderful wind that whirled me through the sky. God, how great it would be to just fly away. I tried to avoid thoughts about Saturday with Dad.

I wondered what Heather was feeling. I imagine this wasn't hardly anything to her. Just being nice to a nice but awkward guy. I knew there was no way we'd go anywhere together, but I blocked that out of my mind as well. Everything was perfect, even if some of it was a dream. I really wanted to feel that great thing called love. To be with a girl who appreciated me as much as I appreciated her. It must be wonderful soaring through the clouds like that, and for a few brief moments I was feeling the freedom of rocketing up through the white and into the sun. I couldn't help but smile as we exited the bus.

Mrs. Wilabough dryly said, "You must like this bus. I can never get you off of it," and a chilled smile froze on her face. Heather and I both laughed and made our way into the school.

I said, "That lady gives me the creeps."

Heather replied, "I bet her favorite holiday is Holloween."

"Yeah, then she fits in." We walked through the main doors and started walking down to her locker.

I asked, "So how long are you going to be riding the bus?"

"Oh, I don't know. At least until I can drive, but maybe longer. We have an old car I could use, but the way my parents are I don't know if that's going to be an option. What about you?"

"Me thinks I'll be there till the glorious day of my graduation. We don't have a car I can use and Dad doesn't allow me the time to get a job to buy my own. I'm stuck. My best friend Dale, do you know him?"

"Yeah, not to really know him, but I know who he is."

"Well, he's got a car, but we're at opposite ends of town. He'd give me a ride, but I don't want to make him run out of his way, but that might be the only way I won't be a senior still riding the bus."

"Come on, it's not that bad."

"For my reputation it sure is, but the people are nice." We reached her locker.

I said, "There me lady. I do believe this is the destination."

"Sure is a bit dull."

"Ahh, but this is the best locker in the whole school."

"Why's that?"

"Because it's yours."

She smiled and playfully replied, "Thanks, Chad." It seemed to me that she really enjoyed my compliment. I thought it was complete cheese. Not that I didn't mean what I said, but it just seemed too much. If I told Dale what I'd just said he would groan. It's the type of thing that would make any guy groan. It seems kind of silly being all mushy like that. That's why I felt really stupid saying it. I wasn't being a "tough guy." I was being a real feeling person and for some reason that's uncomfortable for every guy I know. The worst is being seen by other guys while you're opening your heart like that. I was taking a chance. Someone could hear me, or see me. I tried not to think about the risk. It wasn't too hard because the smile my compliment drew made me soar inside.

I teased her by saying, "Look, you're smiling again. Can't handle compliments?" I wanted to gently touch her cheek with my finger, but that was way too much for me to try. My hand came up a little but I just rubbed my forehead and put it back in my coat pocket where it had been since we left the bus. What a silly thought that was. This wasn't some movie or something. I'd gotten a little too high on all of this. I let my brain remind my emotions of the reality of this situation.

She replied, "Thanks for the compliment. You're really sweet." As far as I was concerned this compliment thing was great. I think she really meant it. I was doing loop de loops in the clouds now. Once again, I reminded myself that it was time for a nice exit so I didn't crash and burn. I needed to give my luck a chance to build back up. So far everything was going well, just too well for anything I could've put together. I had this sixth sense that I needed to get out of there. If I could get away without doing something stupid, the rest of the day would be great.

I said, "Well, I'd like to escort you around all day but I's got to go'n gets me en' edjucation. Mamma always said I's not one for smarts." We both laughed and I took a few steps back.

She gracefully said, "See ya' Chad," and waved a little before I turned and walked down the hall. Holy shitballs, I was in the zone. I have no idea why she enjoyed my company and laughed at my jokes, but whatever I ate for breakfast I was going to do it again and again for the rest of my life. In fact, I took a mental note of everything I was wearing. This was definitely my lucky outfit. The whole thing had gone really well. As I was walking away, I wanted to make sure I didn't trip or slip or do something else really stupid. Y'know, just get out of sight and hold it together. I was flying so fast that the intensity of the speed was starting to scare me. It was working too well. I came smacking into the wall I was worried about because Patrick was waiting a few steps away just as I turned the corner. The vulture was ready to pounce and he had an audience – football buddies, the best kind. I kept walking and he kept following.

Reality and Dreams Indistinguishable

"Oh, my my my Chad I'm impressed. You're moving in on some high-class stuff there. Are you breaking from your homosexual ways?"

I shouldn't have bothered to enter a discussion with him, but I did anyhow. "I'm not gay, can't you just lay off?"

"Ahh, can't you just lay off."

"Why d'you always have to be on my case?"

"I'm not! I'm impressed with your selection in women. We're all impressed. Good luck there tiger. I want the gory details if you hit the homerun."

"I'm not after a homerun. We're just going on a date."

"Oh, a date. Yee haw cowboy. Just take em' some place nice and keep pump em' full of compliments and you'll be getting' some hits, if you know what I mean," He most thoughtfully illustrated his pelvic thrust for me. His goons we're falling apart with laughter. "Well, gotta to go. Good luck there Chippy, and remember, colored trojans." His buddies gave me various sarcastic wishes of good luck. Patrick started to walk the other way down the hall as he said, "Hey, if you're not doing anything Saturday afternoon, come on over. We're going to play some paintball."

"Thanks, but Dad has me working this weekend." He shrugged his shoulders and he and his boys were gone.

At least it was over. I wanted to see Dale, but I needed to get to class right away. I didn't even have time to go to my locker. I raced into English a few seconds late. I was starting to make shocking my English classmates a regular occurrence. I was never late. Once again everyone was looking at me, but it didn't faze me. Nothing seemed to matter. I was already feeling the confidence kick Dale was talking about. It was awesome. I needed to have that track meet right now, I thought. I would be flying. I felt so good, I even talked a little bit in English class, two days of class contributions. The things a girl can do.

Later in the day, I did meet-up with Dale. He kept saying, "I told you so." I had to admit he'd been right. I agreed to make up for his helpful service later on. I really felt like I was on a team with Dale and Randy. When something went well with one of us, it was great for the others. Dale and Randy were friends, but it was more. I was connected to both of them. I loved hearing Dale's women stories. When we could arrange it, one of us would stay over at the other's house and Dale'd always have a good story to tell. We would talk about a lot, at least an hour before we went to bed. Now it was my turn to get to tell a story. It felt cool, real cool. Dale's a good buddy. He was as excited for me as he'd be if he was the one who'd gotten the big break. If things were reversed, I'd be the same way. I guess that's why were such good friends.

I had a lot of things I needed to plan, and Dale was a big help. The two big questions were what movie to see? And, God, what to say? Dale liked my choice of the Outback, even if it was a little expensive. We figured a comedy would be a good movie choice. As for conversation, I planned to start with a simple break the ice hello and maybe a nice compliment about how she looked, you know, something nice. Then I'd try to make some small talk about sports. From there I'd just have to see where things went. I didn't want to be too restrictive with my plan. I'd just have to roll with the punches. I figured I'd probably have to pick the movie because I figured that she figured that since I made the move she would figure it was my job to make the decisions. At least that's what I figured. If she wanted to make suggestions, that would be great. It would save me a whole lot of mental anguish.

The rest of the day seemed a blur, and utterly meaningless in comparison to what was on my mind. I got out of school a half-hour early to leave with the track team to go to our meet. I thought everything over during the bus ride. It's unbelievable. I had to remind myself that it was real. At the track meet I broke my best time in the 100 meter and I don't think it was a chance coincidence. A little stability in my normal life made my athletic life so much easier to focus on. I took first easily in all of my races. After we got back to the school, Mom picked me up and took me home. I did my best to avoid my Dad for the rest of the evening and Friday morning.

I hoped it really pissed him off. He probably could've cared less. He'd gotten what he wanted. When I got on the bus Friday morning I planned to keep everything as low keyed as possible. Patrick would be stirring up enough rumors on his own. I wanted to give Heather her space. When I saw her I gave a smile and took my seat. We talked for a few seconds to finalize our plans. I ran my ideas by her and she liked them. As I'd expected, she didn't want to offer any suggestions. It was my move and my date to plan. She was just coming along for the ride. That made me worry that this really wasn't anything for her. Maybe she'd only said yes because she didn't have the courage to say no. My fears were starting to pull me down from the heights I'd been soaring. I couldn't deny what I feared was the truth. We had different motivations and expectations of this date. It made me want to scrap the whole thing and not waste my time.

However, I couldn't argue with how good things had been going. She did seem like she was appreciating how nice I was to her. It was a start, but I wanted love in the worst way, not sex, but love. Someone to hold and kiss, someone to be there with me watching that ray of gold in a sunset; instead of dreaming what it would be like. I'm not trying to say I wasn't interested in sex at all. I mean, come on! To think about having sex with Heather was like me going to the moon tomorrow. Since I've never had sex, I can only imagine that it's got to be the best feeling in the world. However, that really wasn't my goal, with any girl right now. I wanted to be lucky enough just to be able to talk and hang out with a girl. A miracle would be a steady girlfriend. If that happened everything else would just add to the dream. I didn't want to feel like I was on my own all the time. I wanted someone to be there with me.

Frankly, I didn't know what kind of relationship could happen with Heather. I wanted more than the opportunity to be with a cute girl. I wasn't going to complain if that's what was happening, but I wanted more. I can honestly say now that I didn't know what I felt for Heather, the important and true stuff. She was really cute, but the real stuff was down the road. I was having a hard time separating what was reality and what were my dreams. Part of a dream had moved into my reality and the shift had melded the two worlds together. They were fused and impossible to distinguish. Only in hindsight can I separate one from the other. Having thought all a' this over, I stuffed it in my back pocket and returned to the clouds. Heather was going on a date with me. That was real.

I didn't bother her at all on the bus ride to school. I tried to look like I was doing homework as I was sneaking glances at her. Yes, she was very cute, I thought to myself. There's no doubt. When we got to school, I didn't walk Heather to her locker because I didn't want to push my luck. I was on adrenaline all day long, nothing at school mattered. It felt weird to hear the word date coming out of my mouth. I didn't know how to say it. The bus ride home was group conversations, which was good, once again I didn't want to push my luck. When I was about to get off the bus, I told her I'd see her later. That comment was about the only thing that showed anything was happening between us, just the way I wanted it. I didn't want a lot of people to know that she was going out with Chad Hardly. I wanted a chance to make an impression myself.

I can't possibly tell you how awesome it was to be able to say to her, 'I'll see you tonight.' That carried me on a high all the way through track practice. I worked extra hard. I wanted to feel I had earned my evening with Heather. My coach noticed that I was running the sprints harder than usual and asked about my great performance the night before. I just smiled and shrugged my shoulders. Randy was full of encouragement. We talked about the date to and from practice. As he dropped me off in front of my porch, he gave me a high five before he took off. It's weird, but, in a way, I still didn't believe it was real. I couldn't believe it until we were actually together. Everything still had the feeling of a dream. I was only coming home to go lay down in my bed and enter this new dream I'd created. I shook my head as I walked into the house to kind of get rid of the nonsense. The time was now and it was real.

I raced in the house and up the stairs. I was ready to get myself ready. I didn't have a whole lot of time. I had to pick her up at five. Thank God Friday practices are always shorter. Still it didn't seem like nearly enough time for this big of an occasion.

I quickly threw off my track shoes, shorts, shirt, and underwear onto various areas of my bedroom floor and jumped in the shower. Once I was clean I was ready to get my groove on. I put in my tape of MTV party to go Volume 6 and tried to pick out something decent to wear. I really cranked the first song, as I danced around the room with a bathroom towel around my waist picking out clothes and trying to fix my hair. It was a good time, being stupid. Man, if anyone 'd seen me they would've had one big laugh. As I was still searching for a shirt, Dad came clomping up the stairs.

Definitely Reality

As Dad walked in the room he ordered, "You wanna turn that crap down." Dad was about the only thing that could ruin my mood. I had tried to avoid him, but it looked like the unavoidable was bound to happen.

"Yeah, sure, and I like that crap."

"Yeah, I know. Everyone in the whole valley knows." I focused on finding a shirt. I wanted to scream at him that it's the family that's crap, but I couldn't do it. "There you go. There's that attitude. Well that little blackie singing that music and the one on your wall don't put food in your stomach and clothes on your back."

"Just lay off."

"No! I ain't lay'n off. Things weren't easy for us, but I got in and worked like hell. They're nothin' but beggars. They don't earn a Goddamn thing. 'Give me more welfare,' they cry. 'We need jobs.' I never begged for a damn thing, and you can't even give me the time of day. You don't see me ridin' around in my car blarrin' loud music, with some booze in my hand wearing droopy jeans and gold cryin' about how 'it ain't fair life didn't appear to me on a nice little platter.' Life didn't appear to me on no platter. I worked every shit job there was. It didn't matter as long as I was workin'. I've seen em' work, what a joke. A bunch of lazy ungrateful crybabies, and my boy respects them more'n his ole' man. That's the problem."

"First, it's my music and I like it. Second, he's the best sprinter in the world. Not every "blackie" is the way you say – not everybody's perfect, except you I guess."

"I never said I was; I try hard. That's what I'm talking about. I try hard for you and this family. As long as you're in my house you'll live by my rules and give me the common decent respect I deserve."

"What about me?"

"Look, I'm sorry I had to ruin your plans this weekend, but I need you here."

"I just wish you were still in construction. Farming was just a hobby then."

He replied in frustration, "There ain't nothin' wrong with what I do. It's a decent hard days work. Besides, I couldn't work at that place no more. I learned a lot of things there that I don't care to be around. You wanna know why I left?"

"It doesn't matter."

"I never told ya' the truth. Your Mom didn't want me to spoil you."

"It doesn't matter, OK. I'm not interested."

"That's just like you. I wish I didn't have to depend on you so much, but I don't have a choice." What a bunch of crap, I was thinking. He wasn't sorry at all. Mom probably put him up to it.

"Yeah, well I guess that's just a bummer for me."

"Yeah."

"I've gotta get ready and I want to be in a good mood." I turned my music back on.

"Yeah, whatever you want. Just keep it down. You we're making the ceiling shake."

"OK," I sarcastically finished with, "See you tomorrow." He clomped back down the stairs.

It took me a little to clear my head, but it wasn't long before the nervousness started to kick in, and that got my mind off Dad. I thought to myself, wow, this is going to be wild. As soon as I was ready, I turned off my music and came down the stairs. Immediately, I saw that look from Mom: oh my little boy's going on a date. Uhh, it made me feel like such a loser.

Dad was drinking coffee like usual. He said, "Here," and he threw his keys over to me. "You take good care of that truck, it's the only nice thing I own." Another peace offering I guess. I could smell Mom's intervention all over the idea. Nevertheless, I was glad to be driving something that looked decent. Mom was happier than a lark but Dad was brooding like a vulture. I'd pissed him off, which kind of made me happy. It was a small compensation for the hours I was going to put in this weekend.

I replied despite me reluctance, "Thanks."

Mom gave me a hug and said, "Good luck and be a gentleman."

"Yes Mom." God she was grossing me out.

Dad said, "Show her a good time. That's what I did with your mamma and it sure worked on her." Dad had this wry smile on his face, which made Mom laugh. I was thinking, yeah and I was the result – not the kind of result I was looking for.

I replied, "I better get going before this gets rated X."

My said, "See ya honey," and I walked out the door. Free again and ready to go ride the waves.

Chapter Seven
Surf's Up!

Ridin' the BIG KAHUNA

I jumped in Dad's almost new Ford F-150. It was dark blue and really nice on the outside. It's a sharp looking truck. Dad uses it like a truck, so there's only so long that can last, but he's intensely proud of it. He keeps the outside nice. He must've just washed it because it looked good. The inside is always a disaster area. I swear the only time it was clean was when we drove it off the lot. I quickly tried to make things look presentable, but it wasn't nearly as messy as it usually is. It was time to go. I took a deep breath before I shifted into first and left to pick Heather up. It took about five minutes before I pulled up to her house and walked to the door. I knocked and her Dad answered. He looked kind of worn out like an old glove. His hair was gone on the top and there wasn't much left on the sides either.

He looked me over and said, "Heather will be right out." She came running down the stairs a few seconds later. He stated, "Now, you're going to take good care of my daughter?"

Heather butted in, "Come on Daddy, I'll be fine." She whispered to me, "Let's go before he changes his mind."

I replied as Heather pulled me toward the truck, "Absolutely."

Heather looked even better than she normally does for school. Her hair looked so smooth. I couldn't believe she could look better, but somehow she most definitely did. I was trying to decide whether or not I wanted to give her a compliment. I mean I wanted to but I didn't want to sound too excited or too stupid. I tried to remember the conversation plan Dale and I had gone over. I couldn't remember a thing. I decided what the hell; I'll try nice.

"You look really amazing, Heather. Even better than you do for school and that's pretty amazing." (If you're a guy reading this story you may now groan. Saying stuff like that is like; well it leaves a really bad taste in your mouth. Like I said before, it's not that I didn't mean it. It's just, yuck, like stupid or something.)

She replied, "Thanks, Chad." I opened the door for her and made my way around the truck. It seemed that the compliment was well received, but I also felt I needed to tone it down a bit. I was riding very close to too strong. I backed out of her driveway and we were on our way. I was so nervous my palms were sweating. I did a good bit of grinding the gears when I pulled out.

I said, "Ouch, I'm normally a little better than that."

She replied, "I've never even driven a stick."

"Oh." When I called Dale later that night after the date was over and told him that line, he sure had a laugh. Ha, Ha, it does sound kind of, well, you know. Jeez, I don't need to explain it. Anyways, at that moment I came up with yet another good spur of the moment idea. I decided to teach Heather how to drive stick, and keep your head out of the gutter.

"I've got a great idea!"

"Oh no," she replied shaking her head and laughing a bit. "I'd mess it up. This truck is really nice."

"It's a truck, it can take some abuse. I know you're not afraid to try. You're a go getter."

"Oh please stop." She sighed and smiled some more. I wanted to make her smile a lot more it was such a wonderful sight. It was an infectious happiness. Every time she smiled it made me feel like smiling – what a great disease. She made me forget about Dad and all his bullshit.

"Chad, I mean thanks, but what if I'm terrible at it?"

I imitated John Wayne and replied, "Well, little lady. You'll never know what's on the other side'a that there hill 'till ya' take the horse by the reins and ride on over there and find out." She looked nervous, but I felt a part of her had already decided to give it a try. I could just see it. I smiled and said, "Let's go." I stopped, leaped out, and tried to slide across the hood. It looked dumb and I nearly fell on my butt, but Heather seemed to like the break in the tension. She moved over to the driver side and I climbed in. She looked cool behind the wheel of a truck.

She said, "OK, you got me here, now what do I do?"

"Well, there's a clutch pedal on the far left. You push that in when you need to shift gears. The gearshift is this big stick. Push the clutch in. OK, first is here, then second, third and so forth. You shift when the engine's Rpm's are up a little. The next gear allows the engine to rev. at a slower rate. Ahh, you'll get used to it."

"If you say so."

"Just think gentle. As my Dad would say, 'Trucks may be tough, but they appreciate a soft touch.' Dad actually told me that a truck is a lot like a woman. If you treat it nice it'll stay around longer. Dad's a joker that's for sure. Anyhow, I decided not to give Heather the full brunt of my father's wisdom.

She smiled and said, "What, don't you think I'm gentle?"

"I remember the first time I saw you. You we're playing basketball in middle school. A girl fouled you tough. The next time down the court you busted out a whole gallon jug of whoop ass on that girl. You're tough."

Heather responded defensively, "She deserved it!"

"Yeah she did, but not every girl would've given it to her. You're like the Trojan horse."

"What!"

"You fool people with the outside, all nice and pretty," I couldn't keep my eyes on her when I said that even though I wanted to. I recovered and continued, "But inside there's an army of warriors." (Time for another groan from the guys' section. Trojan horse? Hey, I don't know where it came from.)

She laughed a lot and said, "Is that how I am?"

"I think it's great." I looked away again. It's amazing how you can't even control your own body. I told my eyes to stay focused on hers, but of course they didn't listen.

"You're really sweet, Chad. Thanks for being so nice. Now, let's see what this puppy can do, Yee Haww!!"

"OK. Hold the clutch in and push the gas in a little, then gently let the clutch pedal out while giving it more gas."

At first she revved the engine a lot. She laughed and said, "Oh shit."

"Think gentle, remember?"

"Yeah, yeah, but this is tough." It was fun to watch her try. She was really nervous. It was kind of nice to feel that we had something in common.

I replied, "Give it another try." She revved the engine a little and started to let the clutch out. The engine ground to a stall. "No problem. Just push the clutch in." She went for the keys and I cautioned, Y'gotta take it out of first too before you start it. Now turn the key." The truck started back up.

She said, "I don't know Chad. I shouldn't."

"You just started. You only stalled it once! Keep trying." She shook her head and started to rev. the engine a bit. I smiled because I knew we weren't going to go anywhere. After a couple seconds she looked puzzled.

She asked, "I let the clutch out and were not going anywhere."

"No kidding, you should try putting it in first as well."

"Damn! I'm forgetting everything."

"Don't worry about it. Here we go. Third time's the charm." Sure enough the third time it worked. I thought she might stall it again, but she got it going and ended up ripping out. A cloud of dirt lit out behind us. Both of us started laughing hysterically.

"Nice one!" I yelled as we got onto the road. She banged her hands on the steering wheel and laughed some more. Once she was out of first, I knew she'd be all right. She didn't shift quickly, but she could get it in gear.

After a little work we were going forty-five. I yelled out the window, "Look out, there's a wild women on the road!" It was a great beginning to the evening. If only I could have ideas like this more often. After she had a little fun, we stopped and I got behind the wheel again. She was having a great time and we hadn't even really started the date. Was this a dream? Could this really be reality? It was real. I mean I was sitting right there, but it had all of the perfectness of a dream. It was perfect and real. That was more than a dream because there was this unbelievable intensity to it. I'd had really intense dreams before, but none could reach the thrill of actually riding the roller coaster or shooting through the half pipe. Reality had something more to offer.

You Got to Know When to Hold 'Em...

For the twenty-five minute drive to Deluice and the Gallery mall where the Outback was located, we made some small talk. The conversation was good. At least I didn't put my foot in my mouth or something. The excitement we'd had was winding down, but things were looking good. When we reached the restaurant, I checked with the host and he led us to a table. As we sat down, I felt it was time to switch to the sports idea Dale and I had come up with. The conversation needed a new twist and I didn't feel comfortable with any kind of silence. The driving episode had gone so well. I just wanted to keep it going, but honestly I felt the excitement slowing down.

It was like; y'know when you're riding a roller coaster you can sort of sense the end coming. You've used up your momentum for the big loops and drops and there's just the tiniest drop-off in intensity before, boom, it's over. That's what I was feeling and I was really worried about that boom. There was a lot of time for things to go wrong. I wish I could've just cashed in my chips while I was ahead rather than trying to play for more. I guess I wouldn't make much of a gambler. However, things were still good. The intensity had dropped off, but I could soar anywhere Heather would send me. Nothing held me back, except my own fear that I was going to screw the whole thing up.

After we got situated and talked about what we each wanted to order, I asked her, "So, do you think you'll start varsity next season?"

"Wow, I don't know about starting but I should get playing time."

"You sure seemed tough enough in the games I've seen you play."

"My Dad says I need to keep from fouling out of games. The officials scrutinize girls' basketball. I get called for things that the guys can get away with all the time. I like to play one hundred percent."

I didn't know where to go from there, thank God the waiter returned to take our order. I was running out of safe sky to soar through now that all a' my conversation ideas were exhausted. It was starting to look dark and cloudy where I was headed. After we ordered, the silence returned. Thankfully she filled it with her own question.

"So, what about track?"

"Track," what a relief I thought, something easy to talk about. "Well, I like track a lot. There's a great feeling you get from running as fast as you can. Feeling the wind and knowing that you're responsible for all of that speed. You know there's no bike or skateboard, or whatever, it's your own." I decided not to bring up my airplane analogy of running (you know the pushing the throttle up feeling).

She replied, "That's cool. I love the competition, and winning of course."

"Yeah, I figured you're probably not someone that takes losing well."

"No."

"So, did you punch any holes in doors or break chairs or anything."

She sarcastically replied with a sly smile as she made a fist and rubbed her knuckles, "Not yet, but I've still got three more years." We both laughed. I did all right with the rest of the dinner conversation, but I was getting the sense that this was just a friendly kind of get together. No matter how unequal we are in the social stratum, it was a feeling of equality and empathy I was looking for. That's the sign of love starting its first connection, my theory anyway. I wasn't getting that feeling and it was holding everything back. Without it this was just a one way street for my feelings. However, I didn't know that for sure so I tried not to be too pessimistic, but you know my confidence. At the very least I hadn't been crushed by the wave, yet, but then again I hadn't had the opportunity to drive through a parking lot just yet.

Know When to Walk Away . . .

The food was pretty good, but I was surprised how little Heather ate. We took a doggie bag home. As we were leaving, there are two doors that lead out: a left one and a right one. I tried to go through the left. It was locked so it would only allow people to come in. I hadn't expected it to be locked. I smashed my shoulder into the door. I hit so hard the momentum smacked my head into the door as well. I knocked myself to the floor and nearly knocked myself out.

Heather rushed over and asked, "Are you all right, Chad?"

"Yeah, yeah, boy that's a sturdy door." What a stupid thing to say. 'That's a sturdy door.' God, that was even dumber than actually slamming my face into the door. Just give me a little time and I'll mess things up. People in the smoking section were all looking to see what had happened. I like entertaining when I'm supposed to be entertaining. I hate it when I'm trying to be normal.

Heather replied, "Yeah it must be. Are you sure you're all right?"

I shook my head yes and said, "I try not to make a habit out of crushing my head against doors."

"That's a good policy." I should've seen the doom on the horizon. I was spiraling towards a hurricane and my kite wasn't going to survive the storm. I knew I couldn't make it through an entire date without something going horribly wrong. It had been a good evening, but I was getting that sixth sense feeling again. I really needed to just paddle my surfboard back to the shore before I got hammered. The door was giving me a warning. Unfortunately, there was no way I could do that. I tried to reassure myself. The hard part was over. All I had to do in the movie was sit there. I wasn't going to try and put my arm around her so I should be fine. I was going to make it. That's what I told myself in the moment of silence that had followed Heather's comment.

Heather broke the tension and my thoughts. She said, "Come on. Let's see how fast you are. Race you to the truck!" She took off. I paused for a minute but then I grabbed the throttle and opened it up a little. It was a good idea that helped me to quickly put the door smashing behind me. I met Heather at the truck as she was laughing and puffing air.

"I thought you were speedy!"

"I just warmed the engine a bit. I didn't even crack it open."

"OK. You're sure that your head's all right."

"Yeah, yeah I'm fine." I really wanted to change the subject. "Ahh, how about that movie now."

"That's great. You can drive."

"Oh! Why thank you. That's so very considerate." I seriously added, "Here, let me open the door."

"Thanks, Chad." She climbed in and I went around the back and jumped in my side. She added, "You're such a gentlemen." I think that's what did it. The compliment went right to my head and got me thinking that maybe I still had a chance to find my way onto the two-way street of love and not in a dark alley by myself. The compliment made me turn my surfboard around. I let my guard down. I saw this mirage of Heather and I together. The waves appeared gentler, but they were rising. I wasn't focused on what was coming. Driving through the mall parking lot over to the movie theater didn't seem like something that deserved my concentration.

Know When to Run!

I started the truck and replied to her compliment, "Thanks, Heather. That's real nice of you to say."

"So do you get that from your Dad?"

"No, my Mom. She created the gentlemen in me that isn't in Dad. My Dad's a dirt ball."

"You and your Dad don't get along too well, do you?"

"It's a long story, but to make it simple he doesn't respect me, so I don't respect me. I'm tired of being his slave. I just want to get out."

"What do you want out of life?"

"Wow, that's a big question." I thought for a few moments as I backed up. I replied, "I want to be the best at whatever I do, but not because I think I'm the best, or that I could be."

"I don't get it. If you don't believe it's possible than how can you expect to get there?"

"Why strive for less than the best? It's my job to work as hard as the best, that I control. But, it's not my problem to worry about the outcome, that I can't control. Hopefully if I work like the best, things will work out so I can be the best. One thing my Dad did say I won't forget. He may be a pain but he knows about working hard. When I was about ten and we were having a hell of a time with the tractor he told me, 'Son, this is hard work, but that's what life's about. Just work hard no matter what. You can't go wrong if you build your life on that." I put the truck in first and started to drive.

"Your Dad doesn't sound all that bad."

"Yeah, I guess, but that was then, and things are different now."

"How so?"

"Enough about me," I knew she didn't want to hear about my problems with Dad. "What about you?"

"I like the advice your Dad gave you. I can work hard. I guess I need a goal."

"I think sprinting is my goal. To make the Olympics"

"I want to be someone. That's what I want."

"I want to live like a king for once."

"Trust me, it gets old. My family is pretty well off. It's just junk, y'know. Friendships and respect, they're so much more rewarding."

"Money gives you those."

"Money is good for stuff. Feelings can't be bought. It's like your Dad said. Success is about the way you live life, not what you get from it." That made me think. I hadn't thought of Dad's advice like that.

I replied, "You're pretty smart." She smiled again.

"You're a great friend." I thought, a great WHAT! A friend, I guess I wasn't really surprised. I had seen this on the horizon. I knew there was no chance of anything. I tried to absorb the painful spear that had been thrust through my chest as it slowly wrenched into my heart. At that moment the mirage was gone and I realized just how big the waves were.

I said, "Thanks." She smiled again. She was so beautiful. I couldn't help but enjoy the beauty of that smile. My right hand was on the gearshift, and this is important because she then put her hand on top of mine. It was a wonderful gesture, yet torturous at the same time. Of course I was enjoying and hating that gesture as well as feeling the frigid temperature of her hand rather than paying attention to the parking lot I was driving through. I wasn't going fast but I wasn't paying attention to a whole lot other than Heather. It's no big deal driving through a parking lot. It's a big empty space. You're not going fast. There's just a bunch of parked cars here in there. No big deal, right? Even as worried about messing up as I was, I didn't even consider anything happening during the drive through the parking lot. A parking lot: asphalt, lines, cars, and light poles. Yeah baby, that'd be the one. It was my head smacking off the steering wheel that brought me back to driving.

I didn't know what happened at first. I thought I hit someone's car. There was a loud grinding of metal and

Heather also smacked her head pretty hard off of the dash. I hit the horn with my hands. It all happened very fast. When I regained my senses, I turned the truck off and looked over to see if Heather was all right. Her head was bleeding and she looked dazed.

I asked her, "Are you OK?"

"Yeah, I guess so. What happened?" The way she looked at me said everything. I guess it was dismay. Maybe more like dismay trying to be covered by her good nature. There was coldness in her eyes that seeped through me like a bitter wind through snow pants. I was a fool, a fool in love and a fool in life. It was my job to be a fool. That was my task in life and that's how I felt. The wave came crashing down on me and I was broken and blasted to the ground.

After a few seconds, I had regained enough of my senses to realize that I had managed to drive the right fender of the truck directly into one of the light poles in the parking lot. Each of the poles has a large concrete base. There were about five or six people already looking at us. Two of them were laughing and pointing.

I heard them say, "Holy shit, what a moron. What were you doing you retard?" Another couple came over to see if we were hurt. An ambulance was called, which created a huge audience for my work, my big debut. I didn't know what to say to Heather or how to even say anything, but that was part of the performance, of course. It made everything even funnier. The audience fed off my embarrassment like cannibals. Thank God Heather wasn't hurt real bad. What was hurt the most was her opinion of me. I wanted romance out of the date. I wanted to be able to meet with a girl with true feeling. To feel that connection. What I got was the same old shit; it's who I am. The truck, well who cares about the damn truck, but it had a big dent in the bumper. Of course it's Dad's pride and joy. I bet you can imagine how he was going to react, all part of the spectacle. I probably could've made ten dollars a head to bring the audience to my house to watch the second act. Needless to say, we didn't go to the movies.

After the paramedics took care of our bumps and bruises I said to Heather, "I'll just take you home; if that's OK?"

"Thanks, but my Dad's already on the way. The paramedics called him." I didn't know what to say, how to look at her, or what gestures to make. I felt stupid and I didn't know how to be any other way.

I was looking at the ground with my hands in my pockets as I said, "I'm real sorry, Heather." Like it mattered.

She replied, "I'm fine. It's no big deal."

"I guess I'll see you on Monday."

"Yeah, sure. Are you sure you can drive? My Dad could drop you off?"

"No, I'll be fine."

"Look, Chad, sometimes things happen. It's OK. I had a great time. I'm OK." I tried to smile, but it was hard. I was trying to make sure I didn't cry.I replied, "Thanks, Heather." I give her credit. She could've had a big laugh out of the whole thing like everybody else did. Y'know, she probably wasn't going to even say anything to anybody at school. She wouldn't take advantage of the opportunity. I could only imagine the reviews I'd get from guys like Patrick. He would certainly find my performance an instant classic. However, Heather was done with me. The story was going to get around. She was a nice enough person that she wouldn't join in the jeers, but she wasn't going to stand up on stage with me. I wouldn't wish that upon anybody. She was nice enough to just sit silently in the audience and empathize with my misfortune. I knew I was going to be center stage playing the role that makes everyone else feel better. It seemed I was always the guy who got to play that lead.

Act II

I went home and quietly pulled the truck into the driveway. Mom had waited up for me. When I walked in I could see a little sparkle in her eyes. She was excited to see how her boy had done. It's too bad that what she got was a rock not a star. I could never provide her anything to be proud of.

"Well, how'd it go?" she asked.

"Mom, it was really good for a while." It was too. I felt like just an audience member for once. I wasn't expected to perform.

"What happened honey?"

"The truck and, damn it! I really screwed up just like I always do. I keep trying and nothing works." I had tears in my eyes but I was fighting like hell to keep from crying to top everything off.

"Chad, it's never as awful as if first feels. There will be other girls. Y'know there's this one girl. . ."

"Oh, it's a lot worse than just that. I'm not even talking about making a fool out of myself and having a date turn out sour. Mom, I dented the truck."

"What'd you do?"

"I don't want to talk about it. It was really stupid and everybody got a good laugh."

"Was anyone else involved?"

"No. Things were going really well. I'd taught Heather how to drive stick and it was going really well. We were talking a lot. We're driving over to the Movie Theater and I just wasn't paying enough attention. I hit one of the parking lights. They have big concrete bases. I wasn't going fast but it was enough to probably bruise Heather's head. Everyone in this whole town is going to have a big laugh and Dad's. Man, Dad is just going to flip out." I was just about to the point of crying. I have to admit. It doesn't matter now anyhow, I might as well tell the truth.

"Well, I'll tell you what. I'll give you some money. You leave real early tomorrow and see if you can get the truck fixed. You said you had to go into the city to get new running shoes. So do that and get the truck fixed. You can pay me back later and I'll make sure he doesn't know about it, but you have to promise me that you will try to work things out with your Dad."

"Mom. . ."

"I don't want to hear it. The two of you are exactly alike. You're both as stubborn as the tractor sitting out there. I'm tired of being stuck in the middle. He is your father, Chad. He works damn hard for you."

"Fine." What was I going to say? "Look, I'm going to bed. Just wake me up."

I walked up the stairs and went to bed. I laid there and looked out the window at the stars. The wind was gently blowing through the trees. It just reminded me of the little taste of flying I'd had and the stars reminded me where everyone else was and how far beneath them I was.

I could kill them. They'd respect me then. Just walk in and start blowing people away. Yeah Patrick who's the cool one now? Bang! What, I'm not popular enough for you little miss Cheerleader queen? Bang! Shit, that'd be real stupid. Nobody's gonna respect you when they're dead. There not going to do a thing. It sure wasn't going to get me a girlfriend. The girls weren't going to go for a guy threatening to kill them. They'd go for the guy that saved them from me. Even if I did get respect, I'd probably be dead so what good would it do me. It was just an empty solution like being dead and getting respect. It still felt good to dream about it and pretend people respected me, but it made more sense to save my hated classmates from some psycho than to be that psycho. I guess that's all I need to do.

Just have my small rural school attacked by crazing psychos, then I'd get my chance to be heroic.

I couldn't get the look of dismay on Heather's face out of my head. I couldn't get the excitement I had felt during dinner out of my mind. The contrast of the two feelings created a toxic poison in my heart. It burned with pain. The high made me forget who I really was, and I wanted that so bad. But the low was ten times worse because I'd glimpsed the high. It was a crushing contrast. Dreams are never like that. There's never that pain, this burning in my chest to explode.

I want to be a star, to explode brightly and brilliantly for all to see. But, everyone forces thousands of different chemicals into my soul to keep the energy from bursting into the sky. I just want to run and scream and jump and be able to say 'I did it;' to stand with my fists in the air, to feel those chemicals lose control and a mighty triumphant roar erupting from within me releasing the person inside of me that I know is the real me so he can scream into the night sky. Finally everyone will see who I really am and glimpse the hot fiery ember burning with passion inside my heart. My passion, my honor, my dedication, my power, my power. WHO I AM! It is there tied and restrained. Locked away, and no one, absolutely no one, is looking to find it. I never get my moment. I never get my chance to free myself from those chemicals of fear and failure that strap me to the ground. Those contaminants tear me to shreds. I can't stand it any longer!

I couldn't fall asleep, I'm sure that's no surprise. I gave Dale a call. I told him about the date both good and bad. He did a good job trying to cheer me up. He only really wanted to hear about the good parts. Like I told you before, he got a real good laugh out of Heather's comment that she'd never driven stick before. Hearing him laugh helped to lift my spirits. We talked for probably an hour. When I hung up the phone I went back to looking at the stars.

I gazed at them for hours. It was comforting in a way because I sure couldn't sleep. Every time I closed my eyes the evening would flash through my mind and I'd end with Heather's look of horror. It was so silent outside. The moon seemed so peaceful sitting there glowing in the black sky. It couldn't be going through what I was, but things always look better from a far. Could the moon think I've got it easy? There's no way after tonight. Everyone has a role in life. Mine was to maintain perspective. I'm the joke that makes everyone else realize that their life isn't all that bad. I make people laugh. It would be great if that was what I was trying to do. Look at me and laugh. Forget your worries and smile. I'll gladly take your frustration. I'm always in control. Your laughs don't really affect me, right?

Chapter Eight
Get Back on that Horse, Whether you Like it or Not

Somehow I managed to fall asleep, but it wasn't 'till early in the morning. Mom's wake up call seemed to come right after my eyes had finally found peace. I was emotionally burnt out after last night and now I felt the same physically. My eyes were still sleeping as I put on my clothes and quickly stuffed my knife and matches into my pockets. After I finished slurping up a bowl of cereal, I took the keys to the truck and the money Mom gave me and hit the road. The first stop was a dirt road that turned off about three miles from my house. I drove up the dirt lane far enough that I couldn't be seen from the road. Nobody uses the dirt lane anymore. It used to go up to an old shack, but whoever owned it left and now a bunch of debree had blocked the lane about three quarters of the way up. I made myself comfortable and tried to get some more sleep. There was no way I was going to be able to handle a full day with Dad. I decided that I was just going to sleep and try to at least feel better physically.

Now, instead of just destroying his truck I was also disobeying him directly for the first time. He was going to madder than a hornet when he woke up and I wasn't there.

- 115 -

Who knows how long it was going to take me with the truck. I didn't care.

It felt good to get some more sleep. I slept a bit better in the truck. When I woke up it was eleven. I had slept a lot longer than I had planned, but it really didn't matter. Dad was going to be mad if I was ten minutes late; I might as well make it eight hours. It was time to go to the city and hit the mall. Then, after I'd taken a little time to try and relax, I'd give Louis a call and see if he could take a look at the truck. I knew Louis'd be in the garage all day, so there was no hurry. I tuned in the hard rock station, 99 rocks, and spent forty-five minutes driving and jamming out. I rolled my window down, even though it was a little cool, and let the wind blow through my hair and the tunes rain out onto the highway.

I needed to clear my head. I didn't go directly to Deluice and The Gallery Mall. I drove around for awhile, that's why it took forty-five minutes. Besides, I wasn't all that anxious to go back to the scene of my personal disaster. Normally I'm not a big fan of hard rock, but it clears my head better than rap. The stereo in Dad's truck isn't too bad. It even handles rap pretty good. After I got the anger out of my head with the hard rock, I changed the channel to 102.5, jumping and jivin' one hundred. J and J one hundred is the closest thing to a rap station that we have in our area. It's like a top forty station with a little more emphasis on rap and R and B. I listen to it a lot. So now that my head was clearing, the smooth beats helped to cool me out. That's what's so great about rap music. You can dance a lot to it and get really into it, or you can just be chill and bounce your head. Since I was never much of a dancer, chillin' is what I did.

Some of the guys at my school can dance like MC Hammer. Not nearly as good as Hammer, but they're a lot better than me. If I'd try to dance with them, they'd have a good laugh. To be out on the dance floor you have to first know the secret popularity code or something. If you don't have it, you better be part of a big group of other non-members or you'll be joked right back to the wall. Since I don't know the secret word, I don't get much practice dancing so I'm not very good at it. I usually go to the dances, but rarely am I actually dancing.

I think in life, I'm just not allowed to have any fun. My classmates don't let me and it seems God won't let me either. I've decided there has to be a happy meter for life. Everyone's allowed to have so much and then that's it. If everything's going great for you in high school, you're using up part of your happy allotment. You may even run out by the time you finish high school. Those are the people's whose best days were in high school. I try to tell myself I'm enduring the hardship now and down the line things will balance out so I get my chance to use up some of my happy meter. I guess that's just what I hope. You wouldn't think it's fair if I just got screwed my whole life, but who knows. Anyhow, the slamming beat helped to cool me off. It got my mind off any thoughts and made me forget about everything. I felt ready to jump back into the game of life once again.

Once I made it to the mall, I parked in my usual spot. There's a parking space around the back of the mall next to a big trash dumpster. The back of the mall is where all of the loading docks are for each of the mall's biggest stores. Few people are ever back there and nobody is ever parked in the spot I know. I always have a spot, so I don't have to hunt. Even though it's by the back of the mall, it's just a short walk to the west entrance. It was weird being back at the scene of my dating disaster. It was like going to the filming sight for a Friday the 13th movie. Unfortunately, this movie was my life.

When I drove in I deliberately kept from going by the spot I'd hit. I parked the truck in my spot and made my way into the mall. Before I went in, I couldn't help but look around the side of the west entrance up into one of the main parking lots. Two guys were working on the concrete base. Y'know, it really didn't look that bad. However, I thought about the damage to Heather's head and it looked real bad. That image got me back thinking about everything.

On Monday the story would be out. Everyone would know, and everyone would get their laughs. The meanest people would laugh right in my face; others would get their jollies less directly. Heather would be in the middle of a girl-clucking corner. She'd have to put me down and distance herself or risk joining me as part of the freak show.

I said, "That's enough! Stop thinking about it!" and I stopped looking and thinking about what had happened. I grabbed the two doors, threw them open, and walked in. I walked up and down the mall looking at stuff for an hour or so. It was kind of nice walking around looking at all of the things I'd like to buy. I guess that'll never changes. You can never have enough money to buy everything you want so you might as well deal with it, or so Dad says, if I remember correctly. It was a pretty depressing realization so it was natural that it came from him. I guess I'm pretty good at just looking since it's like second nature to me. Heather thought it was all just stuff. That's pretty funny. I think I'd like to test Heather's theory and then decide. It'd be nice to just walk into Structure and buy what I wanted. Hell, it'd be nice just to be able to walk into Sears and buy what I wanted.

I spent at least an hour and a half looking for the perfect pair of shoes. With the little money I had I knew I wasn't going to be able to get a second pair and I needed a good deal. I found the best deal at Footlocker. I was exhausted after working that hard just to find a good and inexpensive pair of running shoes. I went down to the food café and treated myself to some pizza. Pizza is something I rarely eat. I have to stay in shape, especially now that the season is in full swing and playoffs are quickly approaching. However, I'm an emotional eater. Treating myself helped to boost my spirits. It was almost three O'clock when I finally gave Louis a call from one of the mall payphones.

I heard a lady on the other line say, "Hello?"

"Yes, is Louis there?"

"Just a second." She sounded real dead. After a couple of moments Louis was on the phone.

"Hell-o."

"Hey Louis, this is Chad."

"How y'doin'?"

"OK I guess, I'll have to tell you later. Hey, I banged up my Dad's fender last night and I wanted to see if you could look at it."

"Hey sure, no problem. I see what I can do. So, what happened?"

I replied, "It's a long story. I'll tell you when I get there."

"Will do, just bring it on over. Y'know how to get here?"

"Yeah, thanks Louis."

"No problem." I planned on telling him the story once I got there. There was no reason to try and contain it. It was better if I told it to as many people as possible so they'd hear my side. As for the truck, I knew there would be no way Louis could fix it today. I didn't think there was any way even if I'd gotten it there at six in the morning. The truck was going to need a new fender and that takes time to get. That meant Dad was going to find out. I decided to get some ice cream.

After I bought a cone of twist, I sat down to enjoy the ice cream and to think. Y'know what? I didn't care what Dad or anyone else thought anymore. I really didn't. What I did to Heather was the real worry. She was probably going to have some bruises. It was going to look horrible, and it was my fault. The last thing I could ever do is hurt a girl. Never in a million years could I let that happen. Dad didn't matter. Two more years of high school and I'd be up for release. I'd take care of myself. I'd get an athletic scholarship and I'd be out of prison. I'd be on parole for four years and then I'd be a free man. It was the same way with my life at school. As bad as I knew it was going to be on Monday, I didn't care anymore. I was never going to play the games. I just prayed Heather was all right. Everything else could go to hell. Soon I'd be outta there and I was never going to look back. Every person has their time to shine, and everyone at that school was going to burn out before they reached twenty-five. I hadn't even lit the pilot yet.

I felt pretty good about my situation. As long as you can see a positive, or at least manufacture one, there's hope. I guess that's how I survive. If you don't have hope, that means you've quit and you won't achieve anything with that mindset. Normally I was afraid of being alone, but I felt adamant this time. After the experience with Heather I was determined to bury my feelings and force my life to work out. Nobody was ever going to see anything but my game face from that point on. Only when I'm standing on the top will I smile, I thought. Someday Dad will ask my forgiveness and so will everybody else – someday. It was time to go home.

My life was going to change, but not because of my new attitude. A big change was coming. A monster wave to try and ride. A bigger wave and a darker sky than I could ever imagine. You'd think I'd get a break to recover from everything I'd been through, but God was laughing and saying, "Let's just see what he does with this break."

You Just Play the Damn Game

After I finished the ice cream, I went out the west entrance and around to the back of the mall. I turned the corner and it was just me and the dumpsters once again. Compared to the rest of a big mall on a Saturday, it felt like being in an old desolate haunted house back a long dirt road. But it was a good eerie feeling because I was sick of people. I was thinking about how Dad was going to react. There was going to be a huge fireball at my house tonight. Maybe he'd even throw me out of the house. Anything was possible. Blowing him off was ten times worse than what I did to the truck, and together they were monumental. It was only a little longer and the moment of truth would arrive.

I was about fifty yards from Dad's truck as I past another alleyway. I'd already past several just like it. They were basically the same. Each led down to a particular store's loading dock. The only thing that was different was which store each alley serviced and the numbers used to identify them. I think the one I'd just passed was the loading dock for Sears; I didn't notice what the identification number was. There was a white windowless van that was backed up to the loading dock, which was down the alley about fifty yards. I had hardly noticed it because it was nothing special. There were loading docks all over the back of the mall. It wasn't a surprise to see something being loaded or unloaded. What made this one particularly special was what was being loaded. When you catch a glimpse of the two guys wearing ski masks, business suits, and black gloves opening the side door of an unmarked van, now that gets your attention.

I took a couple steps until the picture had sunk in. I stopped and walked back to the edge of the alley for a second look. I was thinking I'd better go and report these guys, until I peered back down. The plan changed rapidly. Two more guys had appeared from the front of the van. They were carrying a big burlap sack over to the side door of the van, and it was clearly alive and clearly struggling. Something really big was going down.

The smart thing to do was to go get help, but by that time they'd probably be gone. The right thing to do, well that's up for interpretation. I didn't consult fear for an opinion. The right thing to do was to kick some ass!

My new attitude on life was life didn't matter. I didn't care. All my frustrations were going to pour out on those guys. I could feel those chemicals losing control and an explosion about to occur, a release to my frustration and anger. Well, here it comes! Time to ride the half pipe. I dropped the footlocker bag and bolted down the alley. This was the big kahuna. There was no hesitation, no indecision. It's Hardly time! I must watch too many action movies.

    I had run thirty yards or so, almost to the front of the van, when I was spotted. The guy who saw me yelled, "We've got company!" and raised an AK-47 automatic at me. I immediately dove to the ground behind a dumpster on my left. This was a whole lot different than a movie.

    I heard another guy growl, "No weapons! No sound! Take him down quietly." As the guy was giving orders, I pushed the dumpster toward them. The adrenaline was really pumping now. If you could've looked into my eyes, you would've seen the fire welling behind them. I drew every ounce of haybale throwing and years of farmwork outta' my arms and legs and poured it into pushing that dumpster. Then I threw in all my anger and frustration. I had the dumpster on them in seconds. They had little time to avoid it. With a loud grinding, it scraped against the side of the van. Then there was a sharp crack as I knocked two guys over. One was the guy with the automatic. I heard a restrained growl of pain. I had pinned another guy's leg in between the dumpster and the door. He sounded really mad and was already trying to desperately free his leg. Like a ferocious animal I leapt on top of the dumpster and jumped to the other side.

    One of the guys I'd knocked over was starting to get up. I gave him a good kick to the face. I pulled the other guy on the ground to his feet and threw him hard to the pavement by the back of the van. As I turned to take care of the guy who's leg I pinned, I felt the right side of my face smacking against the wall. The blow stunned me for a moment. I tried to regain my senses. I'd forgotten about the fourth guy. I'd forgotten there was even a fourth guy. I was slammed against the van. The force of the blow sent me reeling to my hands and knees. Blood poured into my mouth. With a final burst of everything I had left, I rushed toward the blur I believed was the fourth guy attempting to knock him down. I got a hold of him, but he twisted to the side and threw me up against the dumpster, which lanced my ribs. I immediately yelled in pain. He was a lot stronger than I was.

The guy's who's leg I'd hurt ripped his ski mask off and sharply said, "Shut him up," and looked to see if anyone had seen or heard the struggle. He was really pissed. His long black hair was a strangely mess across his face. It looked as angry as his eyes. With a violent push he slid the dumpster away so he could get his leg free. The guy who had been kicking my ass immediately put his hand over my mouth, pulled me up to my feet, and put a handgun to my head. The guy with the hurt leg looked directly at me as he got to his feet and walked slowly toward me.

He growled, "No gun shots damn it!" Thank God he could control his anger; I'm sure he wanted to put a bullet in my head. He had a Middle Eastern accent, I think. Now that I'd heard him talk a couple of times, I knew it was an accent of some sort, but I was a good bit groggy. If I wasn't being held by the back of my Pittsburgh Steelers jacket, I would've just slumped to the ground.

"What do you want me to do with him?" He had a similar accent.

"Bag him. We'll get rid of him later and get those other two idiots to their feet." The guy holding me took the handle of his gun and whacked me over the head. That was it for me. I wasn't going to be getting yelled at tonight. It was Hardly time all right, like Hardly had a chance. I paddled out to the wave and did a little riding. I almost thought I was pretty cool and then I got crushed, big time. There's a new one for me. Kawabunga!!

Chapter Nine

Alone

    I don't know how long I was out. My body was already beat from not getting a lot of sleep the night before. When I did regain consciousness, I felt even worse. I'd felt sore before, but now it felt like my entire body was sore. The bumps from the fight had gotten good and tight and the back of my head was throbbing. My hands and feet were tied and I was in a burlap bag. It took me a couple seconds to regain my senses and put together what had happened and where I was. At first I thought this was just one of my really real dreams. However, no dream is so real you can really taste blood. My mouth was gagged, and whatever they tied around it was very very tight. This was all real.

    I could see a little bit through the tiny cracks in the bag, but it was dark in the back of the van. My back was against the back door and my right shoulder was leaning against the sidewall. It wasn't very comfortable. There was no carpeting in the back and I was bouncing around a good bit. We must've been moving at a good clip on a road with quite a few curves. Now that I was beginning to come to the realization that this wasn't just a bad dream, my stomach started to twist into a giant knot. I did care about life and I cared a whole hell of a lot more about death.

I had thought things were bad before, but this was even worse and Dad wasn't going to wake me up. Being the laughing stock of my school on Monday seemed like a small punishment. I had a very bad feeling I was going to get a lot worse outta' this one. I was going to be over. Just like turning off a TV. Click and I've been cancelled. I sat for, I don't know how long, thinking about death and all the thoughts death inspires. It gave me a chill in my chest to imagine my last moment. That gun at my head, the cold steel remote about to turn off my show. I don't know what flicked on inside my head, but I started to get mad.

It wasn't fair. It's not like my life had ups and downs. All I had were downs, and now this! Fuck it, I'm not going to die just like wham bam thank you mam. Fuck schools, fuck Patrick, fuck Dad, fuck luck, fuck destiny, fuck God, fuck everything. There's only one person on this earth that gives a shit about me – ME! Sure God's hoping I make it through all this, but he ain't gonna fix if for me. This is my shitty deal and my shitty life and my shitty game; well I'm going to start making my own shitty rules. I'm either getting out of this alive, or I'm going to die with some dignity. I'm not just going to quit. I never quit because of any a' the other crap, and this ain't a damn bit different.

I started to concentrate on getting out of this really bad reality. Focusing my mind on a single goal helped to direct my frustration and control it. I had no plan, no guesses, not even a clue, but I tried not to concentrate on everything I didn't know. I needed to manufacture some hope, and that meant concentrating on what I did know. At this point, that was nothing, so I decided to get stared.

If you're just riding in a car you don't think about using your ears and your body to recognize what kind of road you're on. It's not important, but when it's your only clue, you'd be surprised how much you can learn. I tried to tell myself this was just a science experiment. I was collecting data to hopefully be able to draw some conclusions. I was very rational about the whole thing. I was ready to explode; yet I was calm. I had a new determination.

I started my observations. There were too many bumps and curves for this road to be a main highway. It had to be some kind of secondary road. I didn't hear the sound of flying dirt hitting the van, so I knew it was some kind of macadam. This was all very interesting, but that was about all I could deduce. Where were we, I wondered? How long was I knocked out? The only clue, a winding bumpy road that was macadammed, only made me more curious.

I decided to try my eyes. The other person I saw being thrown into the van was over at the other corner, I think anyways. It was really hard to see. There was a bench seat towards the front with two guys in it. There had to be a driver and I imagined there should be one guy in the passenger seat, I couldn't see for sure, but I remembered there were four guys (this time). There were no windows past the driver's and passenger's seats, and I couldn't see through the bag well enough to see out the front windshield. That was it for my eyes, so much for collecting information.

No matter where we were, I had to get free somehow. I started concentrating on that. They had done a good job taping my hands. It seemed like it was duck tape. I had my Swiss army knife, but there was no way I could get to it. I was so hardly awake this morning I just put it in my jacket pocket. I was too tired to fuss with the holder on my belt. I might've been able to get to the knife if I'd put it on my belt. Well, probably not, now that I think about it, but it didn't matter anyhow. I had to find a way to tear that tape. I also started to listen as my captors started to talk. This was my best chance to get information.

The guy sitting in the bench seat on the side opposite of where I was, I'll call him guy One, was saying, "The get-a-way was clean. By the time they figure out she's gone we will be impossible to find." There was a crazy cockiness in his voice and anger hung off every word.

The driver replied, "You think this place is that good?" The driver was definitely an American. He had a New Yorker's accent.

Guy One replied, "The FBI will be called in. They will think we're trying to get out of the country. We will, however, be blending into the country."

"I don't know, pal. That shit at the mall didn't go down well."

The guy in the passenger seat said in a reserved but sharp tone, "Shut up all of you." I recognized his voice. He was the guy who's leg I'd crushed. It was my impression he was the leader. He'd been giving orders before. In fact, if he wouldn't have, I'd be dead. I'll call this guy the leader. He continued, "Everything is fine and it will be fine. We will give the FBI many reasons to believe we are leaving the country. Leave the planning to me." He had a crisp educated sound to his voice. It was the same accent as guy One, but guy One's voice was more harsh and wild.

Guy One responded, "Well, I'd like to know all the details of this plan."

The driver added, "Yeah, man, when we planned this out we had surprise on our side. Someone had to've heard all of that struggle."

The leader replied, "No one heard anything. If you idiots had fired your weapons then we would be in trouble. They have no idea where we are going, what we are driving, or what we look like. Their best guess is out of the country."

As they were discussing, I noticed that my right leg was lying on something really uncomfortable. During the conversation I felt it with my hand to try and figure out what it was. It wasn't easy to know for sure because it was like examining something with a glove on being inside the sack. However, my guess was a tire jack. That wasn't too important, but there was a square plate with pretty defined corners. If it was a tire jack this was probably the base.

Whatever it was, those corners might be able to tear tape. I had a little hope to keep my mind occupied.

The driver continued the argument. He responded, "You seem so certain."

The leader replied, "Think. We went over all of this before. Our team back home will be making contact and doing all negotiations. It will seem, to the FBI, that the girl and her captors are no longer in the US. Our demands go through Amjad back in Rawalpindi. Is he with us? No. Is he going to be where we're hiding? No. We're giving the FBI what they already want to believe based on their past experiences and their own protocols. They expect us to leave the country and Amjad will appear to verify that assumption. We sit for a couple of days and play babysitter and our brother patriots will be free eating samosas in the streets of Karachi. No one will be looking for us where we are going."

I slowly and very carefully raised myself a little so I could turn the thing and get the plate behind me and close to my hands. I wanted to use my body weight to hold it down once I started trying to tear the tape. Once I got it in position, I was ready to give it a shot. I very carefully started to rip a hole through the burlap sack. It wasn't too hard. With my hands now uncovered I checked the thing out again. It was most likely a tire jack. First, I had to make sure I made a good clean tear and took each layer one at a time. Duck tape is exceptionally strong, but it's also made to be ripped without the need for a knife or scissors. However, if I didn't tear it cleanly and I started rolling the edges, I was in big trouble. With my hands behind my back trying to maneuver the edge of a tire jack to make the tear, I had my work cut out for me. Once the edge of duct tape gets rolled over it doesn't matter how much you want to tear it. If that happened, I was going to be really stuck, so to speak. Plus, I had to make sure I was very quiet. I had a lot of road noise to help mask any sound, and their talking also helped out a lot.

The conversation continued, as I started working. The driver replied, "Well, there have already been complications, as you'd say."

"If you two idiots were paying better attention."

The other guy sitting on the bench seat yelled, "It was not our fault!" Except he wasn't a he. He was a she. So, it was three guys two with Arabian accents or something like that, one guy with a New York accent, and this lady who sounded German or Russian, or something like that.

The leader responded, "Enough!" It was sort of interesting to hear them talking about me. My ears were really focused. I wanted to hear what plans they had for me. The leader continued. "He was an unexpected variable that we will use to our advantage."

"How?" demanded guy One. Exactly what I wanted to know.

The leader replied, "I'm doing the planning. You three do your jobs."

"How's your leg?" asked the driver.

"It will be fine, and so will we."

I wasn't having a whole lot of success with the tape, and I had to work painfully slow so I didn't draw anyone's attention. It was good they were having an argument to keep them distracted. It was still light out outside. I could see that coming from the front of the van, but in the back where this other person and I were it was pretty dark. The darkness was a big plus, but also a double-edged sword. They couldn't see me working on the tape, but it made it impossible for me to see where we were.

The terrorists, that's what I figured they were, had wrapped the tape really well, but after some more work it was starting to tear. I've never been very patient and as terrified as I was it was hard just to hold my hands still. I couldn't even feel them. Everything was numb from the adrenaline. I kept my mind busy to prevent my feelings from taking me through their own personal horror house. I started wondering about the other person who was the real target of all of this. I knew she was a girl, but that was about it. She had to be somebody special because these folks had sure gone to a lot of trouble to kidnap her.

We were still on that winding road because I was being thrown left and right a lot. We hadn't slowed down at all. I was having a difficult time working on the tape because it was so difficult to stay on top of the tire jack. However, the curving road and our speed was actually good because it was harder to see I was trying to break free. The conversation had stopped for the moment. I wished there were windows. I might've been able to recognize a landmark or something.

I kept working on that tape for awhile. Now that they weren't arguing I was even more careful. All my effort was on that tape until I heard a new sound of roadway. We had slowed down and gone around a corner and then started accelerating again only this time the road was much smoother. It sounded like much better highway. I felt certain it was concrete not asphalt. There was a loud clunk as we went over a bump and then the sound changed a little bit again. I had a hunch we were going over a bridge. We hit large periodic bumps every couple seconds, which made the van bounce. It had to be a bridge and that was a big clue if I hadn't been knocked out too long.

If I hadn't been out for like eight hours or something than we were still in an area I generally knew. I assumed I wasn't out too long. The light coming from the windows seemed to confirm that. With that assumption, I started thinking of every large bridge I knew that wasn't too far away. Unfortunately, I realized just how many there were. There were at least eight bridges I could think of. I could eliminate a bunch, if I knew how long we'd been driving. The large clunks continued for about thirty seconds until we hit one final big one. The road sound then briefly changed back to the smooth highway sound before it again changed back to the similar roar of asphalt I'd been hearing since I woke up. I was kicking my brain. It was killing me I'd gotten a sign but couldn't make any sense out of it. If I could've just looked outside for a second, just a second, I might know where we were. However, I didn't need to see; I only needed to listen.

We were only on the asphalt for maybe a minute and then, like a great alleluia, we went over a singing bridge. That sound sang to me exactly where we were. The bridge serenaded me with hope. The hum of its steel frame roadway sounded magical to my ears. I don't know every bridge that well because few are so unique, but I did know the pattern of this one. We had driven north from Deluice up past where I live. We continued north for about another half an hour and now we had just crossed the Tuscan river at Coaltown. At least that's what I thought. I've been over that bridge many a time to go north for hunting and camping trips. After you cross the main bridge there's a smaller one going over a creek that joins with the Tuscan, I can't remember the name of that creek. Anyhow, that second smaller bridge is a singing bridge. Singing bridges get their names because of the sound they make. These bridges have steel roadways that aren't solid. They're grated kind of like wicker furniture. When tires go over them it sounds like they're singing. I felt pretty certain I knew where I was.

It made sense with what the leader had been saying. If they were going to try and convince the FBI they were heading for an airport and out of the country, going north like we were was a perfect deception. The further north you go the more empty it gets. I figured they were planning to hide somewhere in the huge state gamelands area, which was a couple hours further north from where I was guessing we were. I don't know exactly how they were planning on making the FBI buy the airport idea, but I hoped it didn't work. Where we were going, there weren't going to be too many people around to help us get outta' this mess.

I had to be right. I thought it over in my head. There can't be too many bridges with that arrangement. I couldn't think of any that I knew of. I felt a rush of hope surge into my soul. Like I said if you can see a positive or at least manufacture one you have hope. I needed to get back to ripping that duct tape and with hope to ignite my efforts I felt more determined. Honestly, I guess it wasn't really that big of a deal I knew where I was. The real hard part was going to be getting away. If this girl and I could do that, than knowing where we were could be useful, but I didn't think about that at the time. I really needed to have something positive to focus on. It gave me more determination. As I worked on the tape, I started thinking about the road I thought we were on. I wanted to know exactly where it was leading us and any and every little sound landmark, sharp corner, road patterns, or anything else that could keep me informed. I also thought about all the possible turn-offs I could think of, and I tried not to feel too certain. Truthfully, it was only a hunch. The conversation up front started once again.

The lady asked, "Is that boy still out?"

Guy one replied, "I don't know, let me find out." I could make out a blob coming my way. I froze my hands where they were. He grabbed my head and slammed it up against the side of the van. I did everything in my power to keep from making a sound and prayed he didn't see the hole in the burlap.

"He hasn't awaken. How about you little lady?" He moved over to the girl. I heard some whimpering.

The lady seductively said, "You are such a big, tough, mean man."

"Yes, I know. That's why you love me. Don't you love me little girl?" I heard a muffled scream as I think he grabbed her arm or hair or something.

The leader said, "Enough Azi!"

The lady replied, "Come here you mean man." Azi, guy one's name that I now knew, laughed and made his way back to the bench seat. He kissed the lady. At least I think that's what happened. My head was screaming pain again. I could hear the girl crying over on the other side. That made my guts roar inside me. Azi needed to be smashed. She had to be scared to death.

The driver said, "Oh, can you two cut it out. For cryin' out loud you're makin' me sick or somethin'."

Azi asked, "So, Jinnah, what's your plan for our uninvited guest?"

"You ask too many questions."

"Well I'm sorry, but we'd like to know what's going to happen."

"Very well. Before we head west we will head east for an hour. That will make it look like we're heading for the airport. Then we'll kill him and throw him along the highway. He will act like a barrier for the police. They will have to search the area. Then it will be simple connect the dots for them. Two kids were kidnapped in Deluice, which is south. They will figure we came north probably on the road which we are on now, got onto the highway and started going east. For some reason we killed the boy. It won't make sense, but they will easily figure that the girl was the intended target and he was an unfortunate bystander. The next decision will be east or west? The FBI will be on the scene and they will put the pieces together. They will see the connection between this girl's kidnapping and the upcoming trial of my brother and our fellow compatriots. The next most likely dot to connect will be the airport, further east."

"And they will immediately determine, the all knowing FBI that they are, that we are heading for that airport. Thier own sixth sense for terrorist activities will lead them east, and when Amjad makes contact to relay our demands it will confirm their suspicions. Excellent."

The driver asked, "And you don't think that they're going to check to the west at all?"

Jinnah replied, "By the time they find his dead body we will probably have finished going west and will already be going north. We might even be at our camp. Just leave the planning to me."

The lady said, "Maybe we shouldn't be laying our plans out for the girl."

"She is no threat."

So my early exit was already part of the plan. The adrenaline surged through me now. There was no way to control it. It poured into me like water tearing through a harsh channel of rapids. Now I had a time limit on getting free. Fear was free to roam my mind and it made the blood drain from my face and my hands grow freezing cold. I immediately started working on the tape again. I had no clue what I was going to do, but anything would be better than just being pulled out and shot. I didn't want my life to go out with that kind of a bang. The biggest question I wanted answered was why they kidnapped her? What was her connection to these compatriots that were coming to trial? I knew this "girl", whoever she was, probably had some answers. I had a million questions. Azi hopped back over the seat. I thought I was going to get it again, but he went over to the girl.

He said, "So does the little lady like our plans? Aw, don't want to say anything today." I could hear whimpering again. This was no little kidnapping here. These guys and lady were professional and they most definitely had an axe to grind.

"What's a matter you don't like foreigners?" I think he grabbed her around the neck because I heard a very faint scream. "Well I don't like Americans. Why do you Americans pretend to be our ally? Where was our ally when India invaded Kashmir, or when India attacked East Pakistan? You use our alliance for convenience while you support Israel like family. The know-all Americans, you think you're Gods. You revoke aid when you feel like creating a reason and now you attack and murder Muslim brothers in Iraq while marauding as an ally. Your father is going to make the right decision or I will enjoy watching you scream as I chop off parts of your body. Either way, we will have our revenge. Did you ever want to see your intestines? You may get the chance, and your daddy will get the home video."

The lady added, "He can send it into American Home Videos." The two of them had a good laugh. I can't begin to describe how sick it was. I wished that fool would just sit down so I could keep working on the tape.

The driver said, "Man, you two are one sick mother fuckin' match made in hell."

Jinnah said, "Leave her alone. Now!"

"Whatever you say, Syed."

"Let us focus on what we are doing." Azi moved back to his seat. The whimpering continued. I couldn't tell for sure, it was too hard to see, but I think she was shaking. I was so angry I felt like I could just rip my hands right out of that duct tape. I bit down hard on the cloth tied around my mouth. I wanted to kill that bastard Azi right there. He had tapped into a whole well of anger that was buried deep in my soul. You just don't treat girls like that. I was going to get her out of there and if I got the chance, kick his ass. That pig wasn't going to touch her again. He needed his face beaten in. If she could only know how close I was to getting free. I wanted to reassure her. She was going to be OK. She didn't need to be scared.

I was really hot. It took me a few seconds to control my thoughts. I had to calm myself down and focus my anger. I had a certain element of surprise and I needed that surprise. They thought I was out cold and they didn't realize I knew where we were. The leader's talk about a highway seemed to confirm my assumptions. Interstate 67 runs east and west and is north of the bridge that I believed we'd crossed. I couldn't spoil my opportunity by getting all fiery. Surprise was the only weapon I had to get us free. I focused everything on that tape. After Azi had his fun, he jumped back over the seat and gave the lady a kiss.

I had to maintain careful control. One slip and I'd bang the tire jack against the wall or the floor of the van. Once the surprise was gone, I didn't have much of a chance. They'd just put a gun to my head and this time that would be it. The thought of that outcome made me make sure I put all of my weight on that jack to hold it still, while I tried to keep my emotions checked. I'm good at being clumsy, and now wasn't the time. That was the thought that did it.

I hadn't thought about screwing up, not once during the whole ordeal so far. I was too focused on my task, but I had just brought that thought out. This was high stakes stuff, and one slip and it would all be over. Instantly, I felt like a nuclear technician carrying highly toxic radioactive waste. Every movement I made was with complete concentration. I thought about my date with Heather the night before. I thought I was doing OK with her, but I'd had a whoops. I couldn't have a whoops now. I was afraid I had just psyched myself out, but it really didn't matter. I had no other option but to proceed. I just hoped this was going to be the dinner part of my date with these terrorists and not the driving to the movies part.

For twenty minutes I worked in controlled terror. It drove my patience to a cliff not to be able to just rip the hell out of that tape and start kicking the shit out of Azi. I needed to move; all of this secrecy was driving me nuts. When the last strand of tape finally tore, a great relief came over me. I thought to myself, holy shit, I really did it. I really did it. I was free. It was like getting an Algebra 2 final and realizing you could really do this stuff. Now, what to do next? Time to go for trig. Huh? Ever so slowly, I reached inside my jacket for my pocketknife. I pulled it out and started cutting the tape on my feet. About halfway through it made a loud ripping sound.

I held perfectly still. It seemed like everything in my body froze. The beads of sweat were the only things moving. They slid down my forehead and dripped onto my jacket. I froze my eyes on Azi's blob sitting on the bench seat and waited for him to move. I gripped the knife in my hand and readied myself to strike. I think my heart stopped beating. I was going to go for his throat. I could hear the ripping of flesh and his scream as I plunged the blade into him. Every ounce of energy in my body was building inside of me. It was roaring to a peak and I was going to explode as soon as he came back. I waited for a minute, but I guess the sound was loud only to my ears.

I took a few more seconds to cool down. I was more nervous than I'd ever been in my whole life, but I was free. There was a crack in the door to freedom. I had some real progress to be excited about, and that's usually just about the time when I have a big whoops.

It felt like I was playing cops and robbers in a way. Then I reminded myself that I was going to be killed as soon as we hit the highway, or as soon as they realized what I was doing. I had maybe an hour left if that; as long as my guess about the bridge was right. If my guess was right we were still going north on route 425, which connects with interstate 67. I finished cutting my feet free. The main thing now was how to actually get free. It seemed like I'd done so much already, but really all of that was miniscule. How were we going to get out of the van?

Surprise was my golden gun. I knew I should try and get the girl's hands and feet free. I carefully untied my mouth gag. My face leaped with joy to be able to return to normal. I waited until we went around the next hard left. It seemed like the longest time, but thankfully the driver was still going plenty fast around the corners. I let myself fall and sort of threw myself to her side. I banged my elbow hard on the floor of the van making a loud thud. My head was on her leg.

The lady said, "What was that?" I was praying once again that Azi didn't come back.

Azi responded, "Tony's driving so fast he's throwing that kid around like a rag doll."

"Hey, lay off OK. I drive the way I drive."

I whispered to her, "When we go around the next hard left fall my way a bit so I can get upright." I tapped her on the leg and whispered it again to make sure she got it. I think she tried to whisper, "Uh, huh." We waited only a few short seconds this time and the van whipped around another corner. Sure enough she leaned my way so it looked right for me to be sitting up right. I was kind of laying my head on her shoulder.

Azi said, "You never listen do you?"

"Will you just shut the hell up. At least I have a license."

I whispered to her, "I'm going to cut your hands free. Keep them behind your back even after the tape is cut." There was no way I was going to risk cutting her feet free at this moment, but I had gotten a burst of inspiration about how to get out.

Azi and Tony were still having it out about the driving and the lady had joined in. I took the chance to whisper my plan to her. I said, "Listen, we wait until they stop at a stop sign or slow down a good bit and then we go out the back. The van has rear doors. I'll just open them and we'll fall out. The surprise should give us a head start. Then we'll have to run for it."

She must have taken off her gag because she whispered back, "You're nuts."

"You got a better idea!"

"You're still nuts."

"Listen, we're starting to sound like those idiots up there. We have surprise on our side. They think I'm out cold and they certainly don't think we're untied. On top of that, I'm pretty sure I know where we are."

"You're nuts."

"Thanks for the vote of confidence. In case you weren't listening, they're going to be making an early exit for me pretty soon. I'm not ready to trade in this sack for a body bag." I couldn't believe she was so negative. I'd done pretty damn good so far. I was surprised with myself. If she only knew what a klutz I normally am, she'd be ready to run with her luck right now. I didn't care what her reservations were; I wanted to get outta there real soon.

She replied, "Fine. Did you check to see if the doors are unlocked?"

"No."

She replied, "Shit." It sounded like she was going to start crying. She was scared.

I replied, "Look, we're in this together. I'm going to do anything I can to get us outta here.

"I was hoping your were an FBI agent or something." Now, she was starting to cry.

"I'm not, but I'm going to get you out of here or I'll die trying, so I'm committed. We're going to be OK." I carefully slid my hand out and squeezed her hand and then rubbed her back. "I promise I'm going to do everything I can."

"OK."

"I'd also like to kick the shit out of that Azi guy." She chuckled a little. I told myself, I'm not going to fail. She needed me and I couldn't fail, not this time. When I failed my Mom I promised I'd never let it happen again. Here was the chance. I'm not going to be stopped. I'm not going to fail her. I don't know how I'm going to do it, but this time I'm going to get it done. Up front the discussion was dying down so I said, "That's it." Then, Tony slowed down and turned to the left onto a dirt road.

It was an unexpected turn, for the worse. All of the sudden my theory about the bridge, the roads, and the highway fell apart. I had no idea where we were. To get to the highway I thought we were going to, we weren't going to be taking any dirt roads. Maybe the dinner part of the date was over and it was time for me to smash into a parking lot light pole? I'm not going to fail. I gritted my teeth as I remembered just what failure looked like. Not this time!

Syed or Jinnah or whatever his name was said, "Listen up. I want to make this quick. Azi and Katerina you take the kiddies out one at a time to relieve themselves if they need to, provided they are conscious. I will help you. Tony, you fill up the tank with gas. You know where we hid it? That is it. Let's make it quick and without any unexpected events." My stomach felt like a black hole. Azi wasn't going to be too happy when he discovered my tape cutting work. We had to get out now.

Tony said, "This is great! Driving on dirt is a whole lotta fun. I feel like one of those cowboy's or somethin'." We were being bounced all over the van. I had to rap my arm around her just to keep close enough that we could talk.

I whispered to her, "We've got to go, now."

She replied, "I know. The door's unlocked."

"How do you know that?"

"I unlocked it." I was impressed. I hadn't even noticed her doing it. She said, "You say when."

"When we hit the ground, get the burlap sack off, roll onto your back, and lay still. I'll cut your feet free as quickly as possible. Don't try to do anything."

"I'm trusting you." I cut a good size opening in the back of her burlap sack. I had already widened the one in mine. I flipped my blade closed and put the knife back in the holder on my belt.

"I know. I'm not going to fail." It was time for the final test. Were we ready? I could get out of my bag really quick and I'd just have to cut her legs free. I went over the motions in my head probably a thousand times. The time was now. This was a one shot deal. I was waiting for an opportunity, but it didn't seem that Tony was going to be slowing down anytime soon. It was going to be pretty painful if we had to jump out now, but I didn't want to wait until we were stopping at their refuel point. The element of surprise would be lost. Those were the extra seconds we needed. It was going to take me a few seconds with her feet. But there was no way we could risk jumping out at the speed we were going. Azi and Katerina were laughing and giving Tony a hard time. Jinnah was silent. Tony was yelling, "Yee haw," a lot and going even faster. I was getting more and more worried.

I whispered to the girl, "Shit! That asshole is blazing down this road."

She replied, "Please tell me you're not thinking about jumping out now."

"I'm not suicidal. I'd like to get out before we're about to stop for the gas. They'll be ready to get out then. We need all the head start we can get."

"Agreed. You said you know where we are?"

"I don't know anymore. I thought I knew for sure, but I don't know. I could still be right. They migh've just turned off of 425 onto some remote dirt road leading into a state park or something. That way they could gas up without people around."

"Great. What's around here?"

"If we're where I think we are, trees. The area is very remote. Mostly campgrounds are along the highway and they're empty most of the year. The small towns are very contained. Most of the locals live right in the little towns. Basically, once we're out, we're on our own, especially now that we're going back this dirt road." She took a deep breath. I knew fear was running through her veins. She grabbed my hand and held on. I gave it a squeeze.

"I'm not going to fail. We're not going to fail." We drove at off road racing speed for probably fifteen minutes at least. Our friends up front had stopped talking and so had the girl and me. I've never been so nervous in my life, and the waiting made it worse. The build up of energy was killing me. I needed to do something.

Jinnah broke the silence. He said, "You are going to slow down."

Tony replied, "For what?"

"For the one lane bridge you crazy psycho."

"Naw, I was plannin' on going at least a hundred."

"You are just too funny. Maybe you should find another line of work."

"Yeah, yeah I'll slow down. Keep your pants on, Jinnah, I was just fuckin' witcha."

Jinnah didn't reply, but I knew when we'd be getting out of this international terrorist sitcom, what a group. I couldn't understand how some street wise New Yorker, two middle eastern guys, and some German/Russian lady got matched together. And, here I was, the light pole king / Mr. Hardly ever does anything right in his life, in the middle of it, what a mess. I tried to laugh to myself to lighten my mood. The moment of truth was coming.

I whispered to her, "The bridge." I think she knew what I was planning because I could see the intensity of her dark eyes through the burlap. We sat and waited. The van started to slow down, and soon after, we hit the bridge with a hard thud. It was macadammed so I figured that had to be it. We were still going at least twenty miles an hour, but this was our best chance. I started to slide my hand out of the sack. I went over everything in my head. I needed to be lightening fast cutting the tape on her feet, plus, I had to get myself out. I felt like I was coming up to bat for my team's last out down by one; the difference was that a strikeout meant the end of the really big game. I needed them to be really surprised. They had to hesitate. Tony had to hesitate the most. I slid my hand and hers up onto the knob. There was another hard thud and we were off the bridge. It was now or never. Tony would start speeding up immediately. As I looked into her eyes, I squeezed her hand, then pushed the button, and slammed my shoulder on the doors.

Chapter Ten

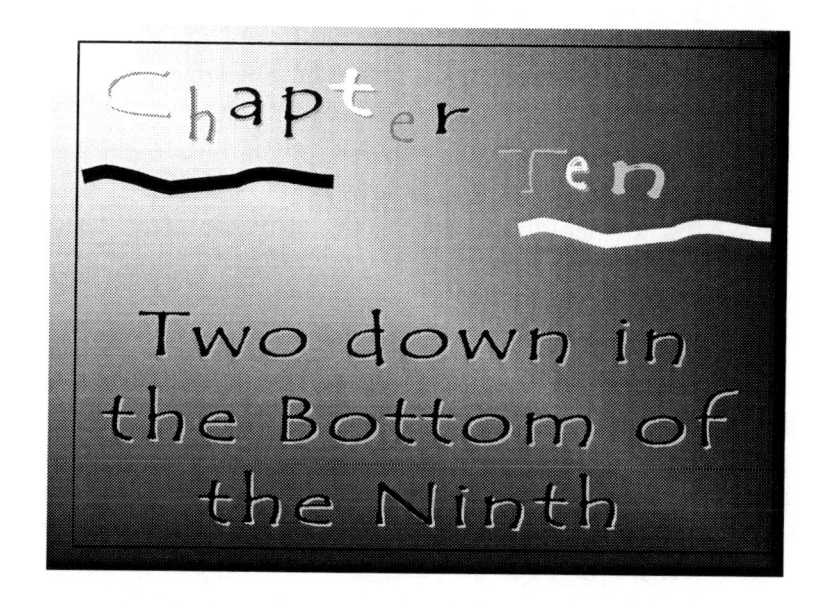

Two down in the Bottom of the Ninth

My hands hit the dirt first. After that, it was a couple bangs and some rolling. I didn't hesitate for a second. I couldn't feel a thing. I flipped open my knife and ferociously ripped through the burlap. I completely forgot I'd already cut an opening in the back. I'd built up so much energy that the burlap didn't have a chance. To be able to move with full force felt great. It's how I felt about my whole life. I never got to move with full speed and feel on top of my life. Now, I had to be.

She was only a few feet from me lying perfectly still. She was already out of her sack. I thought she was dead she was so still. As I moved over to begin cutting, I saw the brake lights flash and the passenger door already opening. The van had only gone maybe fifty yards, unlucky I thought. I ripped through the duct tape.

She yelled, "Come on get my feet!"

"I'm working on it!" I was cutting it as fast as I could. I finished in a few seconds and tore the tape off. I immediately flipped the blade closed. There was no need to keep that out anymore. "I have an idea." They were getting out. Azi and I made eye contact. I was praying that bridge we crossed had a good-sized creek or stream running under it. The water should be high, I thought. Winter snowmelt with spring rains should have the creeks high. As she was getting up she must've realized how close they were because she immediately responded.

She said, "Holy shit, Holy shit. Go! Go! Go!!" and started pushing me down the road. Yeah, no kidding I thought. Who in the hell was this girl?

I grabbed her arm and yelled, "Come on. Back to the creek." We started running back down the road. When we got to the bridge I pulled her off into the brush. We started running around the side of the bridge. The brush around me was smacking my face and trying to grab at my feet. Even nature was working against us. I could hear the sound of their voices not far behind.

She yelled to me, "What in the hell are you trying to do!" As she was yelling at me we almost ran right off the edge of a revine that descended down to a creek. My feet kicked dirt out over the edge. As I expected, the creek was high. It was more like a small stream now.

"Whoa!" I yelled.

She replied, "Damn, now where we gonna go?" Then she looked where I was looking.

I said, "We want to be down there." We were about fifty feet above the creek. The bank was mostly dirt and brush. There didn't seem to be too many rocks. I looked back, saw how close they were, and looked at her and said, "Let's do it."

"I don't know."

"We're out of time." I grabbed her arm and we tried to slide down the steep bank. I tried to stay on my feet but I hit something and I finished at least half of the decent by rolling. My face splashed into the water as I came to a stop. I was dazed but an emergency switch in my brain kicked in and forced me to get up. We had to get into that water. As I got to my feet, I saw she must've had the same luck because she was also lying on the ground and she looked hurt.

I grabbed her around the waist and started dragging her out into the water as I said, "Come on we've got to get into the middle." She was dazed. I yelled at her, "Come on! Don't quit now. We're almost free." We started trudging through the water out to the middle.

She replied, "I'm all right. I smacked my head on something really hard. I think I'm bleeding."

"That makes two of us."

"What are we doing?"

"I'm hitching us a ride."

"You do know what you're doing?"

"If you'd like, maybe we could have a cooperative group session with the terrorists to discuss our ideas." And I thought the terrorists made me mad, I was going to kill her if she didn't back off. We were getting into the deeper water now. I could still stand but the current was good and strong.

I told her, "Start swimming."

"What!"

"Just do it! Swim: breast stroke, freestyle, heck just float. The current is going to get us out of here." She followed my instructions despite her look of doubt. We started moving downstream. "See, a free ride." We were starting to move pretty good. As we went under the bridge, I looked back and saw Azi and Katerina just coming down from the ravine.

Azi saw us floating away and screamed, "The other side, Tony! The other side." His words echoed off the underside of the bridge as we past beneath.

The girl grabbed my arm and said, "Oh shit!" I faced forward and saw Tony making his way into the water.

I asked her, "Can you hold your breath?"

She replied, "Good idea." We both went under. I kept a hold of her hand. I didn't want to get separated, but I smacked a rock and that's exactly what happened. This creek wasn't the ocean. If it wasn't springtime we might've been able to walk across it without getting our feet wet. The big rock must've been just under the surface because I didn't see it before we went under. Once I regained my senses I burst to the surface for air. I grimaced, moaned, and gritted my teeth because of the pain. Then I saw through my squinted eyes that Tony was trying to get a hold of her. That switch flipped again. There was no way I was going to let them get her!

I dove back under and frantically searched the bottom for a baseball size rock. When I finally found one, I raced to the surface. Tony would soon have his buddies. I had traveled ten or twenty yards from where I went under. Tony had gotten her and was dragging her to the shore as Azi and Katerina were running under the bridge along the edge to help him. There not going to get her!

I growled as I violently rushed to dry land so I could get a good throw. As I clawed at the dirt to pull myself out, Tony crept ever closer to the opposite bank where Azi and Katerina would join him. I jumped to my feet and turned. I gripped the rock and yelled, "Hey, Tony!" He stopped for a second and looked toward me obviously surprised to hear me calling his name. That was the moment I needed. I aimed for his head and whipped that sucker. The rock whistled through the air towards him. The girl used his shock to get herself partially free. She ducked down, and it's a good thing too because the rock crashed into Tony right where she would've been. I'm no Oral Hershiser, but Tony was knocked off his feet by the blow.

I screamed to her, "Come on! Come on!" Katerina and Azi jumped out into the water and were furiously splashing down towards her. She was working her way into the middle as I exploded back into the water. With a couple good kicks I reached her, slid my arm around her waist and started doing sidestroke to get both of us going. Azi almost had his hands on her, but I kicked him in the face, which knocked him back into Katerina.

I growled at him, "Get the fuck out!" The kick gave us a little separation, but they were still so close I could almost smell what kind of cologne Azi was wearing. I kicked my legs as hard as I could to get us moving as fast as possible. After a few all to close seconds, we were starting to move away. I saw Jinnah standing up by the van. I just couldn't help it. I didn't need to egg these guys on, but I yelled in his direction, "See ya later assholes!"

He yelled to Katerina and Azi, "Go after them!" but they weren't having much success swimming. Katerina hadn't put down her automatic, so she was having trouble going. Azi found a rock just below the surface like I did and I think it hit him in the 'nads. To see that look of pain on his face made me laugh.

I yelled, "Whoops!" The girl looked pretty scared but even she cracked a little smile. In hindsight I shouldn't have given them any more reason to kill me.

The whole event took less than five minutes, but it felt like forever getting to this point. We'd made it, for now. Azi and Katerina clearly didn't know how to swim or float in a creek. After a few more seconds they were out of sight. We were riding the waves, for now.

Chapter Eleven
Out of the Fire and Into the Woods

The current was strong, which was good because we were getting away and bad because it was hard to maneuver and even harder to stop. I kept a hold of her at all times. We had to stay together. Just after they went out of sight we reached an area that wasn't nearly as high. Once the water had gone down to around mid-thigh we started running. Up ahead more rocks were in the way and the current grew stronger. I kept looking over my shoulder for Azi or Katerina, but they were nowhere to be found. I helped to get the girl out of the water so we could run around the rocks and the rapids created by them. We didn't want to get caught in that bone breaking mess. We rushed through the brush and jumped back into the creek as soon as we were past the rocks. There still wasn't anyone in sight behind us. We were back in deeper water again so we started swimming. For now, anyway, they weren't anywhere in sight. That gave me a little security. Then again, maybe they were already planning to cut us off somewhere down further?

Now that we weren't running for our lives (well at least we didn't have guns pointed at us) I had the time to notice just how freezing cold the water was. I also noticed how sore my shoulder was, how many bruises I had, where all a' my cuts were because they were burning in the water, how incredibly bad my head hurt, and how lucky we'd been. It was the early part of sunset and we'd made it. We floated in silence for about twenty minutes. I watched behind us and all around us very closely. There was no way I was going to blow it now. The girl broke the silence.

She asked me, "How much longer do you think we're going to be in this water?"

"Well, I'm no expert, but I'd say as long as we can stand it. We're putting distance between them and us."

"OK." She didn't sound too thrilled. That was about all that was said for awhile. We were both too high on adrenaline to relax and it wasn't an easy float. I hit another rock. This time my ribs got it. I didn't hit it real hard but it was hard enough to remind me of the bruise I had from being slammed against the dumpster. We also got caught up in some dead trees lying across the stream. Twice we had to get out of the water and walk around the really rocky areas. What little conversation we did have was directly about the task at hand. We were both focused. I must've looked over my shoulder a million times, but they weren't in sight. They couldn't keep up on foot. The brush would slow them down, and there was no sign of them behind us in the water. After about an hour in the water, I couldn't stand it much longer. After another hour, I thought I was going to die. After another hour, we came to yet another rocky area. We probably had to walk around four or five of these rocky spots by this point. Once again she broke the silence.

She said with disgust, "God damn, why're there so many rocks?" It was frustrating. We would usually have to walk through a lot of brush to get around the rocks. Your legs feel like giant logs after you've been in freezing water like that for so long. It's hard to make them work. Any little scratch bleeds like crazy. Once we were out of the water the wind made us shake like an earthquake was occurring. Our legs were tree trunks and the wind made the rest of us rattle like old houses. Even as cold as the water was, it was warmer than that cold wind blowing.

I explained to her, "People put them there." Both of our voices were shaking because of the cold. Our bodies were trying desperately to stay warm.

"What in the hell they'd do that for?"

"Normally this creek would be much lower that it is now. Damming up sections helps to create water holes for fish."

"How'd you know that?"

"My Boyscout troop has done those kinds of projects. If we're where I think we are, I might've even worked on this creek." It felt good to have some normal conversation. It was a release to all of the pressure I'd felt since I was thrown into that van. I decided to keep the conversation going. I said, "I think I've had enough of the water."

"Yeah you ain't the only one. It be nice to feel my legs again."

"Tell me about it. Let's just chill here."

"Oh, funny."

"Sorry, bad joke, but I'm serious. I don't feel like hiking around these rocks again and we don't want to die of hypothermia anyhow." We made our way to the shore and got out. The wind started to work its magic once again. I said, "We need to start a fire or we're going to freeze out here. It's going to get plenty cold tonight and we are plenty wet."

"Now, I'm hoping that you've had some like training in this kind of stuff."

"I disappointed you on the FBI thing, but this time I can fulfill your hope. I'm a Boyscout."

"Great."

"Why does everybody seem to have such a negative view of Boyscouts?"

"Let's just drop it. What'd ya' need me to do?"

"We need wood."

She bent down and grabbed a stick and said, "Well, that's a tough one."

"You'd need a blow torch to light that wood on fire. We've got to find stuff that's not wet and that means most of the stuff on the ground won't be any good." It was really getting hard to see by this point because the sun was almost completely gone, but I started looking for some pine trees. "What we need is firestarter."

"What?" I began looking around. She followed me and asked, "So what are you doing?"

"I'm looking for some evergreens." I found one that would do. I pointed to the small twigs on the tree and said, "These are what we need. They're dead, dry, and small. They'll start a fire. Why don't you start picking some off. I'm going to look around for some bigger stuff to put on once we get it going." She started working on the tree and I walked around pulling all kinds of wood off trees and wherever else I could find it. We were both starting to shiver more violently. It was hard to do anything with my hands. With the first aid training I'd had, I knew that fire had to get started very soon. This was wilderness survival and being wet was not a good thing. I learned a lot with the Boyscouts, but this was the first time under real pressure. The only pressure in scouts was competing for the best time.

After a couple minutes she yelled over, "OK, I got a good amount. Let's do this." Her teeth were really chattering.

I came over and explained, "We need to have more in different sizes, that way when we start the fire we have the wood right there to keep it going. It's better to take the time and make a solid first effort than to have to do it twice."

"This cold is killing me." Not only were her teeth chattering, but her body was shaking badly. That was not a good sign. Shivering is the first sign of hypothermia, but when your body starts to shake uncontrollably, the situation is becoming more severe. I was cold, but I was still under control.

"I know, but we have to do it right the first time. We're not going to have time for a second chance. Here, take my jacket." I only had on a T-shirt underneath, but she needed the jacket more than I did. "Keep working and keep moving. That'll keep you warmer." I rapidly found a good spot to start the fire. We were far enough from the water not to be seen if our friends decided to try and wade down the stream like we did, and the area was well drained. There was a large fallen tree that was on the upstream side and a fair amount thick brush in between the creek and the fire. I figured we'd build a fire reflector and pile some more brush to the downstream side and around the several large trees that were on the woods side of the fire. The trees and brush offered pretty good wind protection. I cleared an area for the fire and began piling the wood I was finding according to size. Working as fast as I possibly could, it took me a good ten minutes to gather a good supply of wood in various sizes. My body was starting to hurt from the cold. Periodically, I yelled over to her to see how she was doing.

After I'd made a fire circle using some stones from the creek I went to over to her and asked, "Are you ready?"

"Take a look," she replied. She had a real good pile of twigs sitting in between two rocks.

"That's good you put them on that rock, it keeps them dry. And placing them between the two keeps the wind from blowing them away."

"Thank you. Before you know it I'll be a Girlscout."

"Well, you're doing pretty good. I think we're cold enough now that we should get this fire going." She was freezing. "How are you doing?"

"Really cold."

"I just want to check something." I took my hand and touched her face.

"Wow! Keep those cold paws off me!"

"Sorry, but I wanted to see how warm your skin was yet. Your lips are pretty blue, but there's still some heat there. I need to get you warm, now." The jacket had helped her, but she wasn't going to hold out much longer. I was surprised how well she was tolerating everything. Being cold and wet is about as unbearable a situation as I've ever felt. We carried the firestarter twigs over to where I had made the fire circle.

I directed, "We start with the stuff you found." She piled all of her twigs in the middle of the circle. I put some little sticks on next. I arranged them in tee-pee style. As I was piling the wood, I asked her, "So, what's your name?" to keep her talking and her mind off the cold.

She hesitated for a second. It seemed she was just as surprised as I was that we had gone this long without knowing each other's name. She replied, "Jasmine Williams. What's yours?

"Chad."

"Well, Chad, how do you plan to start the fire?"

"What's the Boyscout motto?"

"I have no idea. Just start the fire."

"It's be prepared." I reached into my jeans pocked and pulled out the little round metal container of matches.

"You have matches," she said with doubt. "Well they're wet matches now."

I smiled and looked into her eyes and said, "Waterproof," then I shook the container. She shook her head as I started laughing. Soon she started laughing. Laughing was one thing that was easy for us to do; we were shaking so much already. After a few seconds of laughing I said, "OK, OK, I still have to light it yet. As bad as my hands are shaking I don't know if I'll be able to even strike a match."

"I hope you're joking."

"I am, at least I hope I am. We're almost out of the woods. Sorry, bad joke." I knew that a fire was our biggest concern right now. If we got it started, we had an excellent chance of making it to safety, provided we could avoid the terrorists. Fire is that important. I said, "Help block the wind with your body." She moved closer to me. I directed, "Lift up the one side of the wood. I'll light it there." She nodded her head. I think she was getting too cold to talk. It took me forever to open the match container because it was so hard to use my hands. After a great deal of effort, I finally managed to pull out a match with the little piece of sandpaper. I struck the match on the sandpaper and the flame rose. I have never been that in awe of a flame in my life. Both of us watched it like carrion looking for a free meal. I said, "Here we go." I started lighting the twigs. The little flame grew a bit. We were both leaning over it trying to cover it and protect it like two hens guarding a newborn chic from the wind. As it grew into the tiniest flame, we watched intently.

I said, "OK, you can let go." She let the rest of the wood back down and we waited. It started to catch. I said, "Once it catches more of those small sticks we should be OK." The flame grew. We were salivating to feel the heat. The sticks caught. I said triumphantly, "We're ready for bigger wood. I went over to the piles I had laid out and brought more to put on. I arranged them around the tee-pee and waited some more. The fire was almost strong enough that it wouldn't go out. After another minute it was strong enough.

Jasmine said, "Ahh, that feels so good." I put on even bigger wood and soon it was roaring. Both of us sat in relative silence enjoying the heat until we both started to feel warm again. For the first time I felt I could let my guard down a bit. I felt safe for just a second. As I was enjoying the heat, I started laughing once again. I couldn't help it. I couldn't believe that everything had worked. As clumsy, awkward, and prone to disaster as I was, things worked. Jasmine started laughing as well. She came over to me and hugged me as we both laughed and laughed.

I said, "I just can't believe we made it."

She laughed and said, "That was one hell of a throw! You smacked that big fat guy right in the chest."

"You should have seen the shock on his face. It was a good thing you ducked." As she was hugging me and smiling, I noticed for the first time how pretty she was. I mean I noticed before, but there was too much pressure to process it. The hug was like a switch turning on that got me to pay attention and put together: girl, pretty, and hug. I felt warm from both fires. I felt part of something for once. I knew she didn't mean the gesture romantically, but we were a team no matter. She was as excited as I was that we'd made it and she depended on me. That's the kind of connection I wanted out of love. I realized that all my dreams about feeling that kind of love were true. There was no way I could keep myself from smiling.

Just the Typical Me

I wanted to keep the good feelings going so I decided to make some small talk. We hadn't said anything for over three hours that didn't have something to do with our survival. I had only ten minutes ago had the time to even ask her her name. As our laughing died down and we ended our embrace, I wanted to get the small talk started. I was coming back to the normal Chad and I put my foot in my mouth right away.

I said, "Jasmine, that's a different name."

She was leaning her back against a tree. She smiled and said, "How so?"

"Well, it's sort of not a common name." After I said common I felt like I was getting into quicksand. I tried to explain myself better. "I mean it's not like Shaniqua or like Shamalie ala mala afrad," I joked, but trying to move in quicksand only makes you slide down further. I had slid down a long ways.

"You mean it's not black."

"That's not exactly what I meant." To fill you in, I started this whole conversation because I was trying to say how unique and nice I thought her name was. But, (there's always a but with me) I realized after I had already started the compliment that one of the reasons I thought it was nice was because it wasn't only a "black" name. I don't have any problems with "black" names, but I do with the black pride that's usually behind them. I like a lot a' things black people consider "black only" things. Being a sprinter has allowed me to experience a lot of those stereotypes. Since I'm white and I like rap that makes me some kind of imposter. I like MC Hammer; I shouldn't have to be black to appreciate his music. The unique names seem like just another example of "this is our heritage and you're not welcome." Anyhow, I knew I'd offended Jasmine, and now I had to get into all this stuff.

I tried to explain. I decided to say, "Look, I've always felt that the reason black people give their children those names is because they don't want to be associated with white culture."

She wasn't smiling anymore. She replied with more conviction, "We want to take pride in our heritage."

"And that's a black only thing. That's what I don't like. You know, maybe I like rap music and maybe I want to be a world-class sprinter, but those are areas that are "black". I'm not welcome in those groups because I'm white."

"One of the reason African Americans take pride in their heritage is because they don't feel welcome in white groups that they would like to be a part of."

"Great, so we'll form our clic and you can have yours."

"Where do you live, Chad?"

"What's that got to do with anything?"

"I'm just asking."

"I've lived in Canton my whole life." That didn't seem to surprise her. I said, "I can see you've stereotyped me."

"No what you've said stereotyped you. It's the way you bust on black heritage and the way you say 'black people' sounds like you've got some issues."

"When did I start busting on black heritage? You don't even know me. I say one wrong thing and now I'm a racist. How can you make that judgement?" This was getting real bad.

"You said it!"

"I didn't mean it the way you're saying."

"Sure, now you don't. Now, that you know I'm offended."

"I didn't! I'm sorry I got into this, but those names just say to me: you're not welcome. I hate that. You wouldn't believe the stuff I get from blacks when I sprint against them. All of that plus the names forms this big circle that I want to be in, but can't because, 'you just a slow white boy.' Look, all I really wanted to say was I think your name is really beautiful. That's it." God, why is everything such a mess with me. How is it I can make the most simplest of compliments unbelievably complicated?

"OK I think I understand, but no more compliments. Wow, you surprised me."

"Because I've seemed so nice and all of the sudden I said something that shattered your lovely picture."

"Yeah something like that."

"Well, join the club. I have a way of doing that. If you only knew what a screw-up I can be, you'd realize just how lucky we were to get away. I could sure tell you some good stories about my stupidity."

"I'd like to hear them. Other than your blown attempt at a compliment you've saved my life and taken good care of me. I like someone who's not afraid of being human."

"Thanks, but maybe another time with my stories." I almost wanted to tell them to her. I don't know why. She made me feel safe. It was like talking to Dale. I don't know what it was, but I didn't feel like 'chippy' Chad around her, provided I didn't try offer any more compliments. Maybe it was because she was still talking to me even after I made such a stupid mistake. But it was more than that. We were alone out here in nature and there's something about nature that cleanses you of the unnatural within yourself. I've always felt more like me around trees.

I added, "I'm exhausted from this discussion. I shouldn't have opened my big mouth."

"You're wrong. It's always better to talk."

I don't know where the burst of confidence came from, but my next line came out of my mouth before I'd even thought it. I said, "I think you're really pretty and you have a really nice name that expresses that; sorry it took all of this for me to say that." I was probably more stunned than she was.

She smiled, and that's usually a good sign. I think anyways. She said with a laugh, "Thanks. I think you're about the most open-minded hillbilly I've ever met, and just so you know, you did a good job with that compliment."

I smiled, and laughed a little as I replied, "Yee haw. Thanks." I don't know why she believed me and overlooked my mistake. Maybe she needed me to get her out of this whether she could stand me or not. After the horrible first impression I'd made, anything was possible. She, on the other hand, made a great first impression. I'm not even sure exactly what it was, but there was something about her personality. Well, it was more like her essence or her aura but it seemed so, familiar. As I was getting to know her it was more like getting to know someone you knew long ago. Of course the last ten minutes of our discussion was anything but comfortable, but even in my scurrying to explain myself, I felt very comfortable with her. This was all good because we were going to need teamwork to survive. There was so much we had to overcome yet, and I had no idea what that would be or when it would come. Every moment brought the unexpected. I was sick to the stomach from being so nervous for so long. Our discussion was a nice break, in a way.

I said, "You know, you did me a big favor. If I wasn't here I'd be at home getting an earful. I wrecked my Dad's new truck last night."

"Well, glad I could help you get kidnapped by terrorists, fall out of a moving van, roll down a huge hill, and swim in freezing water."

"Yeah, what a blast. You wanna compare injuries."

"Yeah sure," she sarcastically replied, "but we're here, alive and warm."

"And they're out there." It was time to get focused. I was getting more nervous because I felt like we were letting our guard down for too long.

She replied, "Excellent point."

Keeping Temptation Under Control

I felt like a special forces commando as I ordered, "We better start working on a fire reflector and we can pile some brush over here." I indicated to the downstream side of our little camp. "This light can be seen too easy right now. But before we do that we need to wring out as much of this water as possible. Spread my jacket out in front of the fire." She took it off and put it out close to the fire to dry. I took my shoes off and poured about a half a glass of water that had been sloshing around in them. I said, "When we go to sleep we can put our shoes near the fire to try and dry them." She was dumping the water out of her shoes as well.

She replied, "Dry shoes would be nice."

"Well, I don't think they're going to dry in one night. Anyhow, here's the situation. I've got my Swiss army knife and the container of matcher, but we only have about fifteen, if that. I have this light jacket, but I'm only wearing this T-shirt underneath. Then, I've got jeans, boxers, white socks and these old running shoes which are really soaked."

She replied, "Well, no jacket, but this heavy GAP sweatshirt should be all right. Then jeans, these boots."

"Those are good. If you were in some kind of dress shoes you'd be unhappy."

"Yeah, then just socks and, you know, underwear." She really didn't need to encourage my imagination. I had already noticed what a great body she had.

I paused a little while that word worked through my imagination and then tried to quickly keep going. "We have, ahh, plenty of water; although it's not purified. We'll have to take our chances. It should be all right because the creek is moving pretty good. Food, however, is going to become a concern if we're out here too long. I'm hoping we won't be."

"How long do you think we'll be out here?"

"Like I said before, if we're where I think we are we should follow this creek south and we'll hit something. There's a Boyscout camp up here somewhere. It could be really close by. I know there's a creek that runs through it. Maybe this is the one."

"Are you sure?"

"I'm pretty sure, but either way we follow the creek south. Where there's water there's people. If the scout camp is down there somewhere, I'll recognize the surroundings."

"Things are looking up."

"A lot better than a few hours ago. I just have one more huge question, do you have any idea why they tried to kidnap you?"

"That's a good one, and I know the answer. My father is a respected prosecutor. He's the best, and he just got a really big case. Y'know that bombing of the number 9 line in New York?" I nodded my head yes. "They arrested four people who are members of a new and very active terrorist group called Al Jaala Juloh or The Winter Flame. My father is the lead prosecutor."

"So, where do you come in?"

"I think I was going to be an incentive for him not to do a good job."

"Why didn't you have protection?"

"I did."

"Well, he sure did a good job."

"I ditched him in the mall."

"No way! You are a little hellion. Why the hell did you do that?"

"I hated not being able to just be a normal person and I didn't believe all the concern for my life."

"How did they get you out of the mall and around back?"

"A man came up to me when I was in The Wall. He asked me if I was Jasmine Williams. I said yes and he told me that someone had a gift for me and I was to pick it up at loading dock 3A which was around back. He was wearing a Mall customer service uniform and everything. He told me there should be another customer service representative with a white delivery van. Then he smiled and said the gift was a surprise from someone who was, 'working hard and missed me very much.' My father had been away for almost a week working on the case, so I figured it was from him. I went around back and the next thing I know I'm in a burlap sack."

"Maybe you had some help losing your bodyguard?"

"What were you doing back there?"

"I was going home. I always park back there. A spot's always there and it's only a little walk to the one entrance. I had bought a new pair of running shoes and was done cruising the mall. I did a good job on two of them. The guy called Syed or Jinnah, they called him both names, won't be getting around well. I crushed his leg pretty good before they knocked me out. I was one finger away from being dead. Azi was going to shoot me right there, but Jinnah made him stop. He whacked me over the head, instead."

"You were nuts to come running at them."

"I didn't think about it rationally. I just reacted and did the best I could. It seemed like the right thing to do."

"I guess I haven't really said thank you yet."

"I haven't really finished the job."

"You make me feel like you will. I thought I was screwed when I found out you were just some kid my age, but you've taken good care of me. Thanks for saving my life." I wanted to tell her that I'd save her life any day, but I didn't have the guts.

I simply replied, "You're welcome." It was still nice to hear her being so sincere. "We should get started with our clothes. So, if you don't mind I'll need a little privacy." I indicated to my jeans and she got the hint and walked over behind a bunch of trees and turned her back. Now that she wasn't close by, for some reason I felt more comfortable thinking about her. She was something. I always figured a city girl wouldn't do to well in the country, but she was all right. Then again I didn't really know she was a city girl. That sweatshirt and pair of jeans were from The Gap, however. Her look wasn't one of roughness, so I had a feeling she had to have some pampering and it takes the green stuff to make a softer pillow. I finished squeezing as much water out of my clothes as possible and then I put them back on. I said, "OK, you can have the fire now."

She laughed, "Have the fire, why thank you."

I decided to ask her about my suspicions. "You're not a wilderness girl are you?"

"I've never been camping, but that doesn't mean I don't like it. I think I'd be having a good time if my life wasn't at stake." I laughed and went over to where she had been standing. Now, what had she meant by that I wondered, 'I'd be having a good time.' I didn't want to get too hopeful and think that I was the reason, but maybe this was my lucky day. I had to have bonus points for saving her life. That's what all the big stars do in those romantic movies and the girls love them for it. I hadn't really thought about her in a girlfriend type of way, but after her comment the thought grazed my mind. Another switch flipped on and I could feel my romantic side powering up. The date with Heather then flashed to put the 'do not operate' sign back up.

I wasn't going to go through that feeling of loss again. I decided to make a pact with myself, no romance, which would probably be easy to keep since I could see little chance that she'd give me the chance. How hot she was, was only a warning sign of how impossible it was going to be for someone like me to touch her. Jasmine and I only had one conversation and I'd almost made her run for the terrorists.

Anyhow, you know how you've got a good side that says one thing and a bad side that says another. Just like my emotions said this could happen but my rationality said no romance. I'm trying to tell this story truthfully, so I must admit that I caught a glimpse of the fire when I was supposed to looking into the night sky, if you know what I mean. I hope you don't think less of me. I couldn't help it, and frankly I wasn't really sorry I did it. Now, I'm sure you think less of me. I only peeked for a second, but it was the right second and plenty long enough.

On her, those were more than just white silky panties. With her wearing them, they came alive. They danced and glittered in the firelight as she was working to get the water out of her jeans. The light from the fire made her glow like a bronze statue. As I looked up into the sky I wished more than ever I wasn't such a loser. Patrick would have a chance with her. I had a chance she wouldn't run away thinking I was a complete idiot. That wisp of a thought that we might have a relationship grew to a strong gust for a few seconds. I imagined us together. I have a good imagination. I've got lots of practice. Before I started to enjoy that notion, I quickly reminded myself of the pact I'd just created. No romance, that was the rule. It would just blow up in my face. Besides, it was just lust, right? Then again there was something about her. I felt I actually knew more about Jasmine than I did Heather, and we'd only been together for a few hours. Unfortunately, while Heather was cute, Jasmine was hot and that didn't mean good things for me. Besides, there was no time for these kinds of thoughts. When your life is at stake you're not supposed to be worried about falling in love, right? Romance is so stupid.

She called over to me, "OK." I exited my thoughts and came back over to the fire.

"Feel better?"

"Yeah, I guess. I'm a little bit dryer, but everything is still wet."

"It'll dry eventually. Come on I'll show you how to build a fire reflector."

"How about explaining what it is."

"Just what the name says. Normally you build one to reflect the heat from the fire back to where you're sitting, but we also want to help block some of the light."

"You know a lot about this stuff."

"Yeah, I guess, but I've all ready had us break the golden rule of survival camping."

"Which is?"

"Don't get wet. Let's get to work." We spent the next couple hours concealing our location. We talked a little, but it wasn't anything important. I asked her what kind of music she likes and movies she's seen. She did ask me a little more about my Dad. I don't talk about him with even Dale all that often, so I kept it pretty thin. I only told her how much I couldn't stand him. That wasn't too personal. She was a good listener.

Saying No Makes Yes Impossible to Refuse!

After we finished, it was time for us to get some sleep. We were both exhausted. We each picked out trees. Mine was to the left of the fire and hers was to the right. We tried to make things as comfortable as possible, but sleeping on the ground with tree roots for a pillow is generally uncomfortable. We said good night and then I tried to fall asleep. I wasn't falling asleep, so I looked up at the moon and stars. It's the peace of camping that's beautiful, being alone with your thoughts. To top it all off, I was also alone with the person I was falling in love with, but making sure I didn't fall in love with because this was a no romance falling in love kind of thing. I kept reminding myself to deny it was happening. I started thinking about her sleeping over there. She was probably as uncomfortable as I was. Why shouldn't I take a chance and make a move? She could lay her head on my shoulder and that would be a whole lot more comfortable. Plus, it wasn't any big deal or anything. Well, it would be for me, but I was denying that to myself at the moment.

I asked her, "Are you comfortable over there?"

She replied, "Yeah, I'll be fine." That sort of ruined my plan. How in the world could she be comfortable? Maybe she thought that I was making a move and she was trying to cut it off before it started. She was a really nice girl and she wanted to stop things before I started pushing too hard and she had to knock me down. No, it was not a good idea to ask her to sleep with me. What a stupid idea that was. I hardly knew her, but, the gentleman thing to do was to make her more comfortable. My jacket was still drying by the fire. That would make a really nice pillow. So, I'll give her the jacket to be a nice guy, I decided.

It took a little extra coaxing to get my body in motion. When I got up she asked, "What are you doing?" I thought to myself, dang she was really trying to shut me down.

I replied, "Oh, just getting in a new position. There's a rock over here that's driving me nuts."

"I know what you mean," she replied. So much for my gesture of kindness. She was being evasive. And she had just agreed that she wasn't comfortable when a few seconds earlier she told me she was fine. This is part of my problem with girls. I just don't understand what's going on in their heads. My guess was she's trying to avoid an uncomfortable advance from me and she's trying to be nice about it. That made me sort of mad about the whole thing. I hadn't done anything. I mean I couldn't have been so bad she would want to avoid me already. The name thing was bad, but I thought we patched that up. I decided I just wasn't going to quit. She was going to have to be a man about it and just knock me down.

I asked her, "Are you sure you're comfortable?"

"Yeah, don't worry about me. I can handle it." Well you're not getting out of it that easy.

"Well, you can have my jacket to lay your head on if you'd like."

"No, that's OK. You can use it. I'll be fine." I couldn't believe she was being that stubborn. What could I have done that pushed her away this soon? Maybe we hadn't patched-up my poor name compliment as good as I thought, but I'd just saved her life a couple of hours ago! I was getting pretty pissed off. She was going to take that jacket and like it, or she was going to have to come out and say that she didn't like me. I wasn't letting her off easy, no way God damn it. How could she have gotten a negative impression already? I thought things were going fine. I was showing her all about living out in the woods and she seemed to like it. But, that's all part of my problem. When I think I'm doing OK I'm really striking out. If I was a dentist I'd be dumb enough to believe that people really meant it when they said hello to me as they came into my office. Maybe the whole thing was just a cover. Underneath she was dreading every moment. That was probably it I thought. Well, she's not getting off easy.

I got up and grabbed the jacket by the fire and walked over to her.

I nicely said, "You'll be more comfortable."

"You didn't have to do that for me." Yeah, no shit. I'm trying to be nice. God girls drive me nuts. I'd have more fun smashing my head with a sledgehammer.

I replied, "Just trying to do something nice," and I walked back over to where I was sleeping.

She said, "Thanks, Chad. You're taking good care of me." I guess she felt obligated to be nice now. She could tell I had seen through her evasion, and she was trying to make it easier for me. It wasn't working this time. I knew what her true feelings were.

She said, "Goodnight."

"Goodnight," I replied, as I was thinking yeah right. As much as I wanted her to like me, I would've appreciated a little honesty. I looked up into the night sky. Everything looked so peaceful up there. There was an organized beauty to everything. Organization in my life would be nice. It'd be much easier to get a girlfriend if I just had to complete a training course and pass a few tests. How can you be good at something when you don't know what to study? I just couldn't believe I had blown it already. My thoughts instantly ended. I nearly jumped up to the stars when I heard a twig break close by. I quickly rolled over and jumped up facing the direction I'd heard the sound. I was ready to strike, but it was Jasmine.

"Holy cow you scared me!"

"I'm sorry."

"What'd you want?"

She paused for a second and then said, "Nothing, nothing at all. I was just wondering if your tree was as comfortable as my tree?"

I laughed a little and said, "Oh the rocks do wonders for my back." She laughed and gradually meandered back to her tree. Now what was that all about? Maybe she had realized that I had realized that she was trying to keep me from realizing what her true feelings were. That made sense. She needed me around. I was the one who was going to get her out of here. That made me even angrier. Not only had she already put me down, but I was also being used. I rolled on my side so I didn't have to look at her and decided to force myself asleep. After a few moments I heard more moving around. I rolled over to see Jasmine up again.

"Whats'up, Jasmine?" I asked.

"That one was just uncomfortable. Do you mind if I try this one?" She indicated to the tree closest to me. It was about ten feet away. What in the hell was going through her head? There should be some kind of gender translator so guys can understand what a girl is really trying to say. Why couldn't she just come out and tell me she really would prefer it if I kept things on a friends kind of level, or as a business relationship, or whatever? Why play the games?

"Sure. Whatever makes you more comfortable." I rolled on my side once again so I was facing away from her. I said, "Goodnight."

"Goodnight, Chad. Thanks for everything." Yeah somebody's got to be the loser; it might as well be me. It took about an hour for me to fall asleep, but if felt good to be back in my dreams. I had a hard time sleeping. I didn't feel secure enough to let myself really fall asleep; besides, as uncomfortable as I was there was little chance of that happening anyway. I also needed to check on the fire and keep it going. The sporadic moments of sleep I did get, I had some good dreams. I have a lot of dreams. They make the waking hours tolerable. My enjoyment of life is largely from my dreams. They keep me going. If I didn't have them, I'd probably just commit suicide and be done with it.

Chapter Twelve
The Melding

Eventually dawn started to light the sky. As it grew brighter between sleep and waking, I finally decided to get up. The sky was ripped with orange and red. It was really impressive. I realized how much I missed camping. Because of Dad, I hadn't been able to go for a couple of months. I sat and just listened and watched for awhile, very quiet and very beautiful. Being in nature reminds you of your place in the world. It renews your ties with creation and the link to the wonder and quiet purity all nature posses, including us humans. For some reason, being alone with the sun and the dirt makes the truth easier to find for me. It's easy to get twisted up in my life. The right thing to do, well that depends on law 238 and provision B and C. Then, there's the Supreme Court case of New Car vs. Donation. Plus, wrong, well that depends on your interpretation of wrong. It's just circles within circles within circles. In nature you can't avoid the truth. When you give out here, you don't get a tax deduction. When you have a question the green leaves and soft dirt point you to the westward setting sun. There you can see the truth emanating from the golden rays. Once you see that, the truth is apparent everywhere, pouring out from the leaves and the water and the grass – all around you.

I felt very calm. I went out into the woods to get some more wood for the fire. I was starting to get hungry. That was a feeling that was going to drive us crazy over the next couple days or weeks. I hoped it didn't take weeks. It wasn't going to be easy to get food while trying to cover a lot of ground quickly. Well it wasn't going to be easy to get food that we would want to eat. Now, bugs, worms, and various plants were a different story. I remember working on my wilderness survival merit badge. When we went over this stuff and the camp merit badge instructor had shown us how to find this survival food we all grimaced. I never thought I'd need to actually do it for real. As I was working on the fire, Jasmine woke up and came over to me.

She said to me, "The sunrise is beautiful."

"Yeah it sure is." The calmness I'd found helped me to forget last night like winter snow melting under the morning sun. Dreaming always calls the birds to return, the flowers to bloom, and hope to emerge again.

"It's going to be a great day."

"Actually, that beautiful sunrise may be a bad sign. That red could mean a storm is going to move through. We'll have to keep a good eye on the weather."

"Did you learn that as a Boyscout?"

"No, Dad taught me that. Red at night sailors delight. Red in the morning sailors take warning. It doesn't always hold true, but it's something to watch."

"What're we going to do if we get a bad storm?"

"I know how to build survival shelters. We'll just have to nigger r. . ." I don't know if my brain was too calm, or if I'm just so used to using that expression, but this was a real bad time to use it. I put my head down. I didn't want to even look at her, so much for the good morning.

She didn't say anything for a few seconds. We were both a bit stunned. She finally said, "The name thing was one thing, but that was on an entirely different level. Now you tell me why I shouldn't believe you're racist: a white kid from Canton who doesn't like black pride and uses expressions like. . . like what you just said?"

I didn't know what to say. It seemed she had all the evidence she needed. If she only knew (now if she only could believe) how much I liked her. I offered, "It's just an expression for me."

"Well, it's not for me."

"I know; you don't have to explain it. It just slipped out."

"You just can't tell me, to my face, how much you hate African Americans."

I replied, "That's not true. I mean, I saved your life."

"You probably did that because you didn't know 'till we fell outta the van. Then, it was either me or the terrorists."

"It wasn't like that! Damn it! I'm such a freakin' fool. Look, I don't know what I should say. I know how it looks, but you can't make that judgement."

"I can't?"

"Do you really think who I am is contained in those two words?"

"Don't pull the intellectual card on me again."

"There's a person inside all a' that. He's not racist." She was about to offer her protest. "I'm not! It's so far from the truth. I'm a social idiot. I am what I am. I always say the wrong thing. It's a bad expression that I use a lot at home, but I just say it, it doesn't mean anything to me. If I wasn't so stupid, I wouldn't have said it around you."

"Why shouldn't I believe you're trying real hard to hide the real you, but these slips ups tell the truth about Chad Hardly?"

"I don't know, but it's you who's putting together your own stereotypes of white and rural to choose between those two options. Guilty, I don't live around black people. That means I'm going to put my foot in my mouth. I always manage to say or do the wrong thing at the wrong time; it's the story of my life. I can't help the idiot I am. I try so hard not to have that stuff happen, but it always does especially when I'm around girls, especially very attractive girls." I naturally looked away as I said that, but I wasn't consciously aware I'd just given her a compliment and a major glimpse into how I felt about her. I just kept going. "If you judge who I am by a couple of words, I don't have a chance. Look, it's just you and me out here. There's no reason for me to try and hide my racism if I had it. I want you to see the person I really am. It's just like in *Huckleberry Finn*."

"Huck lived in the 1860s, you should know better."

I turned and looked at the sun. "I'm telling you I've admired black people my whole life: rap music, the style, the attitude, the walk, my idol is Michael Johnson. I know racism. I see both sides of it: white to black *and* black to white. I've heard African American sprinters say things to me like, 'Come on whitey, you ain't got nothin. Maybe I'll slow down so I don't lap you.' The guy that said that made me so angry, but is he racist? Maybe he's just reacting to the frustrations he feels. It's not an excuse but it is something to understand and even respect. People are rarely contained in the words they express. That's why words are as full of deception as they are explanation."

"Who do you know that's a racist white person?"

"My Dad."

"So why aren't you a racist?"

"Because I see it in my Dad and I see it in those black sprinters, and I see it as wrong and stupid either way. Besides, if I was, I wouldn't have thrown that rock at Tony. Racism is hatred; my problem is social stupidity, there's a big difference."

She replied, "Just so you know, that tone in your voice is still there."

"What?"

"It's the way you say black."

"Is that all you listened to?"

"No, you said you're not used to being around African Americans, well I'll teach you how to not put your foot in your mouth. Not everybody would be able to see your viewpoint. I had a hard time reading *Huckleberry Finn*, but a lot of my friends wouldn't read it at all."

"I can understand that, but racism is a lot more than one word. Besides, just because someone doesn't use those expressions isn't a sign that everything's all right. People can be real good at putting a chocolate coating over their real feelings. I couldn't be like that even if I wanted to. If we die or live we're doing it together, that's how I feel. I'm going to do everything I can to get you back home. I could care less what color you are. I'll try not to be such an idiot. This is like three times I talked and I've struck-out twice."

"I believe you."

"Why?"

"It's something about you. I trust you. I feel safe with you."

"Thanks, that means a lot. How'bout we change the subject? Are you getting hungry?"

"Good change of subject, I am. Are we going to pass a McDonald's or a Dunkin' Donuts along the way?" It was good she made the joke. It made it a lot easier to put the conversation to rest.

"Maybe." I put on my best hillbilly accent and said, "I think if we take a left about three hundred trees down and the right at the big green bush it should be around there somewhere."

"Seriously, what are we going to do for food?"

"Seriously, you don't want to know. I've been camping a long time, but I've only learned about eating the stuff we'd have to eat if it comes to that. If we're not out here too long we won't have to worry about eating. Water's the main thing our bodies need. You can survive for about thirty days without food, but only three or four without water. Unfortunately, we're going to be doing a lot of physical activity. We may be able to survive for thirty days without food, but by tomorrow we're going to be feeling the fatigue. If we're out here for too long we'll have to eat things like worms, bugs, and bushes, oh my!"

"Umee." We both laughed.

"It's actually not that bad. The problem is I don't want to spend the time trying to get food. We want to cover ground as quickly as possible. Normally in survival camping you don't have crazy Arab terrorists trying to kill you. That factor changes the variables a bit."

"Yeah, just a little." We warmed ourselves by the fire for awhile. The anger I had felt towards her from the evening before and the frustration of trying to explain my stupid slip of my dumb tongue were already into the past. I was still upset with myself, but what did it matter. Yesterday I didn't even know she existed and when we got out of here I wouldn't see her again. I might as well make the whole thing as enjoyable as possible, which was probably what she was thinking as well. Jasmine was on a different level than me. She had class. I could see it in her. It was a look she had. She was someone important. We would never've met me if it weren't for our misfortune. That had nothing to do with her color but everything to do with my scrubby life and poor family.

After about a half-hour of enjoying the morning and the fire, it was time to start hiking. We put the fire out by throwing dirt on it. I made sure to do my best to hide that a fire had been there. I didn't want them to be able to track us. We took the remaining partially burned pieces of wood and threw them in the creek. The rest we buried. Then, we tried to make the area look as natural as possible. We did a pretty good job. It was time to walk.

Walking was all we did for the rest of the day. We followed the creek south. I didn't want to jump in the water again, so we hiked along side. The brush was tough, but I thanked God we weren't into the full swing of spring. It would've been real thick. Thinking about the brush made me worry about another problem.

I asked Jasmine, "Have you even had poison ivy, sumac, or poison oak?"

"Yeah, it makes you really itchy."

"Yeah."

"I've had it a couple times. I've never heard of sumac or poison oak."

"They're just more potent versions of poison ivy." I looked around and pointed at a little poison ivy plant. "That's poison ivy there. I don't see any sumac around, but that stuff's supposed to be the worst. It's like a small sapling that has red berries on it and long thin leaves. Poison oak has leaves that look a lot like oak tree leaves."

"Have you had sumac poison?"

"No, I've never had any poison."

"What, as much as you've been out in the woods."

"I'm immune to it. I can roll in the stuff and I don't get it, but I was a little worried about you. We're going to be walking through a lot of brush. I can keep us away from sumac, but regular poison is harder to avoid. Do you have a strong reaction?"

"I can't believe you're immune to it."

"I just am. It's like the one break I got in life. But, how do you react?"

"I really don't know. It's been awhile since I've had it. I don't remember it being real bad."

"I imagine you haven't been around it a lot. There's plenty out here. Keep your eyes out for poison ivy plants and steer clear."

"Damn straight I'll steer clear."

"You should be OK since you have long pants on."

"You're not playin' with me, you really don't get poison?"

I laughed. "Hey everyone gets a couple breaks. I'd gladly trade in my inability to get poison for some coolness." We continued walking. For the rest of the day I was sort of like a tour guide in a lot of ways. I pointed out trees and plants I recognized as we past. Teaching is a big part of Boyscouts. I've spent a bunch of years learning a lot, but the other part of scouts is then teaching what you've learned. I've been called on more and more to be a teacher now that I've made advancements in rank and hold the position of patrol leader. In a way Jasmine was like a first year scout I was teaching. As I showed her things, I began to realize just how much I knew. I'd never considered myself the best scout, but I knew a lot more than I realized.

When we stumbled on a deer path, I explained to her how to identify deer footprints, and why we found those footprints near the creek. Deer need to get to water and they will often follow the same route to a safe watering hole. We took breaks now and then and we used the time to have a little fun. We had a skipping rocks contest, which she won. She told me she didn't know how to skip stones so I spent a few minutes showing her. Then she whooped my butt. She told me afterwards, as she laughed and gloated over her victory, that she'd lied about not knowing how. I'm not one for losing, but I got a good laugh out of how much fun she had beating me. She was even trash talking when we were throwing.

As I was laughing out loud, inside I was realizing just how much I liked her. The more I got to know Jasmine the more I had to fight to honor my personal pact. I loved her cockiness, and how perfectly balanced it was. She listened and learned from me in a way nobody had done before, girl or guy. I felt she respected me, and this is after I'd given her two good reasons to believe I was racist. Jasmine was fascinated by everything. She seemed like a girl born in the wrong place. She was dying to become a country girl. She hardly talked about her home or where she lived, or really anything about herself. I liked sharing my experiences with her. So few people had taken a real interest in my life, but she appreciated everything. She gave me the respect I never felt from anyone else. That respect was a feeling I'd been searching for for a long time. She was a sign of joy and renewal in my life, like the first flower that blooms in the spring, very delicate and wonderfully vibrant. I was thrilled to have her with me. All I needed was the emotional connection. That would be true love. Of course that meant she would have to feel the same about me. Sure, whatever.

For the first time I realized what love truly is. It's not some wonderful la la feeling. That's a crush. I had that for her as well, but what Jasmine made me feel was even better than that. I realized Heather was probably just a crush. Heather and I didn't connect through respect. She was really cute and that's what made me want to know her, but I never really got to know her. Something was different about Jasmine. She was a crush and so much more. Jasmine and I were connected; unfortunately, our connection was for our survival not for love, yet I realized just how powerful love could be. I wanted it more and more.

The Uniting Force of Nature

As the sun was beginning to set, we were resting on some big rocks by the side of the creek. The weather was looking worse. It had been a nice day, fairly warm, but that was going to change. The sky was amazing. On one side was the warm glow of the sunset and on the other an ominous black. It was like nighttime was literally rolling across the sky. The wind was already starting to pick-up.

I got Jasmine's attention, pointed to the sky, and made the Indian sign for sunset."

"What's that mean?" she asked.

"It's the Indian sign for the setting sun. I went to an Indian signing class last year at long term camp. It's pretty cool, huh? There's such reverence in Native Americans, especially for nature. That comes out in these signs. The Indian that taught the class had this amazing calm look when he made them. It was like poetry." As we sat and watched the sunset I showed her how to make the sign.

After about five minutes, I said to Jasmine, "Well, it looks like we're going to get wet again." I made my boots squish. "We made good time, but those clouds are telling me to stay put. Why don't we camp here?"

"Hey whatever you think. You're the nature boy."

"OK, me build em shelter. You pick berries."

"I said nature boy, not cave man."

"Sure, we need to get working on that shelter."

"That sounds like an excellent idea because those clouds look mean."

"They're going to be. We're going to make a debris hut. It's the best survival shelter around. Time for work," I made the Indian sign for work.

"What can I do?"

"We're going to need two long sturdy poles about two feet taller than you are. I'm going to build this shelter a little different than normal since there's two of us. Those poles are going to be the ridge poles."

"I'll hunt for those." While she was looking for the ridgepoles, I searched around for a door location – a rock or log, or some other kind of strong prop. I wanted something that was about crotch high. I found a rock that was just about right, now I needed another one since we were making a kind of double debris hut. I wanted to allow more room inside so we didn't have to be all over each other. Of course I wouldn't have minded the closeness, but she would and that would make things awkward. I looked around a bit more until I found a good log I could drag over to use as the second prop. Jasmine was waiting by the rock when I came back dragging the log.

I said, "Those look good." I put the log in place. "We want to put the entrance so that the wind doesn't blow into it." I faced downstream. "Water runs south, so this direction is generally south. Facing this way east should be my left and west my right. The wind blows from west to east, but sometimes it will blow from the north as well so let's face the entrance a bit to the south." I checked the wind direction by throwing grass in the air to confirm my theory. It was going to get pretty gusty when that storm hit, so it was going to be difficult to pick any direction that wasn't going to get some wind.

I continued, "Lean each of the poles on the props so the higher end is on the south side."

"OK."

"Next, we need to put a ribbing of small sticks close together along the sides. Normally there's one pole and you put ribbing on either side, but we're going to connect the two ridgepoles by putting ribbing across the top from the one ridgepole to the other. We should have more room then." This was kind of a new creation for me. I never tried to make a two-ridgepole debris hut. I was straining just trying to remember how to make a plain old regular debris hut.

Jasmine and I both walked around picking up sticks and arranging them on the construction. When we had a good skeleton I said, "Next, we need to dump lots of forest brush on top a' the whole thing. I'll rake and you can pile."

"So, you brought a rake along, too."

"Never doubt nature boy." I looked around and pulled out a dead tree limb from the brush. It still had some of its branches. "This is almost as good."

She smiled and said, "I guess. It's a good thing you're out here with me."

"My pleasure," and I made the Indian sign for work again.

"Well, I'm waitin' on you. Get workin' boy," I laughed as I started to rake.

"We need about two feet over the whole thing."

"Damn, by that time we'll be ready for winter." I just shook my head. "I know, I know, but it's necessary." She made the Indian sign for work. I gave her a sarcastic smile and started raking as she dumped the stuff on. It was one hell of a work out to pile the two feet we needed over the entire structure.

When we finished I said, "That looks good." I had worked up a good sweat. As the sun was fading you could tell it was going to be a little chilly that night, probably forty or fifty and with wind and rain it was a good mix for hypothermia, again. There was a loud crack of thunder and the sky flashed. We both looked up.

There was a little fear in Jasmine's voice, "Wow, that just made me feel really far away from civilization." The wind was starting to blow stronger. I could feel and smell that the rain was soon to come.

"We need to finish this up soon. Don't worry. Once we have this built we'll be fine. We want to put a layer of small stick over all the debris to help hold it all down. Then the last step is using evergreen branches for the final layer."

"Sure, so why're we doin' all this?"

"The debris insulates the inside and keeps us warm. The sticks will keep our shelter from blowing away and so will the evergreen branches; plus, the evergreen branches will act like shingles and help keep the water out." I was worried about that wind. I didn't know how well our shelter was going to hold up. It was going to be a long night if it didn't. "I'll get the evergreen branches. You can pile the sticks on." Another loud crash exploded from the sky. "Let's make it quick."

I walked out into the woods to my left. It was getting near impossible to see. I made sure to keep careful mental notes of how to get back to the camp. When I found the kind of trees I needed, I pulled out my pocketknife and opened the saw blade. The branches I could rip off the tree I did, the bigger ones I sawed off. Cutting off live branches from trees is normally a big no-no, but we needed the live needles and the weight they provided. The wind was really starting to blow. I started to feel the first couple drops of the storm. That hurried my work. After twenty minutes, I put my knife away and piled the branches on top of each other. I could hardly see my own hands it had gotten so dark. As I bent down to grab the branches, the whole sky lit-up. In that one flash I could see all through the woods, and I thought I saw a face!

Tony or Katerina, I thought for sure it was a person. Everything in me froze. A crack of thunder roared like a thousand jet engines behind the flash. It sent a chill down my spine. I listened intently for movement, but the eerie wind rushing through the trees was all that could be heard. It was a heart-throbbing sensation knowing that someone could be standing with a pick axe two feet from me ready to chop my head off and I couldn't see it. It made the wind that much more wild. I stood perfectly still and listened until the next flash of lightening ripped through the woods. I spun around checking my blind sides, but I didn't see any one. My sixth sense feeling was telling me people were all around. Maybe my mind was playing games with itself, but I would've felt a lot better if Jasmine was with me. I was going to wait for one more flash to make sure no was around, however, things instantly changed.

"Chad, Chad, Chad!" I dropped the branches and spun around. In a flash, I took off back to the debris hut. I tore through the brush, ripping past bushes, and slamming off a couple trees because it was so hard to see, but I remembered my way back. As I got closer, I tried to be quieter. I quietly pulled my knife out and flipped open the blade. I didn't call to Jasmine so I could surprise whoever it was that had her. I readied myself to explode on anyone that was there, but I couldn't see a thing. I stealthily walked around the area carefully looking and listening. The lightening was soon going to flash. I readied myself to strike. Someone was around here. With a bright flash God turned on the lights for a second. I looked around, but there was no one. Where was she?

The rain was starting to come down and the wind was blowing even stronger. I was starting to get cold. God, I hope she didn't go looking for me. She could easily get lost. The wind, rain, darkness, and your own crazy mind can easily disorient you. I listened for a little longer and then I moved over to the debris hut to check for her. Maybe she'd gone in to stay dry. Why did she yell for me? It was her voice. I knew it. As I got close to the debris hut, I heard something. I bent down and looked in as another flash of lightening illuminated everything. There was Jasmine.

"Jasmine." I put the knife away and crawled in. "Jasmine." She was huddled in the back and she was crying. I put my hand on her shoulder and asked, "Are you OK?"

She took a deep breath. "Yeah, I just don't want to be alone out here. It seemed like you were gone forever." I wiped the tears out of her eyes. "I thought you were lost or hurt or they got you, or they were gonna get me. . ." I cut her off because she was getting more worked up.

"It's OK. I'm fine and you're fine." I felt pretty awkward and I didn't know if I should, but I put my arm around her and held her for a couple of moments. She seemed to calm down with the embrace. Caring for her and seeing how much strength she gained from my caring just melted my heart. It felt so good, I almost started crying. As I was holding her I said, "We're gonna be OK. I think we'll both feel better if we stay together until this Steven King like storm goes away." She nodded her head as it was still buried in my chest. "I need to go back out and get those branches. Why don't you come with?"

"I like that idea." We got the branches and came back. We also got pretty soaked in the process. I arranged them on the debris hut and we crawled back in. Jasmine was feeling better, but I wanted to keep her mind off the storm. All I could think about was how hungry I was, so I thought it was a good idea to compare what each of us was going to eat once we made it home. Besides, it seemed like every minute took as much time as eating a three course meal. She was getting closer to me, emotionally and physically. Hope was starting to creep like a sneaky mouse back into my mind, but as soon as I started to think about those wonderful feelings, I became paranoid I'd end up eating rat poison.

I wanted to be an actor not a person. I wanted an army of people to make sure I did things perfectly. I wanted to sit with Jasmine and discuss what would be a good thing to say and how I should say it. When I messed up I wanted to hear, "cut," not, "I think we should just be friends." I wanted a make-up artist, a hair stylist, a clothing designer, and someone to construct my image and build my persona. Who cares if I'm fake?

The rain kept coming. Even the clouds wailed for my bum life. The rain was cold and the wind was relentless, but we were prepared. Our construction helped keep us dry and helped keep the wind from blowing as hard. There wasn't much else to do but try and sleep. I laid on the left side inside the hut and she was on the right. I couldn't fall asleep. The lightening and thunder were intense and I was secretly waiting for the shelter to blow away.

I started thinking about Jasmine. She had to be cold; although, it was pretty warm inside our shelter, but even so it would be great to have her sleeping on my shoulder. The very moment I had that thought the tension returned to my stomach. At least there wasn't a chance of indigestion. I tried to be rational about my decision. Not only was asking her to sleep closer to me the emotional thing to do, but it was also the rational thing to do. It was cold, windy, and rainy. We would both be able to stay warmer if we were closer together. Besides, our relationship had been building. It was the logical choice for me to make a move.

As I was going through hell trying to make this decision, I began to see how nice it must be to be a girl. Why doesn't she make the move? Well, she doesn't want to, but supposing she did, she still wouldn't have to. She should be the one to make the move. She's the more confident person anyways. What a luxury, all she had to worry about was whether or not I was going to make a move, but she didn't have to try one. The social code was for me to do it. But she's the one who looks like a supermodel, probably has a lot of money, is popular, and has a father who's a nationally known prosecutor.

As I was lamenting my lot in life, she whispered, "Are you asleep?"

I replied still bumming about my indecision, "No." I heard her shimmying over to me.

When she reached me she said, "This thunder and lightening is unbelievable." I was wondering what she was trying to get at, but it was nice to have her sitting close by.

I replied, "Nature can sure be noisy. It's good we built this shelter."

"It's still windy and cold enough for me." What was she getting at? "I was wondering. . .?"

I broke in and said, "If you could use my jacket? It's no problem."

"Yeah, thanks." She took the jacket and turned to crawl back to her side. She stopped for a second like she was going to say something else, but then she moved over to her side and said, "Goodnight, Chad. Thanks for the jacket."

I replied, "Goodnight, I hope it helps you sleep."

Now, I hope you can see what I just ruined. Don't feel bad if you can't, it took me a couple of minutes to figure it out myself. I wanted to bash my head against a tree, once it dawned on me. I had gotten my wish. She made a move. I'm not sure exactly what she wanted, but she didn't just want my jacket. I think she wanted was to sleep closer to me. It made sense. That explained why she beat around the bush when she first came over and why she seemed unsure when she left. She was deciding whether or not to come out and ask me. She was probably hoping that I would get the idea and offer to her. Ahh, what a moron I am. I'm like a dumb cow. You lead me right to the water and the stupid animal still won't drink. Now was my chance. I had to go over there and say what I should've said when she opened the door. Once again, the moment that thought entered my mind, my indecision flared up like dumping a can of gasoline on a fire. It didn't matter, however, because I was so mad at myself, disappointed, and frustrated I said what the hell.

I whispered to her, "Are you asleep?"

She replied, "No." I got up, moved over, and sat down next to her.

"Y'know, I think my side get's a lot less wind and rain," that was a lie, but I was trying to appeal to her logic. I wouldn't have to take it so personal if she said no.

She replied, "I thought it was a better over there too." Well, I knew I just lied even saying that, so she must've been lying too. That was a good sign, I think.

"You could come over, if you'd like to, ahh y'know over to my side, but only if you'd like to?" There, now it was going to be personal.

"I'd like to." A warm glow from my eyes started to illuminate the darkness as an irresistible smile pulled at my cheeks. Yeah, who's the man? Wow, she said yes. God she was cute.

I said as I was smiling, "That'd be great," I added in my hillbilly accent, "Come on over. There's plenty a' room. You just make yere' self at home." She laughed and we both moved over to my side. I laid down and she knelt next to me.

She asked, "Since you're being so friendly,"

"Shoot honey you're family."

She laughed again. When she stopped laughing she was quiet for a second, and then she looked me in the eyes. She asked, "Could I put my head on your shoulder?" Oh my God! Let me think about that one for a few hours; OK I'm done, sure you can. That'd be a yes. I thought I was going to explode right there – instantaneous combustion.

I looked directly at her and softly said, "That'd be great." We paused for a second as are eyes were locked and then she laughed a sweet little laugh that made her whole face beam like someone had just plugged in a neon sign.

I said, "Here, put your head here." She laid right next to me with her head on my shoulder. I asked, "Where's my jacket?"

"I put it above my head."

I grabbed it and said, "I'll put this over you to keep you warm." I spread the jacket over as much of her body as I could cover. I rubbed my hand on her shoulder and said, "That should keep you warm."

She replied, "Thanks, Chad. This feels a lot better."

"I hope you'll be able to sleep, now."

"I will. Goodnight, Chad."

"Goodnight, Jasmine."

I fell asleep soon after our goodnights. Dale was right, again. All I could think about was how bad I was going to feel if she said no. I never considered how great I was going to feel if she said yes, and it was great. To touch her was unexplainable. My heart had been an iceberg with layer upon layer of frozen defenses. In that one connection I felt it all melting to form an ocean of joy. The happiness flowed all throughout my body. She saw me for who I was and that was enough for her. I was good enough.

"Don't Stop me Now"

I dreamt the most wonderful dream that night. Jasmine and I were together and alone having a picnic on a beautiful clear spring day. Our picnic basket sat on a worn picnic table that was under a lone enormous oak tree at the end of an empty field. The smooth refreshing breeze brought wisps of new grass. We were standing, holding hands, and leaning against the end of the picnic table. I gave her a hug and spun her around as we both laughed. Then I gave her this crazy look and I started running. She chased after me calling my name and laughing. We ran through a wheat field and then reached a cornfield. The clear blue sky and bright sun watched are joy intently as the gentle breeze made the tassels sway in the wind. I hid in the corn and waited. She came in and walked right by me. I snuck up behind her and scared her. She jumped and screamed. I laughed and went running again as she tried to grab me. I ran out of the cornfield and over to a creek on the other side of an empty field. She came running after me and tackled me onto the soft grass by the creek. We both rolled in the fresh grass and laughed. I stood up with her and gave her a big hug and a kiss and then looked her in the eye and gave her a wild smile. I jumped onto a tire swing that was hanging out over the creek and went flying through the air. I put my arms out and yelled as I took a couple swings. When I jumped off I hugged her again. She returned my embrace and gave me a wild grin. She followed it with a good shove that made me fall into the water. She laughed like crazy at the look on my face. I made myself a cannonball and made a big splash. When I came back up I waived for her to jump in and she did. We both splashed each other a bit, until I wrapped my arms around her and let out a sigh of complete happiness. I moved us over to big rock and rested there with her in my arms as we both gasped for air and enjoyed the love that flowed between us.

She was so warm and real. To feel her breathing made me amazed by the power of life I was holding. I relished that dream all night long. The rest of my dream world seemed so empty now that a real person was apart of it. Waking up and actually feeling her breath was intense. Maybe I'd been wrong about dreams. Maybe they aren't better than reality. A dream is a vision that opens a tiny crack to reality. When you really experience it you're standing in the light. I think I smiled the whole night.

Chapter Thirteen

The Weed

We woke up pretty early to scattered clouds and an orange smeared sunrise. Both of us were glad to see the sun. We packed up camp, which took awhile since we had to take apart and scatter the shelter we'd spent so much time building. Once we were done, we began walking again. I was so hungry I didn't feel hungry anymore. At some point we were going to have to start eating some of the survival food I learned about. I was feeling more and more confident that I was right about where we were. It shouldn't be too much longer until we reached that Boyscout camp. Even if I was wrong about being near the camp, we should run into something soon. There had to be something around this creek. I tried to remind myself that we had only walked one day. We shouldn't get discouraged, yet, but Jasmine was depending on me.

I was encouraged that we hadn't run into our terrorist buddies at all. At the same time that made me even more worried. What was their plan? What were they doing right now? They couldn't be good woodsman, but they had guns and probably a map. They could be waiting for us. They didn't know where we were for sure, but we didn't have weapons, supplies, transportation, or any concrete idea where we were. I wasn't counting on the police or any kind of search. I'd been debating with myself whether or not to build a helicopter signal. The signal would help someone find us, but it would also help the bad guys find us. For the moment I'd decided the chance that someone would see it in such a remote area wasn't worth the risk. We just had to be patient and cautious.

The fatigue was starting to wear through both of us. I was in a great mood because of last night, but my body wasn't. I'd been running on empty for too long. We hadn't said a whole lot to each other for most of the morning.

That is until Jasmine asked, "Do you know where we're going?" What an appropriate question considering the turmoil I had with that question. Should I lie to her to keep her confidence up, or should I tell her the truth?

I replied, "I can't guarantee anything. I'm going on a hunch." After last night I felt I had to be straight with her. She could handle the truth.

She replied, "That's not what I wanted to hear."

"Yeah, I know, but I can't lie to you. We're equals out here no matter how much more I know about this stuff. You need to know the situation."

"So why didn't you tell me straight out before?"

"Well, it's not that I didn't. I tried not to talk about it. I didn't know how you'd handle it."

"You figured I was a stuck up little rich girl didn't you." I don't know where her anger was coming from, but it shocked me.

I replied, "Whoa! Cool your jets there. At least I didn't assume you were poor because you're an African American. It was easy to tell you hadn't been in the woods much before. I didn't assume you were stuck up and rich."

"Oh come on."

"When I first met you, I assumed you didn't live in a rural area. Once I got to know you I realized your family had money, but I also realized that you weren't some wimpy stuck up girl from the burbs."

"I'm from the burbs!"

"Are you paranoid or something? I didn't make that judgement. If I'm so bad, what about you? What did you assume about me?" She didn't say anything right away. "You figured I was the end of your life. You said it earlier. You were hoping I was a FBI agent and what you got was a dumb redneck. So who made more assumptions, me or you?"

"Now that I know you, I've changed my opinion."

"Me too. Gosh dang what made you so angry?" I wanted to ask her just what her opinion was of me, but I didn't think now was a good time, not that I would've been able to ask if it was a good time.

She replied, "I don't know. I just don't like being treated unequal."

"That's why I told you the truth." Jeez it's a good thing I did. She would've killed me if I lied.

She asked, "So what's the real deal?"

"I only have a hunch where we are. If I'm right we'll run into a Boyscout camp along this creek."

"And if you're wrong?"

"I have no idea what we'll run into, but," I paused because she was looking angry again, "we will run into something."

"What makes you so sure?"

"Where there's water there's people. I was taught that in scouts. It's one of the golden rules of survival training. Look, I'm frustrated too, but we've only been walking for a day. It might take us a lot longer than that."

"I know. I'm just irritable."

I laughed, "Yeah, well we haven't eaten for awhile. That probably has something to do with it. We might have to start looking for food if we're out here a couple more days."

"Let's just look now."

"Bugs, worms, and other tasty treats."

"I remember you telling me. OK, we'll wait." We both focused on walking for awhile. We were a lot more serious than yesterday. The newness of the woods had worn off as we became dirtier. Every now and then something interesting popped up and I'd show it to Jasmine, but survival camping wasn't as much fun as plain old camping. At least it wasn't raining. The weather was nice. It was a bit cool in the morning, but by mid afternoon things were much nicer.

As we were walking I debated whether or not we should talk about last night and our relationship. As Dad always says, 'Nothin' means nothin' until you'd signed papers.' Last night was unbelievable, but I wasn't going to hope for anything until it was really there. Once again, I chickened out because I was afraid of pushing the issue. I didn't want to blow what I had been lucky enough to get. Let's just say I am completely gutless. However, I decided to surprise her with a gift.

I started looking around for this one kind of fern. Spring wasn't in full bloom just yet, but there was a fair amount of undergrowth. I finally found one and broke off one of the big leaves. I'll try to describe this fern leaf for you so you get an idea of what I was going to do. Each fern has several leaves. Each leaf has a thin stem that runs up through the middle. This leaf wasn't too long it was only about a foot; they get a good bit bigger once they have more time to grow. From the stem, long thin leaves spread out to the left and right. At the bottom of the stem the thin leaves are the longest and at the top they're the shortest. The fern is light green in color. With those long leaves it makes it look a lot like a feather in ways. And, the leaves aren't solid. They're like a green mesh kind of like the way steel wool looks only the leaves are soft and light green. I hope you get the idea.

Now, what you do is grab at the base of the leaf you've pulled off and pinch your thumb and index finger along the base. Then, you slide your fingers all the way to the top as your other hand grabs the bottom of the stem once you get started. The long thin leaves will break off and slide up. If you keep pinching, you will have all of the thin leaves held together by your two fingers. It looks like a flower.

So I did all that and stopped and said, "Jasmine, hold up a second. I have something for you." She stopped and came back. "Here's a flower for you." She smiled and went to take it. I said, "Wait a second." I held it up in front of me and told her, "You have to hold the base." She reached out and pinched where my two fingers were. We were holding it together. I added, "This is a special flower. In order to give it to someone you have to work together which is the essence of a relationship. The flower is only beautiful because of the thought behind it. That is the true beauty of a flower and a relationship." That last part is supposed to be, 'That is the true beauty of a flower and true love,' but I didn't want to press my luck. I said, "Let go of the base." She did and the leaves went fluttering to the ground. "You see. Without our effort," supposed to be, without our true love, "it is not beautiful." I thought for a second this tough girl was about to cry. Bingo, that one hit the heart.

"Thanks, Chad. That was really. . . nice. Where did you learn that?"

"It's an old Indian story I learned in Scouts."

"Really?"

"Well, the truth is I made the whole thing up."

"You made that all up!"

"When I first joined scouts as a little kid of eleven, Mr. Enders, my scout leader, showed me those ferns on my first camping trip. I sort of came up with my own Indian legend for it." When I created that whole story I promised myself I was going to give that fern to the first girl I could finally get a chance to love. I was going to treat her better than any other guy could possibly imagine. I was going to care about her more than even her own parents did. That way I could overcome my lame personality and innate ability to look like an idiot. I didn't want to admit to Jasmine that I made up such a sappy story, but that wasn't a good reason to lie. Lies always have a way of coming back to demand the truth. I was hoping she wouldn't appreciate my gesture any less.

"That's the most thoughtful and nicest thing any guy has every done for me." It seemed to me she liked it even more because I'd created the story myself, which just goes to show how well I understand girls. What she said made me curious about her past boyfriends.

I asked her, "So you've had a couple boyfriends?"

"Yeah, a few in middle school, but that was more of a social thing than anything real. I dated a senior named Rasheed as a Freshman." That's always bad news, I thought. "We lasted a couple months. I thought my father was going to kill him before then. Then there was Tyrell Simpson. He seemed so nice, but he was really just very smooth. He wasn't going to take care of me even if he knew how. I broke up with him after about six months." I could sense the end of her story and I was worried she was going to ask the dreaded question. "So, how about you Mr. Hardly?" Ahh, and there it was!

I chuckled a little. I was going to tell her the truth and that made me laugh. "Well, ahh, I'm sort of a good joke at my school. I'm one of those useful people the popular people use to prop themselves up on to reach the popular girls. Then you add in the shack I call home, the loud-mouthed man with barely an eight grader's education that is my Dad, and the fact I run track instead of playing grrrrrrr football, and one can see I'm untouchable. I do have the unique ability to ruin anyone or any situation I'm in. For instance, I had a date with a very beautiful girl a couple nights ago, which is like a once in a lifetime occurrence, literally, and I managed to ruin that."

"This is one of those stories you didn't want to tell me?"

"Circle get's a square! What'd she win, Chuck."

"It can't be that bad."

"Oh yes it can."

"What happened?"

"Naa, I better stop before I make you go running for the terrorists."

"You're not going to send me running anywhere."

"It's funny, but that really means a lot to me. You're the only girl who really listens to me. However, we are out here and the civilized world is waiting."

"So?"

"I'm comfortable out here. Nature isn't judgmental. There are no social rules. There's no one to tell you who you are and how you should be. If we were back there, what are the chances we would've even met? Nature says come on in. Out here if you want to fly you just do it; back home you need a license, a flight plan, and (before you can do any of that) money. Money rules everything back there. In nature all you have is your real self."

"You're right. No parents to tell you what to do. No narrow people to get frustrated by. So, how about that story?"

"I'm not getting out of this am I?" She shook her head no. "You asked for it. After I finally got the courage to ask Heather out on a date, I made it a disaster. She was just humoring a very courteous and polite guy. Heather was nice enough not to avoid me. Anyhow, we went on this date. Things were going pretty well, which just made me worried something bad was going to happen."

"What kind of mentality is that?"

"That's just how it is for me. I was right to be worried. We had eaten at the Outback and were driving over to the movie theater through the parking lot. I wasn't paying attention and bang; we hit a light pole. I was nearly knocked out and I think Heather will have a huge bruise on her forehead."

Jasmine started laughing, "No shit, you hit one of those light poles. It must've been the one they were working on."

"Yes, please enjoy my stupidity."

"Damn, how could you hit a light pole?"

"Yes, yes, thank you thank you," I replied as I took a couple bows.

"She must've had her groove on and put the love hex on you."

"I can only imagine what it's going to be like when I get to school. The story will have gone around ten times."

"I'm sorry." She calmed her laughter. "I know you feel bad about it, but it's funny. Just try to laugh about it. If people can't appreciate you for how nice a person you are than so what. I'm having fun, even though we could die, that's because of how caring and brave you are."

Her compliment made me embarrassed. I replied, "Thanks, you're really different."

"Look at you. Can't you even look me in the eyes?"

"No."

"Oh please, come on. Look at me." I tried but I just couldn't. She came over and put her hands under my chin and held my head up. She said, "Thanks."

I still avoided eye contact. I replied, "You're welcome." This was a really good sign. I told her I was an absolute social dud and she still felt like she was having a good time. I think talking had brightened both of our moods. I felt better that she knew the truth about my hunch, and I felt even better about two of us. We walked the rest of the day and into the waning moments of sunset, before we found something.

Chapter Fourteen
A Little Dose of Reality

I was following Jasmine, not paying attention too much. That's why she saw it first.

She turned to me with a hopeful smile and said, "There's a person up there!" We both stopped and I looked up ahead. Sure enough there was another bridge like the one we had crossed when we jumped out of the van.

"Good eyes. Follow me." I started sneaking up closer to bridge. We moved slowly keeping low and staying behind trees and brush. Daylight was starting to slip away, but we could still see good. We got pretty close to the bridge and hid behind a group of trees and bushes. There was a car sitting just past the bridge that looked like it was broken down. The guy had walked out of sight once again, but I was waiting for him to come back.

Jasmine whispered, "Whats'up?"

I whispered back "I want to check out this guy. Keep out of sight."

"Where you going?"

"To get a better look. Just stay put." I got down on my belly and crawled up closer to the bridge. I moved up another 100 feet. Now I could get a good look at him. I waited for a few seconds until he came back to our side of the bridge. My hopes swelled inside of me. This could be our way out. Sure enough, it was Azi, not exactly who I was looking for. I crawled back to Jasmine with the bad news.

She whispered to me, "Let me guess, terrorists."

I whispered back, "It's even better than that, Azi."

"Oh great! Just damn great."

"Well, at least the rest of the crew isn't there. They must've broken up to cover different areas."

"So what're we gonna do now?"

"I think we should wait until it's night and then try to sneak by him."

"That's a bit daring. We could go around him."

"That might be what they're planning."

"Maybe, but you could be overanalyzing it. Do you think sneaking past him is worth the risk?"

"I've played capture the flag many times in scouts. You can sneak past people, especially when it's dark."

"I believe you; I don't know why. In fact, why am I excited to do this?"

I smiled and said, "We'll have to sit tight for a couple more hours."

* * *

Jasmine and I sat and watched the bridge until it was too dark for us to see Azi from where we were.

I whispered, "It's time."

"Let's do it."

"I need to get ready." I took off my jacket and turned it inside out so that only black was showing. The gold of the Steelers emblem was too reflective. Then, I moved down to the creek bed.

"Where you going?"

"I need some camouflage. I'll be right back." I went down and smeared some brownish black clay from the stream's bank on my arms and face. We both needed to be stealth tigers. I've played capture the flag a million times during campouts. A stealth tiger is the name we give to the group of scouts who are essentially like the navy seals of the team. My troop's strategy was to create a diversionary attack to get our stealth tigers into the other team's territory. Once they're in, they're on their own. The mission is to sneak deep behind the other team's front line looking for their flag. Sometimes I had the stealth tiger's job, but I hadn't completely earned the designation because I'm too clumsy so I would get caught too often. I crawled back to Jasmine. We were ready.

When Jasmine finally realized I was right next to her she said, "Wow, it's hard to see you now."

"And it's hard to see you as well. We need to be as dark as night. Let's go. Keep low and be as quiet as possible." We started moving slowly through the brush. I couldn't see well enough to find Azi. I stopped and held my hand up for Jasmine to stop. I grabbed a stick just in case things went bad. We started moving forward once again. My heart was already pumping hard, swirling the adrenaline around my body. We only made the softest rustle through the brush. It was too quiet.

After a tense meandering walk, we reached the bridge. This was the dangerous area. Just a few crickets chirping broke the still of the night. The peaceful sound of the water rushing though the creek seemed such a contrast to our tenuous situation. The moon wasn't exceptionally bright tonight. That was good.

I paused by the side of the bridge to listen. Jasmine and I were worthy of the stealth tiger designation so far, but we still hadn't seen Azi. I was worried. He should still be up top somewhere, but I was hoping to confirm that hunch. I motioned for Jasmine to follow and we started going under the bridge. I had an eerie deju vu feeling being back under a bridge. I could almost hear Azi and Katerina's voices echoing to Tony on the other side. I walked carefully along the edge of the water. Where was Azi!

There was a loud thud and a splash. Something was wrong. I spun around and saw Jasmine struggling out of the water. She had slipped on something I knew it. She was terror-stricken. She looked like she was going to explain what happened, but I quickly put my finger over her mouth. With my eyes I told her to freeze where she was. I listened intently for a few seconds and then I heard what I was afraid I was going to hear: footsteps walking on the bridge. Shit, shit, shit. We needed to get out of there right away. I listened to try and determine where the footsteps were moving, but when a deer spotter flicked on I knew we had to get the hell out.

I yanked Jasmine's shirt and said, "Let's go. Quick, quiet, and low." I grabbed a big rock and whispered, "Now." I threw the rock as far as I could back up stream. We were out from under the bridge in a second as the loud splash and clunk sounded the other way. It didn't matter if the diversion worked or not. We needed to move quickly. I never looked behind me to see if the deer spotter had turned upstream, but no light had found us so far. We were making a lot more noise than before. Azi was going to hear it soon, even if he did fall for the diversion. Once we cleared the bridge we moved as fast as we could while still staying low with the brush. I led us up into the brush rather than along the side of the creek to give us more cover. The deer spotter started scanning the creek. We kept moving until the light started to sweep more towards our area.

I yelled in a harsh whisper, "Hit the ground and take cover!" I slid in behind some bushes and made myself into a ball trying to use the undergrowth to mask myself as best I could. I had no idea where Jasmine was. The light scanned over where I was hiding. I held every muscle perfectly still, yet ready to explode away the moment it seemed like I had been spotted. All I could think about was whether or not Jasmine had concealed herself well enough. The light scanned back and forth several times, then went over to the other side, and came back to our side once again before it switched to scan up stream.

The moment it went the other direction, I got up and whispered, "Jasmine." There was no response. "Jasmine." I wanted to put some distance between that light and us. I started moving back towards the bridge. She had been behind me. "Jasmine." Shit, maybe she hadn't been behind me.

"Over here." I scurried over.

"Jasmine."

"Right here." I almost stepped on her she was buried in a bush so well.

"You OK?"

"I guess."

"Then let's go before the," but before I could say before the light came back, the light came back making a broad arc over where Jasmine and I were. I immediately hit the ground and tried to get behind a tree. We were far enough away that he couldn't hear us talking but he could see us. The beam moved back and forth over the area I was trying to hide at. I felt the beam shine in my face. I wasn't going to wait much longer.

"We're soon going to jet out of here. I think he might see me."

"Shit," I heard her reply.

The beam came back over where I was and then it started to disappear. It was still wobbling around in our area, but it wasn't panning back and forth anymore. I looked up to see what was going on. Azi was moving. The light was coming down around the side of the bridge.

"That's it, we're out of here." I jumped up and so did Jasmine. "Stay as low as you can. Get back down to the edge of the creek. Then, run like hell." She took off. I wanted her to be ahead of me, so I waited for a few seconds. Then I exploded toward the creek. I looked over my shoulder to see where the light was going. He was on our side of the creek and searching up into the woods. He was coming downstream. I forced my way through the brush diagonally towards the edge of the creek. I had no idea where Jasmine was. I burst through onto the edge of the creek, and took off as fast as I could run. I hoped she was still up ahead of me. The splashing of water was soaking my jacket and even hitting my face. The light was searching the other side of the creek now. Maybe he hadn't seen me? The creek went around a bend to the right. I jumped back up into the brush to cut across the meander and because there wasn't anymore dry shoreline for me to run on. As I was ripping through the brush, I heard my name.

"Chad!" I stopped right away and came back to where I heard the sound.

"Jasmine."

"Yeah, over here dummy. Don't you see me?"

"No I don't." She stood up about twenty feet off to my right. "There you are. I was hoping you were up ahead of me somewhere."

"I was afraid Azi got you when I didn't see you behind me."

"I was watching where that light was going. He might not've saw us."

"I'm so sorry about slipping. . ."

"Forget it. We need to keep moving and worry about everything else later. Besides, I'm usually the one that klutzes things up." I gave her a goofy smile, which made her laugh. I took her hand and we went running downstream some more. We ran until we were both beat, which wasn't all that long because we were already exhausted. We kept walking for the next two or three hours, until the adrenaline started to wear off. The cool night air was starting to give me a chill. I decided it would be best if we stopped and tried to get some sleep for the night; she agreed.

I built a very small and well-concealed fire to keep us warm. I sat with Jasmine by the fire for a while. We both stared into the flames. The silence of the night and the cracking and flickering of the flames helped to relax me. I told her to get some sleep; I was going to keep watch. She eventually fell asleep leaning against my shoulder. I felt a lot of pressure to keep her safe. Despite the danger, another evening with Jasmine was further proof how much I loved her, but we had to find help soon. I gently carried her to a more comfortable place for her to lay down. Thankfully I didn't wake her up. She stirred a little, but she was still asleep. I took off my jacket and put it around her shoulders. I almost let my fingers gently slid along her face, but I didn't want to feel I was taking advantage of her. Instead, I looked at her for a few moments before I returned to carefully watching for Azi.

The evening had reminded me of the life and death nature of our situation. This wasn't a little camping trip turning into a date. While I was sitting and watching, I had a lot of time to think. I reevaluated my plans. It might be a good idea to split up. I could head downstream and Jasmine could remain carefully concealed and much safer. But even that was too dangerous. If I got caught or if something went wrong on her end and she had to make a run for it, she didn't know enough to take care of herself. I felt like the cage door was closing around us. A part from my scare during the thunderstorm, I had felt a relative amount of safety in the woods. But now, they knew where we were.

Chapter Fifteen
Chocolate and Milk are Better Together

    I hardly slept so the dawn's first rays didn't come as a waking "there's the sun"; it was more like watching a slowly rising curtain going up. Once Jasmine woke up we went through the same routine we'd been doing the last two mornings: put the fire out, disguise where the fire had been, walk down to the creek and have a drink, maybe wash off our hands and face, and start walking. That was it. As we walked that morning, Jasmine could see I was tired because she mentioned it several times. She thanked me for being so kind to her, I think to try and lift my spirits. That wasn't an easy thing to do. Around every tree I was waiting for a terrorist to jump out and grab me. I'd been using luck like it was going out of style the last couple of days. It was bound to run out. Despite my worries, it felt good to hear her say that. Caring about her came natural to me. All I ever wanted was to opportunity to care for a girl.

    Finally Jasmine asked me straight out, "You look worried. Don't keep it to yourself. We're in this together," she put her arm around my shoulder.

"I feel like we're running out of time. They know where we're at and that means they probably know where we're heading. I don't like it at all. It feels like they're all around us."

"Maybe we should hide for awhile?"

"I've been thinking about that possibility. My gut tells me to get to help as quickly as possible, but that might not be the best idea. That was too close last night and you better believe they're going to try again. Then again it could be just as risky trying to hide."

"Then we keep doing what we're doing."

I smiled at her because her conviction surprised me. I replied, "Yeah."

"Why don't I tell you a little bit about my life. I'm sure you're curious and I know we could both use a change of subject."

"Yeah, you don't talk about your family a lot. I'm the motor mouth."

"It's a nice quality. So, my life: my mother and father are complete opposites. Father is the rational one and mother's the psycho, but I get along with both of them; although, Mom can be a pain. We live in the mostly white and really ritzy Bambridge development."

"How were the natives when you moved in?"

"Worried to say the least. Either because black people were moving into their community or just because a black family had been able to reach their economic level. The first year I always felt like people were looking at me like I forgot to comb my hair or something. But, my father could be discouraged by nothing. He saw the neighbors as just another challenge. One of the families seemed very open so he had started there and after a year or two people were a little more accepting. At least they'd say hello to us.

"Noticing your different is one thing, but not being able to say hello, that's just stupid. That's how my Dad is. How are things now?"

"Satisfactory. I still think some people are shocked a black family can have their kind of money. It shakes up their notions of privilege. Rich people don't like to think that hard work can bring others up to their level. They see their status as unique, almost appointed by God, like royalty in a way."

"Well we've got one thing in common, rich people turn up their noses at us. Your black and I'm trailer trash. God, I can't stand snobby people."

"I hope I'm not like that."

"You're not even close. Don't ever worry, you'll never be like that. I think you'd enjoy doin' some hillbilly stuff, like ridin' four-wheeler and horses. Too many people would find those things to plebian for their refined tastes."

"That stuff sounds awesome to me. Your world is like a whole new thing for me. I can't wait." We had very different lives, that was for sure. She may've been excited to jump into mine, but I felt very nervous about being around an upper class neighborhood, let alone what her parents would think of a white farmer's son from Canton.

"We've just got to get home?"

"Yeah."

Our discussion lighted up the day and made it go quicker. I was hoping to find the Boyscout camp on that day, but my luck didn't pan out. That made me even more edgy. In the late evening we stopped to make camp for the night. Before we started working on the fire we sat on top a boulder that was perched above the creek. We just sat. I didn't say anything and neither did she. It was peacefully calm. Too calm because all I could think about were those terrorists. The orange sun was glowing against the mountain in front of us. It was only moments from hiding. The rays painted onto the bottoms of the puffy white clouds that hung overhead. A beautiful purple developed on the outer edge. Gradually, as you looked towards the other side of the sky, the colors faded to the moon. The water sliding through the banks of the creek in front of us reflected this painting for the sky to see.

We sat and enjoyed the scene until Jasmine said, "You're still concerned." She sensed my feelings well.

"You're very perceptive. I was hoping to find the camp today. We're not safe until there are fifty FBI agents around us with sawed off shotguns and automatic machine guns."

"When I see you concerned, it makes me feel sick to my stomach."

"I'm sorry I'm not more reassuring. I guess if I was Rambo you would have nothing to worry about."

"There's nothing to apologize for. I can handle it."

"Yeah, I know you can." I noticed a little movement to my right. Jasmine was on my left. There was a snake on another rock about five feet from me. I looked carefully to see what kind. It was a black snake; they're about the easiest kind of snake to identify.

I said, "Look over there." She leaned forward and looked.

She replied, "Get out! I'll get a stick."

"Hold still! It's just a black snake. They strangle their pray so they don't have fangs or any venom." I concentrated for a second and then I jumped to grab it. I got just below its head. He wasn't a big one, but he still hissed like crazy and wrapped his body around my arm. Jasmine jumped back.

She yelled, "Damn! Are you trippin'?"

"He can't hurt you. The most he could do is put a little cut on you. He's the one who's afraid. If I sat him down he would get out of here as fast as he could slither. Do you want to hold him?"

"Hold him!"

"Yeah, it feels really cool."

"You've been out in the woods too long."

"It's all right to be afraid. Here," I grabbed just below his head with my other hand and pulled him off my other arm. "Just grab him right below where my hand is." She was going to give it a try. I could see it in her eyes. She didn't say anything. She turned her head, and slowly moved her hand over then she slid it around the snake's body.

She moaned, "Oh, God what am I doing?"

"You're fine. Do you have a good grip?"

"Yeah, sure whatever."

"He's all yours." I gently released my hand. Her eyes got real big as he hissed and coiled around her arm.

"Oh, too much fun with nature." After a few moments I could see she was relaxing a bit.

"It feels cool doesn't it?"

"Yeah, he's got one helluva good grip." She laughed a little bit and rubbed his body with her other hand. "I thought snakes were slimy."

"Common misconception. I think it's because slithering and slimy seem to fit together so well. That guy would do a good job keeping mice out of your house. We never kill a black snake on our farm."

After about a minute of playtime she asked, "So, what are we going to do with him?"

"Are you hungry?"

"What! You just said you don't kill them."

"Well, that's because we have food in the house to eat. If you know where a stocked refrigerator is out her just let me know."

"But. . . you can't kill him now. I mean, I like the little guy."

"Oh, will you look at this. Have you forgotten how much food you've eaten in the last three days?"

"No, but I'm not into killing cute animals."

"A few seconds earlier you were gonna beat it with a stick."

"Well, I. . ."

"I was just kidding, anyhow. I have another idea for some food." I wasn't kidding, but I could see there was no way she was going to give in. It took some coaxing to get my stomach to go along with the idea. That would've been some good eating. I said, "I'm confident we're going to be out of here soon, but if I'm wrong, finding a snake like this guy is going to be like eating gourmet food."

"How do I let him go?"

"I'll get him." I grabbed him and pulled him off of her arm and then set him down a couple feet away. As soon as he hit the ground, he took off.

"He's got some speed."

"I caught him sleeping."

"How do you know he was sleeping?"

"When it's cool outside snakes will sun themselves to raise their body temperature. He was catching the last rays of sun before going to hunt. Snakes are active during nighttime and sleep by day. He uses the heat of the day to warm his blood up enough so he can hunt through the night. We, however, are warm-blooded. Warm-blooded creatures maintain a constant body temperature, but a cold-blooded creature's body temperature fluctuates with the temperature of the environment. If he gets too cold he can't really do a whole lot."

"That's interesting."

"Since we need to maintain our temperature, we better start working on a fire." I had decided it was time to get some nourishment, plus cooking would keep my mind off terrorists and dying.

After we got the fire going, I announced, "Were going to do some cooking. Grab me that log over there.

"Sure, what's this for?"

"That's going to be the pot."

"It's going to take you awhile to carve that out."

"I still have some tricks up my sleeves. We need two long sticks yet." She looked around and found two. She handed them to me. I brought the log and sticks next to the fire. I moved the coals around with one of the sticks until I found a nice sized coal. Using the two sticks I lifted it out of the fire and set it in the middle of the log.

I said, "We can take turns blowing on it."

"So, the coal is going to burn a hole in the log,"

"Making a pot. It'll take a few coals, but we'll have a pot and we certainly have the time." We started taking turns blowing on the coal. It was burning pretty good.

She said, "You know so much about camping."

"It's no big deal. You could learn it too. When I started scouts I didn't know any of this stuff, but I learned. After this little adventure, you'll be surprised just how much you know." We spent half an hour burning out the bowl. Then, we scraped out the ash with a rock. Jasmine went and rinsed it out, filled it up with water and got two small rocks. I found some pine needles and brought a bunch back.

I instructed, "Make sure you grab pine needles like this, not evergreen branches like we used the other night. Those are poisonous." I pulled off the needles and put them into the bowl with the water. "Now put those two little rocks into the fire, and we'll wait until they're hot." After twenty minutes I figured they were ready. I took the two long sticks and lifted one of the rocks into the bowl.

Jasmine said, "That's ingenious. The rock boils the water."

"That's what I thought when I learned it."

"Why don't we just eat the pine needles?"

"Good question. I asked the same thing. Because our bodies can't digest the plant matter like, let's say, a cow or deer can. However, by boiling the needles, we can remove the nutrients and drink it like a tea." After our meal, if you want to call nutrient rich water a meal, I needed to get some sleep. Jasmine agreed to keep watch for awhile. I think she enjoyed the chance to look after me. I had been wondering how things were going to work after that night in the shelter had been. She didn't hesitate or even ask. As I started to lie down, she came over to me and put my head in her lap. I fell asleep for awhile. When I got awake, Jasmine was still holding me and still watching into the woods. I sat up and moved behind her. I wrapped my arms around her and we eventually ended up lying down. We were practically one. I ran my fingers through her hair and she snuggled into my chest even more.

All I could think about was how real she was. The way her hair felt. The way she was breathing. Everything that was behind her eyes. The way she smiled. When she smiles she looks amazing. Her eyes seem to glimmer like stars and her face lights up like the moon. She sparkles like a ray of sun shimmering off the surface of a crisp lake on a majestic spring day. It was remarkable to hold life in your arms like that. Holding her was a great comfort as I looked out into the woods trying to find those eyes trying to find us.

Now I was thinking about kissing her, when I should tell her I loved her, and asking her the big question – would she be my girlfriend? As I thought about those words they seemed so unnatural. Like that question was in another language. I never did anything with a girl, and here I was holding the stars. I wasn't going to kiss her tonight or ask her to go steady. I was afraid, but that wasn't it. I wanted to just enjoy a real dream. We looked like white and dark chocolate melted together. It felt like we were a hot glass of chocolate milk.

Chapter Sixteen
Reckoning with the Past

When morning rose, I opened my eyes almost expecting the whole thing to've been a dream, but there she was once again. She hadn't gotten awake yet. I watched her for some time. She looked as peaceful as the sunset we'd watched the previous night. I let her sleep awhile longer before I gently woke her up.

Once we were up and completed our usual morning routine, we started walking. We walked till about noon when we stopped for a break. I had been thinking about asking her how she felt about me. I had been thinking about telling her how much I loved her, but even as certain as it looked, I still felt hesitant. I don't know why. It wasn't that I was skeptical of the signs so far. Everything seemed perfect, but that was out here. If we got outta here alive things were going to be more complicated. The real world is different. The thing we were praying to get back too was the very thing that was burning down the forest where our love could flourish. Out here I could almost believe we would fall in love, but in the captivity of some zoo, I had little hope. I decided not to express to her my feelings. During our break, we started skipping rocks again.

Jasmine said, "So, Chad." For a moment I thought she was going to bring up the big question. That made me both excited and worried.

I replied, "Yeah."

"What's up with your father?" She brought up a different kind of big question. I was wondering if this was some kind of final screening. She liked me, but now she wanted to make sure everything else was good. This was exactly the kind of thing I worried about. Out here it was just us. Back home there were a lot of other factors. I felt this was the only chance I was going to get to stand for myself. She didn't know a lot of the other stuff.

"My Dad, ehhe," I replied with some trepidation.

"Yeah, I know you don't get along and you think he's a racist."

"They go hand in hand. So, what do you want to know?"

"Why don't you get along?"

"We can't see eye to eye."

"That's it. Come on, Chad, I've trusted you with my life. You've got to trust me with yours." She was right. There was no sense in trying to hide it from her. Our relationship wouldn't last once we got back anyhow. It was better for me to tell her now.

"You're right. I just don't want you to think I'm like he is because he's my Dad."

"Everyone is prejudiced about things, including you. I think you still have a bunch of prejudices about African Americans."

"That's not true!" It was blowing up in my face.

"Listen. You do, but my father taught me that just as you shouldn't be prejudiced about race you also shouldn't hold prejudices against those people you assume to hold those views. 'Wanting to understand the truth, whatever your prejudices, is the spark of equality', as my father would say. I know you have some prejudices. I know I have some prejudices about the prejudices I think you have, and about the area you're from, and the type of people I assume live there. Our brains work because of connections. It's natural for us to link things together. But, you can't just look at people, hear a couple things they say, and determine who that person is. People aren't equations. I learned that first hand through you. People are more complicated than even the most difficult Calculus equation. I'd be on crack if I expected you to never utter something I felt was prejudiced towards African Americans. Like you said before, there's a real person behind those words. You have been so open to me. You've taken care of me. You have what my father's talking about. I know who's behind the Xs and Ys of your life."

"Here goes." We started walking again as I began telling the story. "When I was a little kid I loved Dad more than anything. He'd take me for tractor rides and he was always in the mood to do something crazy. Dad was working mainly as a construction worker for a big contractor down in Deluice. Just two years ago he quit and started farming full time. That's when things got tough. I guess ole' pops made a good bit of money in construction. Nobody knows why he quit except for Mom. I wouldn't have known because we weren't talking by the time that happened, anyways. But, I've gotten ahead of myself.

All through Elementary school, up to sixth grade, I adored him. He was the coolest person around. Farming was nothing more than a hobby from the past for Dad. He did it sort of for fun. Gandpap was a full-time farmer and he had milk and beef cattle. It was a big operation so Dad and my other four uncles did a lot of work on the farm. That's how he knew so much.

During those years he was the best. He had this John Deer hat I used to love. On the weekends if he had that hat on I knew I was going to have some fun. As soon as he'd see me, he'd hoot and hollar, 'it's time for a wild ride.' It's hard for me to even explain it to you. He would dance around the kitchen, bathroom, and living room screaming, 'yee haw,' like a madman. I thought he was the greatest thing to ever walk the earth. We'd go running out and he start up the fourwheeler and he'd slap that hat on my head and we would go tearing out through the fields. Mom always scolded him about getting me hurt, but even she was laughing at him. Dad made everyone laugh.

One day we went out to eat at a smorgasboard. It was Dad's birthday. To make a long story short he got drunk and made a fool out of himself. I saw Dad in a new light that day."

"So that's why you don't get along?"

"I wish it was. It got a lot worse. Something really bad happened."

"What happened?"

"Something happened." I stopped walking. Jasmine came up to me and looked into my eyes.

"What?"

I started walking again. "I just can't. I trust you a lot, Jasmine, but the only person I've told is my best friend Dale. We've been friends since I was five, and I didn't even give him a lot a' the details. It was bad, and it destroyed every good image I had of Dad. I never saw him the same again. From that day on we were on two different sides of a war. Dad never talked with me about what he did. It was just like our family to shuffle things under the rug. It didn't matter. I think Dad and I would've started to grow a part naturally anyways. I was going a different direction. I wasn't going to be a farmer. Science classes were starting to get my attention. I joined track my freshman year and found a dream. I realized I had the brains to go to college and the wheels to maybe get a scholarship. I started listening to rap and hip-hop in seventh and eighth grade. I hung up my first poster of Michael Johnson the summer before this year. Now, the time I spend with Dad is because I have to. When he quit his good job in construction, I was in eighth grade. He turned to farming. The last I'd heard he was up for a promotion to foreman and the next thing I knew he quit. The extra pressure on the family money wise and Dad's need for me on the farm made a really bad relationship even worse. I don't need my Dad anymore. I don't want him in my life anymore. I'm planning on taken care of myself."

"Did he ever try to make peace with you?"

"Sure, hundreds of times. Mom keeps reminding me all the time. We have our fights, but Dad tries."

"You've got to give him some credit there."

"He's never said a word about what happened, never explained a thing."

"Did you ever talk to him about it?"

"That's not my place. I'm not going to let him off the hook. He fucked up, big time, and I'm his reminder every day that he did fuck up. Mom's told me a hundred times it kills him he's lost his boy. I hope it does."

"I know you're hurt, but it seems to me you're holding on to a grudge you'd be better to get rid of. Maybe you need to be the one to open up?"

"My family isn't open with our feelings. We get along and have a good time, but nobody talks about feelings. He's the one that needs to open up. I'm not doing it for him. I don't need him."

"Sure maybe not to go to college or to run track, but he's your father."

"Sometimes people lose their Dad early. Mine died four years ago and he made it worse two years ago when he quit his job."

"You're sure you can't tell me what happened?"

"I learned a lot that night, a lot about life, a lot about failure. That's why I'm going to get you out of this. I'm not failing again."

"It would feel better to get it out."

"Thinking about it makes a thousand different emotions burn in my heart. It's so vivid. I can smell the smells and hear the sounds just like I'm there, again." I started looking at the creek and studying the trees and rocks to get my mind off of the whole event. I was starting to think about everything again and it was ripping open my dams. Telling that story rekindles the fire that consumes my thoughts. Jasmine was saying something but a flash of familiarity burst from my memory. Those pine trees and the big rocks over on that side were, unique. I started looking around me more. Those rocks were, familiar.

I started yelling and jumping up and down. I said, "How about talking about the break we've been hoping for!" I started running in circles around her.

"Have you lost it?" I stopped running and gave her a big hug picking her off the ground. "Down boy. You just need to calm yourself down."

"We're here!"

"Where?" She asked with a sarcastic shake of her head.

"The Boyscout reserve."

"You aren't playin' with me?"

I looked her in the eyes and replied, "I shit you not."

Chapter Seventeen
Whoops!

It took a few seconds for it to register, but this was the place. We weren't in the camp just yet, but we were close.

I said to Jasmine, "You see those rocks blocking up the creek?"

"Barely."

"That's because the water is so high, but I helped build that during one of our campouts."

"So, we made it."

"Not yet. We're not in the Scout reserve yet. We have a little more walking until we will reach the northern section. No one will be there. The northern section is closed during the winter and I'm pretty sure it won't be open just yet. But, once we're in that section all we'll need to do is follow the road down to the main section. Then, we are outie! We're going to McDonalds!"

Everything was still settling into Jasmine. It took a little for reality to work its way into her consciousness. After a few seconds she started smiling. She yelled to me, "Damn, we did it." I started jumping up and down again and running around. She remarked, "You are one weird white boy."

"Oh yeah, well I'm pretty fast too. Bet you can't catch me?" I tore off through the woods.

She started chasing after me and yelled, "Your speed better be able to pay for that check your mouth just wrote." She was keeping up, but I was running full speed. I checked back over my shoulder to see where she was and to make faces at her. It was a lot of fun until I hit a hole.

I didn't see it. I couldn't have. There were leaves all over the ground, which hid it like a mine. My foot slid in a couple inches and my body twisted and began to fall. There was a really nice crunching sound and then the back of my head hit the ground. I immediately rolled over onto my stomach to stop the twisting and tearing. I ripped my foot out of the hole. Once it was free, I curled in a ball and rolled around. I didn't want to look at it. My ankle was throbbing with pain and there was also pain in my knee.

Jasmine had laughed at first, but she must've seen the pain on my face because she immediately asked, "Are you all right?"

"It's bad I think," I managed to reply between gasps and grimaces of pain. "I really twisted the hell out of it."

"You sprained it?"

"I don't know. I think it's worse than that."

"Let me take a look at it. Come on, you've got to let go." I didn't realize I was protecting it that much. I moved my hands. She pushed my jeans up to my knee and tried to slide my sock down. "Well, I can't see much with this sock here. Where does it hurt?"

"My whole ankle is throbbing. I'd say it's mostly to the outside. We should take my shoe and sock off and put my foot in the creek."

"Good idea. I'll help you over." She helped me up and I started limping over to the creek.

I said in disgust, "I hope it's not broken. What a stupid thing to do. The one ability I do have is doing something stupid. I'm such a goof."

Jasmine laughed and replied, "Yeah, and I slipped on a rock with a terrorist a few feet away. Shit happens. I hate to see you beat yourself up so much. Perfect people are predictable and boring. I'm not afraid of people who are different."

"I wouldn't call possibly breaking your ankle while trying to get away from terrorists that want to kill you as different."

"Yeah it was a stupid thing to happen."

"Well, stupid things always seem to happen to me."

"All you can do is laugh about it." We reached the creek. We found a good spot for me to sit. She helped me remove my shoe and sock. I put my foot in. It was really cold. I had to will my foot to stay there.

She said, "Don't feel so bad. I like your uniqueness, and accidents go along with that. You shouldn't try to be anyone but yourself." Now would've been a good time for me to ask her how she actually felt about me, but I didn't have the guts to ask. There's a new one, huh? I forced my foot to stay in that water until I could hardly feel it. I had Jasmine get two medium sized sticks that were about a foot long. When she came back I had gotten my sock and shoe back on. I couldn't tell just how bad my ankle was, but it was a lot sorer than any sprain I'd ever had.

I said to her, "Now you're going to learn a little first aid. Because there's a good chance this ankle is broken we need to immobilize it." I took off my jacket and then my T-shirt and put my jacket back on. "We need to cut some long strips out of this shirt."

"What, you brought scissors along too?"

I pulled out my pocketknife and opened the little scissors. "This knife's got lots of useful parts."

"Sweet, I'll cut. How should I do it?"

"Cut in from the bottom about an inch and a half up and then cut all the way around the shirt. Once you've cut one, do the same with the next. Cut as many strips as you can get. I'll be sunning myself." She started right away.

"At least I'm learning some first aid now."

I sarcastically clapped my hands and said, "Yeah."

"Come on. Y'know when I was little I decided I was going to cook for my parents. I got half a ham out of the freezer and plopped it in the microwave. Little did I know the aluminum foil it was wrapped in was going to be a big problem. I turned it on high and hit the start button. I was picking a vegetable when the microwave basically exploded. The microwave was destroyed and when my parents came home I thought I was going to be destroyed. My mother was gonna whoop my ass, but my father calmed her down. He told me how much he appreciated my kindness, and explained why I should've done a better job thinking my idea through. I'll never forget what he said. 'Creative ideas always come with risk. In this case your idea failed. Your failure was not thinking things through. However, people who are too afraid to try new things will never create. Creative minds are always in demand no matter what fields, despite the risks and disasters. Creative minds create the future.'

"Wow, can we trade homes?"

"Well, after the talk I learned that disasters have negative consequences. I got a good spanking and I was grounded for a while. My father created a point system for my chores so I could work to 'repair my error.' But I didn't forget what he said."

"You have such a great Dad. You have everything my parents are never going to get. You're pretty rich aren't you?"

"I don't like to admit it. I grew up most of my life thinking I wasn't rich. My parents were careful not to spoil me or to lose the ties back to our more humble beginnings. I have a very negative attitude towards the stereotypes of being rich: stuck-up, thinking you're better than everyone else, arrogance. A lot of the people we live around are like that. It's been difficult for me to deal with the fact that we are rich. The last thing I want to be are those stereotypes, but we do have money."

"You're not like those stereotypes." She was a star that came down from the night sky to brighten my lifeless existence. There was no doubt I loved her, but true love never works one-way. Everything was great now, but all to soon we were going to be back in the real world. I was going to be a good friend, I just knew it. I did manage to say, "You're really great."

"You are too." There was silence for a moment. Our eyes met for a second. She grabbed the strips she had cut and asked, "So, what now?" I had the same question.

"Ahh, you need to put the two sticks on either side of my foot. I'll hold them. Now tie the strips around everything." She started wrapping the first one around at my shoe. "Make sure you tie the knot on one of the sticks."

"You mean tie it to the stick?"

"No, tie the ends of the cloth together so that the knot is on the stick. Pull it tight."

"I get it now." It took her a few minutes to tie all the strips.

When she finished I said, "Not bad. That should hold pretty well. Let's get going. We should be able to reach one of the northern camps by the end of the day. Then you can go get help."

"What?"

"I'm no good for traveling. It's going to kill us just to make it to the camp. All you'll have to do is follow the road to the main section. It won't be hard. I'm just going to slow you down and possibly re-injure my ankle."

"I don't want to split up."

"You'll be fine. Let's just work on making it to that camp."

"You'll know when we're there?"

"You'll know too. There are tents set up. They're up all through the year. Let's go."

We started walking. It was probably around one in the afternoon when we started again. It was a pretty slow go. We had to get there before I could be dropped off so Jasmine would know where to go. She couldn't just follow the creek. Well, she could, but that was the long way. As sunset was beginning, we came to the hill I was looking for. The creek went to the left. For the first time we were going to separate from our guide. We needed to go to the right. The hill was to that side. I got confirmation of my memory when we saw a sign for the Susquehannaux Boyscout camp. No hunting or trapping, it said. There were a lot of pine trees on the hill. I was pretty sure there was a trail somewhere but I couldn't remember. We had to hurry because daylight was fading. Getting up that hill was pure labor. My good leg was dead tired. My whole body was dead tired, but we made it eventually.

After we reached the top I said, "It should be around here somewhere." There wasn't much light anymore. It was probably seven o'clock or so. We kept walking to our right. We went down a little bit and then the ground leveled off. We walked probably another hundred or hundred and fifty yards until I saw something.

I smiled and pointed, "Look over there." There was a small brown building.

"What's that!"

I laughed and said, "The shitter. The camp area is straight down from there. Let's go before I fall over."

InterDependence

Before long we found the tents. We picked out one and pulled out the wood loading crates that were in it. The crates are in all the tents. They're used as a solid base to put the army beds on. When the camp was in use, each tent would have two army beds in them. The army beds are canvas foldouts, a luxury in camping. All they did was hold you off the ground. There wasn't a mattress or anything, but it was nicer than sleeping on the ground, which was where we were going to be sleeping once again. I flopped down and rested. Jasmine worked on the fire.

She was a good student. She'd make an excellent scout. A good scout doesn't need to know a thing about camping, wilderness survival, or nature when he starts. All he needs to know is how to listen. You learn everything you need to know if you listen, and Jasmine was good at it. I watched with a certain pride as she built the fire. I had to caution her not to build it too close to our tent, but she remembered what I'd taught her.

As she was working I said to her, "You're pretty good already. Next I'll have to show you how to fish and shoot a gun."

"You hunt?" she asked with clear shock.

"Yeah, a little. That's right, you're not into killing those cute little furry animals."

"Yeah, what's so wrong with that. They don't have guns."

I laughed a little, "Don't worry I'm not really into the killing part. Dad used to be when he had the time. I'll tell ya' deer jerky and deer bologna are excellent."

"Ah, I don't wanna hear it."

I laughed some more. "I told you I'm not into that. I trap shoot and target shoot, and I don't do that a whole lot anymore. I just don't have the time. My Mom can shoot. She's a good shot."

"She doesn't hunt?"

"No she doesn't, but she's tough enough to gut a deer. To live with my Dad, Mom needs to be that way. That's their idea of a date. Go shooting."

"This is going to be a culture shock for me when I meet your family."

"You'll like Mom. You already know about Dad. You'll have to teach me how to act civilized if I'm going to meet your parents." That statement was about as much courage as I could draw from the well.

"It's no big deal. My parents didn't grow up with the life we have now. My father lived in the projects for awhile when he was younger. We just look like we're civilized." She laughed a bit. "I'm ready to light this baby up."

"Go for it." I felt encouraged by her answer. She wasn't afraid to introduce me. I wanted to believe it was going to happen. We'd start dating. Simply an unbelievable thought for me, but I didn't want to doubt anymore. I wanted to lose control. I wanted to just let go and tell her my feelings and hear her say she felt the same, and hug her tight to my chest, and kiss her. I wanted to kiss her. I'd never done it before. It would be unbelievable. It would be unbelievable to be able to release my feelings with open arms, and not feel like I had to sneak around protecting them. But it was the knife to my unprotected heart that made me keep them chained in the shadows. Tomorrow when she left to get help would be the day I lost her. There was no sense in making it more difficult for her and more crushing for me. Her voice brought me out of my thoughts.

"How about that? Come on now. Show me some love?" How ironic her statement was.

I softly replied, "That's great, Jasmine." She was really great. She took care of me the rest of the evening. She tried to make me comfortable and she propped up my leg. I think she enjoyed the opportunity to take care of me. She had depended on me so much the last few days. Now I depended on her. I was glad for everything she did, but I didn't want my time with her to end. She made me feel comfortable around myself. Our worlds had collided so suddenly and now just as suddenly and remarkable they were leaving; just like the stars leave from the sky as day and night trade places. I'd tried to prevent my emotions from becoming too involved, but I fell in love with her star. I wanted to be up there with her. Why shouldn't I ask? I was losing her anyways.

Instead, I went over the directions for her journey in the morning. I said, "Tomorrow when you leave all you have to do is follow that road. You'll pass the pool and a large open gathering area used for big campfires. The road bares to the right and you'll go across a bridge. Just keep going and you'll eventually reach the mess hall and the main offices. That's it."

"Sounds easy enough. We're almost outtie, as you'd say." She laughed. It was a bitter sweat moment for me. She asked, "What's wrong?"

"Nothing."

"Are you sure?"

I hesitated. Then I replied, "Yeah."

We slept apart because of my leg. I didn't sleep a bit. It was eerie sleeping in an empty camp. Desolation hung like the cobwebs. It made me think of all the fun I'd had at these camps. My troop camped here at Susquehannaox probably twenty times since I joined. There were always people around, except for tonight. The wind blowing through the trees reminds you how alone you are. It's so quiet.

Jasmine had fallen asleep. I watched her for awhile. My heart wanted me to wake her up and tell her all that I was feeling, but of course I didn't. It didn't seem that Jasmine felt leaving tomorrow was going to affect us in any way. Maybe she didn't feel things were going to be different once we got back. She probably wasn't really thinking about a relationship with me once we got back. We'd be friends who shared one hell of an experience. I eventually closed my eyes and put all of my thoughts to sleep. I dreamt about Jasmine and me.

We were dancing under the moonlight just behind the tent. Her eyes sparkled against the sky and her skin seemed to shimmer with the light of the moon. She rested her head on my shoulder and we gently swayed together as I softly wrapped my hands around her waist. No one was around. Only the wind acknowledged we were there. I could feel her against my body. Having her arms wrapped around my waist made me feel like a God. I stopped dancing and she lifted her head. Our eyes met. I lifted my hand and ran the back of it gently across her cheek. It made her smile. Then, we kissed. There were no more questions. There were no more doubts. It was so real, and when I opened my eyes there she was laying just across from me. How I wished to bring those two worlds together. Only the stars and the moon were next to my bed. She was a fallen star that landed in my life, but it was misfortune that brought her violently out of the sky. She had to return to her place and me to mine. Could it be possible that she loved a dreamer like me? I doubted that. Only gods can play in the stars. Gods don't need to dream.

As I watched the rising dawn hide the moon once again, I knew that Jasmine would soon be in her constellation. She would disappear with the day and only be a sparkle in my dreams by night. When she woke up, she yawned and stretched a little before getting ready to go. Every little movement she made I watched intently. Even yawning she was perfect. She asked me if I was going to be all right as she held my hands. I shook my head yes. I tried to ask her, but when I looked into her eyes I couldn't get anything to come out of my mouth. We were both looking at each other for a couple seconds before she said she'd better get going. I paused for a moment and then wished her good luck. She backed away and then turned and started walking through the camp to the road. I watched her the whole way. It took about fifteen minutes before the road curved out of sight. Before she turned the corner, she waved. I waved back and she was gone.

There was nothing I could do to try and get my mind off of her. I could hardly move anywhere with my bad leg. I dragged myself behind the tent under the shade of the trees. I laid down and tried to get her out of my mind, but all my dreams were about her. Nothing else would do especially now that she was gone. I tried to fight it for a little but eventually I decided to just enjoy what she had become for me. I closed my eyes and little by little she came back to life in a world where we could be in love.

It was a huge ballroom. I was dressed like a prince. As I entered, I caught the attention of everyone. However, there was only one lady I was looking to find. As I scanned the ballroom I saw her. Jasmine was standing next to a huge floral arrangement of golden daffodils. She was dressed in an exquisite Victorian gown of a deep regal blue, white ivory, and gold. Her hair had fresh flowers in it. She noticed my gaze and smiled my way. Her smile was more beautiful than ever. I walked over to her and asked her to dance. She graciously bowed and held out her arms. She was flattered by my pressance. It was her heart that was hoping to be accepted into love. I motioned over to the musicians. They immediately noticed me and changed the music to a gentle melody. I took her hands and once again we were dancing. We spun all around the ballroom. Everyone watched as we floated with regal grace. Her eyes signaled the joy she was feeling inside. If only I could fly. When I was a little kid I thought I could, but I soon found out you need a license, a flight plan, and money.

Chapter Eighteen
The Rose

I dreamt for the rest of the morning and fell asleep at times. It was mid-afternoon when the guests arrived at my party. I had my eyes closed and I wasn't really awake. I heard footsteps, which started to get me awake. I figured it was the rescue team here to rescue me from living the dream I always wanted to become a reality. I started to sit up and open my eyes.

I heard, "Well, well, look what we've found." It sounded like Tony. My frustration with my girl problems instantly disappeared. I opened my eyes, and it was Tony. They were all there.

Tony said, "Looks like you were right, Jinnah. We had a feeling you'd follow the river."

I was pissed about everything. This was just perfectly appropriate for my pathetic life. Not only did I lose Jasmine, but because of my stupidity I also got caught, am probably going to die, and I'm endangering Jasmine. I hate life.

I replied, "Nice to see you guys again, but I imagine you're not really looking for me. How'd you find me?"

Azi replied, "We checked some other places that were closer just to be sure, but when we didn't find you there, we knew you followed the river. You tried to sneak by me the other night didn't you?"

"It looks like we did sneak by you?"

"I thought I wasn't hearing things. We started checking out this camp right away. I figured this would be your next stop.

"That's really bright of you Azi. Did you come up with that all by yourself?"

Jinnah replied, "Easy Azi."

"How did you get up here?"

Tony replied, "We drove to the entrance, but the guy at the front gate wouldn't let us drive up. He said this part of the camp was closed, and that this was a Boyscout camp only for Boyscouts. I guess we don't have that scouting spirit. So Azi and Katerina here told em' they had a kid who's a scout thinkin' about commin' here, and 'could he give us a map, please.' Ahh, you two were great. The jerk gave us a map and told us to leave, and we did. We went right out to the road and took our four-wheelers right up here."

"How's your chest?"

"Just fine."

"I guess I knocked some sense into you. You guys did a good job."

Azi replied, "You're a cocky little son of a bitch. Well, I hope you have the answer we're looking for."

I replied, "What'd you mean?"

Azi grabbed me by my jacket and yanked me to my feet. Then, he pulled my face up to his. "This isn't a game. We want the fucking girl!" Jasmine had been gone for awhile now, but I didn't really know how long it would take her to get to the main camp. Plus, it would take some time before the police could get there. None of the dumpy hillbilly cops from this area were going to be able to handle these guys. She would have to wait until the FBI got up there. I had to stall. If these guys stopped at the gate, the people who run the camp had to be suspicious. When she got down there she'd hear about them and get people up here in a hurry. I could depend on her to get help as soon as possible.

"The Girl!" Azi yelled at me as he cracked me across the face with the back of his hand.

I replied, "We split up the morning after we got away. I haven't seen her since."

Jinnah asked, "Where did she go?" I was really trying to pull this story out of my butt. I had no idea what I was saying. I needed more time to think it through to make it sound more accurate.

Katerina yelled, "You better start talking a whole lot faster."

"She headed west."

Azi replied, "You're full of shit! We've checked to the east, west, and north. Besides, she would no nothing of surviving out here. You'd never split up. Now, I'm going to ask again. Where is the girl?" I was running out of options, but telling them the truth was never going to be an option. I didn't reply.

"You can do this the easy way or the hard way."

"Well you take a left about five hundred trees down and keep going till you see this one pile of logs. Make a right there. . ." My explanation was cut short by Azi cracking me across the face.

He said, "Do you think this is funny?"

"Would you like to kiss my ass?" That comment got another smack across the face.

Azi yelled, "We need that girl right now. Where is she?" I didn't reply. I was regaining my senses.

Jinnah had said very little but he stepped forward. "It is unfortunate you became involved in all of this, but I need that girl. A lot depends on it."

"So you can get your terrorist friends free and kill more innocent people. Fuck you!" Jinnah lowered his eyes and motioned to Azi as he walked away from the group.

Azi said, "Good, it's going to be the hard way. It looks like you hurt your foot." He pulled out a big knife and cut the strips off and threw the sticks to the ground. "I bet it's really tender."

Tony started laughing and said, "Hey, you little prick, how's this feel?" He started yanking my foot back and forth. I screamed in pain and tried to drag myself away from them, but Azi and Katerina grabbed both of my shoulders and held me there.

Tony said, "Let's try side to side, Daniel son." Once again my foot was screaming in pain. After he went back and forth for a bit he pushed hard and continuous to the one side. It hurt so bad I almost broke free from Azi and Katerina. Tears started streaming from my eyes, and I screamed at the top of my lungs. I could feel my skin ripping on the other side of my ankle. I had broken my ankle.

"Does that hurt a little. I'll stop when you tell us where the girl is." I can't believe I didn't pass out. I looked down towards the road. No one was there. God, how much longer? Finally the bone broke through my skin to the outside, and blood started to run down into my shoe. It shocked everybody, especially Tony.

He stopped yanking my foot and said, "Holy shit!"

Azi ordered, "Back away Tony. Let's see if he's ready to talk now." I rolled onto my side and covered my face in the grass. The pain was intense. "OK, boy, this is all over when you tell us where she is?" I didn't reply. Azi got really mad. He yelled to Tony and Katerina, "Get him up. Stand him up against that tree over there." They grabbed me and started dragging me over to the tree. I punched Tony with my elbow and kicked Katerina with my good leg. I tried to hop away, but it was hopeless. Azi quickly grabbed me and dragged me to the closest tree slamming me up against it.

Jinnah came over, looked into my eyes, and said, "Talk, for your own sake." Azi and Katerina each held one of my arms behind the tree, which pinned me against it. I looked to the road again, nobody.

Katerina said, "This is going to get even worse."

Tony laughed and said, "Yeah, there's plenty more comin', and it doesn't hurt us. Like, I'm sorry about your foot."

His smug face and laugh made me really mad. I smiled and said, "Yeah, sorry about the rock, but we had places to go," and I spit at him.

"You little piece of shit. I'm gonna kill you."

Jinnah ordered, "Hold. Are you going to give us the information we desire?"

I replied, "Sorry about you're leg. I was really bummed out about it."

"I see." He motioned to Azi. Tony grabbed my arm and Azi moved in front of me. He whacked me with a punch across my left cheek. Then, he punched my hard in the stomach. I wasn't ready for it and it knocked the wind out of me. I was gasping for air. Azi moved aside and Tony came over and punched me in the face to the right and then left. Then, he hit me with two jabs and finished with another blow to my stomach. I think my nose was now broken. There was a lot of blood in my mouth.

Azi said, "So, now. Have you anything new to say?" I didn't reply. "Where is the girl?"

I replied, "Fuck you," and spit the blood in my mouth at his face. There was no way on this earth I was going to give up Jasmine. I just prayed she was hurrying the help. I wasn't sure how much I could take, and I wanted to see her again. I had to tell her how I felt. I knew it now.

Azi was furious. He stepped back and said, "You are a little bastard. Tony, go and get the fire going again." I was pretty delirious, but I was regaining my senses in the ten minutes they were getting the fire ready. I used the break in the beating to fix my ankle.

Compound fracture, what to do for a compound fracture? I tried to dig out first aid training from my dazed mind. I worked on getting the bone back to its normal position. It was incredibly painful, but I eventually slid the bone back to a more normal position in line with the rest of my leg. Then I tried to wrap it to slow the bleeding. I had blood everywhere and seeing it made me terrified. Azi and Katerina were simply keeping an eye on me while they helped Tony with the fire. Tony had pulled one of the metal tent spikes and was heating it up.

He motioned to Azi and Katerina and said, "Bring him over here." They had to drag me because I was beat, literally. There was no fighting this time.

Azi looked at me once again. He said, "Have you ever been burned little bastard. I'm telling you, you better tell us now, because I'm going to make you feel pain beyond anything you can imagine."

I replied, "I'll never tell you anything."

"Why?"

I should've told her. I paused for a second and looked him right in the eyes, "I love her." It's what I truly felt.

Tony replied, "Oh, you fell in love.

Jinnah slowly moved over to me. He lifted up my face and our eyes met. He said, "If you love her than stay alive to see her again. We are not going to harm her, I promise you that. As long as her father does what we tell him to, she will be returned unharmed." In a way it was tempting, but I didn't believe him. They were going to kill me either way. At that moment I realized I was going to die. Nobody was going to get up here to save me. I wasn't going to see Jasmine again. Whether I told them where she was or not, it didn't matter. I was going to die, and I loved her. I started to cry.

I said, "I love her." The tears poured across my face like rain from a thunderstorm down my window. I looked to the road once again. There was nobody.

Azi replied, "Very moving. Bring the stake, Tony."

"Wait!" ordered Jinnah.

Azi snapped back, "Wait for what?"

"This is out of control?"

"Do you want your brother free or not!" Jinnah paused for a moment and everyone looked to him. Azi added, "He is an infidel."

Jinnah lowered his voice and slowly replied, "He is a boy."

Azi replied, "He is an American." Azi looked ready to fight. Then, Jinnah nodded his eyes at Azi. Through the tears in my eyes I could see the hot glow of that tent spike, but behind it I saw Jasmine's face. Through the hot red she was saying, "I love you." She smiled and I started to smile.

Azi said, "I will give you another chance to answer my question," but I wasn't listening. Her smile seemed to mesmerize me like the flame from the match the first night we were together. Katerina held my arm and Tony burnt a spot on my arm black. I screamed in pain.

The torture went on for at least a half-hour, maybe more. They burned more spots on my arm black with the hot tent spike. Then, they dragged me back over to the tree where they punched me some more. They would stop periodically and ask me the same question, and I would say nothing. Then, the torture would start again. I looked to the road and there was nobody. I was starting to lose consciousness. The pain wasn't really affecting me anymore. I was numb to everything except how much I wanted to see Jasmine again. That was the real pain. My heart burned with a flame a thousand times hotter than that tent spike. I begged God for her to come. I begged God for one moment in my life that I could enjoy, just one moment where I could stand on top and feel good.

I lied to them at one point and told them she was in the outhouse. That bought me maybe five minutes before they came back madder than before. They yanked me up against the tree and the beating started again. This time one of them grabbed a stick. I don't know how much longer it was, but for some reason they stopped hitting me. It took a few moments for me to figure out what was going on. I had fallen to the ground. It took great effort to raise my head. Azi and Jinnah were arguing.

Jinnah sharply commanded, "This is going nowhere."

Azi replied, "It will soon!"

"I did not come here to kill an innocent child."

Katerina broke in, "Getting sentimental on us."

"I need not remind any of you who is in charge here. I say enough!" That was the first time I saw his full anger. He looked mystical to me. Like he was a powerful sorcerer or something. There was a tense silence as Azi and Jinnah looked eye to eye. I was still very delirious, but I noticed something in front of me. It was the flower. Yes, there it was. That leafy fern, gentle and beautiful like her. I weakly reached out my hand and pulled off one of the branches. The sound of engine noises broke up the argument; although I was only interested in the fern.

When one of the terrorists yelled, "We've got company," I focused what little attention I had left in me on the terrorists. I kept that fern leaf in my tightly clenched hand.

Another one of the terrorists yelled, "Let's get the hell out of here." The SUVs drove right through the camp over the fire to where I was. My Dad was the first to burst out, much to my surprised. He threw down his hat and ran and tackled Azi. I'd never knew Dad could run that fast. I guess I know where I got my speed. Once he had a hold of Azi, he really kicked his ass. After he'd knocked him down, he grabbed his head and slammed it against a tree. Dad was swearing up a storm. People in suits were also jumping out of the SUVs, but then everyone froze. I was being dragged away from all the good guys. Where was I going? Then, I saw her: her eyes, her beautiful face. Where am I going? I love her. I need to tell her.

"Jasmine!" My voice was barely a whisper. Her father was standing with her holding her back as she screamed my name with tears in her eyes. Her father stood proud and strong. I had to tell her. Our eyes were still locked, but I was moving out of sight. Why do they just stand there? I have to tell her. I made the Indian sign for love. I did it over and over until I was dragged onto a 4-wheeler and Jasmine was whisked away from me once again – always like a star. It was too early in the day for me to be with her.

A flurry of thoughts went through my mind all at once. I thought about Dad and Mom, school, and Jasmine all at the same time. I was jumping into twenty different memories all at once, but one face stuck out.

Where was she? I wanted to see her. Why did I want to see her? No more tractor rides with Dad. Why was he so mad? Mom's right. Dale's right, I need to take more chances. Jasmine – the star. Her eyes, that smile. Why am I here? Jasmine, I wanted to say something to her. What's that in my hand? Jasmine should be here. She called them and they came. I don't know where I am. I'm lost. Where's that star. I need to go back over to those people. I can't. I'm going so far away from them. This fern in my hand, the flower for Jasmine. Where is Jasmine? I want to tell her I love her. I wanted to tell her I love her. I'm dying.

I weakly lifted my hand and gently rubbed the leaves. My fingers smeared them with blood. As I focused on the blood-smeared fern, I remembered I had told her; someone would tell her what that sign meant. For some reason I all ready felt she loved me. I saw it in her eyes. For some reason, I felt happy – even as my life poured onto the forest floor. I stared at the blood red fern until I couldn't see anything anymore.

Instantly I was riding the waves, the sun was out, and it felt amazing. The wind blowing through my hair and the mist of the seawater splashing onto my face felt cool and refreshing. I whipped my board into the half pipe and went shooting through. When I opened my eyes, I could see only black. The End.

Chapter Nineteen
Living by your Principles

Just kidding, but that's what I thought happened. When I regained consciousness, I don't know how long I was out, I expected to see the pearly gates or something. After I took a few moments to reboot my brain, I was able to convince myself that I was still alive. I took my pulse to be sure. I had a pulse. I looked around. I was underneath a rocky overhang. It was like a cave, except it didn't go back very far. I tried to wipe the grogginess out of my eyes and mind. After a few moments I had regained enough reality to remember vaguely what had happened. It all had the feel of a freshly ended dream. Maybe it was all a dream? The pain throughout my body sure seemed real enough, though. I looked myself over. My wounds were bandaged? My ankle was back in a brace and the burns on my arm were covered. I tried to sit myself up, but my ribs and stomach hurt really bad.

"I see you are awake." My head immediately turned to my left as I tried to slide myself closer to the rock wall on my right. I wanted to get as far away from that voice as possible. "Try to lie still." It was difficult for my eyes to see who it was. He was masked by the darkness on that side of the overhang. "I have done my best to treat your injuries."

He moved out of the shadows closer to me. "I can only offer my apologizes for everything else." It was Jinnah.

"You fucking bastard!" Tears streamed down my cheeks. "Are you feeling guilty now? Now that I'm dying!" He grabbed me and put his hand over my mouth.

"You must keep your voice down." After a moment, he slowly removed his hand and walked a few steps to the mouth of the overhang. I glared at him the whole time. He turned and looked back at me for a moment before he sat down. We both stared at each other for a few more moments. Jinnah then said, "You are very brave. You would make an honorable Pakhtun."

"I'm honored. Is that where your from?"

"I am from Pakistan, my heritage is Pakhtun. Pakistanis are a people of peoples all united by Muslim, and Pakistan."

"Thanks for the geography lesson you terrorist."

"I am not a terrorist."

"Bullshit." I started coughing very harshly. Jinnah moved over to me, but I fiercely shook off his hand. "Fuck off!" Jinnah moved back and sat down clearly frustrated. Once I got control of my coughing, I reached down for some more strength and quietly and intensely said, "At least I have the comfort of knowing that Jasmine's father can do his job and send your terrorist buddies to the chair."

"I am not a terrorist. My name is Syed Jinnah."

"So you're not the leader of Al Jaala Juloh? Y'see, you can't play games with me. Jasmine's filled me in."

"You were told Al Jaala Juloh is a terrorist organization?"

"Yes, just look at me, I'm proof!"

"There is a lot you do not understand."

"You're all terrorists. You ride around your deserts with assault rifles trying to plan the next innocent people you're can kill, all for Allah." Jinnah laughed and shook his head.

"So, you already know who I am?"

"Yeah." I started coughing hard again.

"You must save your strength. Why don't you listen to me for awhile? Can you place your fears and opinions aside and listen to me?" I thought this was gonna be good. A terrorist was going to try to convince me he wasn't a terrorist. I nodded my head yes with a laugh. "Good, no speaking. You need your strength and I need a great deal of time to explain. I suppose you do not know what Al Jaala Juloh means?" I shook my head no with a sarcastic nod.

"It is not a terrorist organization. The best translation is, the winter flame, but the flame doesn't do it justice. In Baluchistan, another province of Pakistan, there are scorching summer winds that are so dry and hot they can almost burn your eyebrows off. These fiery winds are called the Juloh. However, unlike the assumptions of most American's, Pakistan is not a big desert. Not every Muslim lives in a desert with assault rifles. The province of Punjab is a land of much farming and extensive irrigation. The city of Lahore has beautiful gardens and several universities. There are also the Northern areas that hold most of Kashmir, a land in dispute with India. This is an area of some of the highest mountains in the world. It is an area very different than a desert. That is where Jaala comes in. It means winter. Al Jaala Juloh is the whole of Pakistan, both desert and mountain, fire and ice."

"Great, just wonderful."

"You promised you would listen."

"I don't care."

"You Americans need a great deal of enlightenment about the world you control in ignorance. The American way is the only way with you."

"Look who's the terrorist."

"Al Jaala Juloh is a political organization seeking the unification of Pakistan under a peaceful and prosperous government. I am here because I feared many American's would perceive us as terrorists. It is my brother that is in an

American prison awaiting trial for the bombing of the New York subway. I cannot allow my brother's life to hang on the whim of American stereotypes."

"You're saying he didn't do it?"

"Yes."

"There's a new one."

"My brother is innocent, but he is also Muslim and a member of a political organization. It matters little what our real mission is or who my brother really is. To an American he is a terrorist riding around the desert with assault weapons, as you say."

I thought everything over. "Why should I believe you?"

"Why should I lie? I am deeply sorry for all that has happened."

"Sorry! You were going to kill me if we hadn't've gotten away!"

"You were very wise. You did a very impressive job escaping and surviving. I did say that, but it would not have happened. I was trying to keep Azi under control. I came to save my brother, not to kill people. Azi is the killer."

"So how'd you guys all get together?"

"Azi is my Brother's son's son."

"That's not much of a bond."

"In Pakistan it is. Family is very important and much larger than in America. Azi moved to America several years ago with my brother. He hates Americans very passionately. Your country does not make friends well, you know. America was our ally at one time, or so we thought. When India attacked in Kashmir, American help was no where to be found. We were not an ally, but a political convenience. Pakistanis do not forget the past. Azi is also a fundamentalist Muslim. American policy and Azi's strict religious views create a deep hatred in him. America is the greatest of all enemies. Azi met Katerina during his time here. She is from Leningrad in the former Soviet Union.

She has no love for America either. They are a couple. Tony was hired help. I was not excited about bringing him, but Azi insisted we needed someone who was familiar with this country. For the right price Tony agreed. I should have seen that such a plan would only result in the mess I now have."

"Yeah sure, it's a great story, but I'm dying." I didn't believe him. I didn't want to fall for some trick he was planning. However, Jinnah had sincerity in his voice. There was concern in his eyes. There was a dignity to him. It's not something I can immediately point to, but I knew it was there. It's like the elegance of a racehorse. Some are just horses, but then you will see one that just says 'I'm the best'. It's not one thing you can point to, but you know it's there. Jinnah was either one awesome actor or very sincere.

"All I want is to unite my people. My concern is not with America."

"Well, not all of us Americans are that bad, y'know. I live on a big farm. We've got lots of space. It's real peaceful. The mountains are beautiful."

"I would enjoy seeing it. The unknown creates much fear, but it is the curiosity that brings one back to look again that saves us all." I started coughing again. "You must rest."

After the coughing subsided I said, "What are you going to do?"

"I am unable to save my brother, thanks to your intervention, but I must also hope that there are more Americans like you. I do not belong in the middle of this. I need to go home."

"Yeah, me too."

"Rest. I will tell you stories of my land. Stories that painted my dreams with wild wonders I'm sure you never imagined." Whether I believed him or not, I needed to rest and there was little I could do but listen. "I remember my father telling many of them when I was a boy. He could make my eyes grow wide the way he told them. I will attempt to be so vivid. Pakistan did not exist until the middle of this century. Before then Pakistan was a part of India and Muslims and Hindus ruled together. This cooperation is no longer. Pakistan exists for this reason. However, a Muslim and Hindu India has over two thousands years of history.

Fate brought the two vastly different cultures crashing together when the warrior Hulagu led armies through the Middle East murdering entire cities. Muslims fled to India. At this time Hindu Sultans ruled India and most Muslims were on the bottom of this feudal system. The Mughal Empire began when Muslims overthrew the Sultans and began to rule India.

Babur, a Muslim, was born to become king of a small kingdom called Fergana at age eleven. He lost most of his kingdom in his teens, but he was a strong leader and regained his power. He then looked to India. Babur met Sultan Ibrahim at Panipat north of the capital of Delhi. It is said that the Sultan had over 100,000 men and some 1,000 fighting elephants trained to crush anything in their path. You must imagine the roar of 1,000 elephants. Babur had only 25,000 well-trained men.

However, those elephants had never heard cannon fire. When Babur's men fired their cannons the elephants became frightened and out of control. Sultan Ibrahim was killed along with 20,000 of his men by his own best weapon. Babur took control of India. It is said that in the Sultan's treasury there was a jewel, an enormous diamond called the Koh-I-Nur (mountain of light) big enough to buy enough grain to feed the entire world for three days. Babur now had it and for the first time Muslims controlled India. Babur ruled with wisdom. He learned from the Hindus and appreciated their culture and art. His appreciation led the way for cooperation.

When Babur died, his son Humayun took the throne, but was soon driven out of India, for a time. Broken and with little, he headed for Persia to raise an army. Along the way he fell in love with an amazingly beautiful girl named Hamida. He was a beaten king wandering the desert and much older, but Hamida fell in love with him." My mind drifted to thoughts of Jasmine. "With his new-found love he raised an army in Persia, using the Koh-I-Nur as payment, and retook India only to die falling down the stairs of his newly regained kingdom." Now, tell me that doesn't sound like me?

"Are you listening?"

"Yeah, I was just thinking that Humayun's luck is like my life's story."

"After he died, his son Akbar then began his very long rule of India. Akbar, which means great, was a skilled warrior with a keen mind. His strength was in his wisdom. It is said that to train his army he would go on massive hunts. Some 50,000 soldiers would bang pans with sticks in a circle 60 miles wide as they walked inward. Stags, antelope and even tigers were scared into a center pen that the emperor would hunt in. One time Akbar even grabbed a stag by the horns. As he fought with the beast he was knocked down and gorged. Akbar was respected for his bravery but more for his compassion.

He brought unity to Hindus and Muslims. He married a Hindu princess and ruled with compassion and strength as both of his allies. Akbar encouraged architects, painters, musicians, and all other artistic endeavors. He wanted only prosperity for the whole of his kingdom, both Muslim and Hindu. After his rule, never again would India's Muslims and Hindus live under such an air of cooperation and understanding.

Some thirty years after Akbar's death and the brief rule of Jahangir, Shah Jahan took the throne by defeating his brother. He fell deeply in love with Arjumand Banu. She soon became Queen of India. Shah Jahan trusted no one as greatly as he trusted her. She was greater to him than even his kingdom. He changed her name to Mumtaz Mahal (the chosen one of the Palace). After less than four years together she died giving birth to her fourteenth child. Shah Jahan was crushed. For two years he mourned and even prohibited music at court. A man of so much joy was now very plain and beaten. Have you heard of the Taj Mahal?"

I had to wake myself up to answer the question. My imagination was running wild with such an amazing story. I replied, "Yeah, I think. Doesn't Donald Trump own it or something?"

"Ha, ha, you Americans. The Taj Mahal in India is far grander than any casino. In his beautiful wife's memory Shah Jahan gathered his finest architects and commanded them to build a tomb "as beautiful as she was beautiful." 20,000 craftsmen and laborers worked for sixteen years in Agra to build, "the dream in marble" the Taj Mahal. It is as amazing and overwhelming in its mammoth size as it is in delicate detail. It is the pride of every Pakistani, despite it's location in India. Shah Jahan built many more beautiful structures. He created the Shalimar Gardens of fountains, gardens, and marble and when we would hold audience in Delhi he would sit on the peacock throne, a jewel-laden chair of diamonds, emeralds, gold, rubies, and pearls. *His son* would rise to power of his own accord. Shah Jahan grew ill . . ."

I drifted off to sleep as Jinnah's gentle voice lulled me to sleep. I dreamt about all that he had told me: mighty kingdoms of elephant armies and a huge jewel as big as a mountain. I imagined myself as the ruler of this kingdom with Jasmine as my Queen. She was indeed beautiful and wonderful enough to sit in a chair of jewels. I pictured myself at her side riding an elephant decorated in our kingdom's colors. To live in my dreams!

Jasmine was such a star. When would it be nighttime so she could join me again? I wanted to talk to Jasmine. I wanted to talk with my Dad. I wanted to be back home getting ready for the next track meet. I wanted to stay alive.

Chapter Twenty

The Ending

The next thing I remembered was waking up in a hospital room with about ten thousand tubes coming out of my body. I felt horrible. Did I really sit and listen to stories with Jinnah? Who was Syed Jinnah? Did all of that really happen? Nothing seemed real to me anymore except that my body felt kinda like I'd been beaten up real bad. At least I knew that that part of my memory was real.

Everything that was in my memory was too unreal for it to be a part of my life. It was crazy and wild like my dreams: terrorists and lands of elephants and burning my arms and a girl who fell in love with me, no way. It was too unreal. I looked at my arms. They were covered with bandages. How much of my memory was real? How much was my own creation?

Eventually, a doctor came in and told me about my condition. I was lucky to be alive at this point, but there was a lot more to come. Those were essentially the highlights. The technical stuff wasn't important. He told me I'd been unconscious for a day, which was mainly because they'd kept me sedated. He also told me it was morning, I couldn't tell the difference, anyways. There were no windows in intensive care. After he left I had a lot of time to think. I wasn't in good shape. The white walls made me paranoid. It just reminded me where I was and how far from home I could go. That's what I thought about until my family came in later that afternoon.

Mom was the first through the door. She said, "Hey, honey. How'd you feel?" She sat down on a chair next to me and rubbed her fingers through my hair.

"A little beat up." Dad walked in behind her followed by a man in a black suit I didn't know. Dad was holding his hat in his hand. He stood along side Mom by the side of the bed. Dad always took off his hat in a building. He looked more concerned than I'd ever seen him.

"We've worried about you a lot. When the police found the truck at the back of the mall, they figured that you and Jasmine were kidnapped together. They didn't have a clue where you two were. They couldn't figure out why they took you."

I said, "So, this is all real?"

"Yeah."

"I was alone with one of them?"

"Yeah, when the FBI got up there the one guy put a gun to your head and took you with him. He had on a black ski mask. I was so worried about you. You were so close to us."

"How'd I get here?"

The man in the black suit stepped forward and said, "Agent Snyder, it's a pleasure to meet you Chad. You got away from him somehow, I know I'd like to hear the story. I bet it's as good as how you and Jasmine got out of the van. You'd make a good agent. Once you got away, you made trail markings to show us where you were. We found you unconscious in a small cave. Those trail markings probably saved your life, as did all of your ingenuity." Wow, was all I could think. The reality and the dream were beginning to come into focus again. It all did happen, to me, and I made it. "Don't worry if everything seems a bit groggy right now;

you'll feel better. After you get a chance to chat with your folks, I'd like to talk with you for a second."

I mumbled a reply almost to myself, "I was an unexpected visitor. I ran and tried to play hero, and I made it." I coughed for a good bit and grimaced with pain. It hurt really bad to cough.

Mom replied, "You just rest. You can tell us the story later."

"Mom, did Jasmine see what I signed to her?"

"I'm not sure what you mean."

"How is she?"

"I'd say she's in love. She wants to come in to see you, but only immediate family can enter intensive care. You also need to be sixteen. That's why Becky couldn't come in. She hopes you're feeling better. She wanted me to give you this card from the school. All of your classmates signed it. Everyone hopes you get better." She handed me the big card. I couldn't believe it. Everyone signed it. When did these people start caring about me? I looked to see if Patrick's signature was there. He wrote, 'everyone's rooting for you. Get well.' It was signed, PP with a circle around the two Ps. It threw me for a loop. I didn't think most of these people cared I existed.

I said to Mom, "Wow, this is really unbelievable."

"I thought it was really nice." Throughout the conversation she was trying to smile and keep things light, but I knew she was really concerned. Dad had been fidgeting with his hat and sort of standing in the sidelines.

Agent Snyder asked, "I hate to break in, but any information you could give us about that last terrorist is crucial right now. We have some ideas, but none of the other terrorists we caught are saying anything. Jasmine couldn't remember, but she said you knew the guy's name that got away. I also wanted to know if you have any idea what his plans were?"

I paused for a moment as I thought everything over. "His name is Akbar, ahh, Jahan. Yeah, the last name was Jahan. Akbar Jahan, I remember I got him to tell it to me. He was always pretty talkative about what they were going to do. I guess he figured I couldn't get away twice."

"Never underestimate a Boyscout, huh?"

"Yeah, ah, I believe he said he was going to take me to Mexico where he was going to ransom me. I don't know if he's still going that direction, but that was his plan."

"Hmm, well I'll get some people working on that. We hadn't heard of an Akbar Jahan. I'll get an agent in here who can do a composite drawing as soon as possible." Agent Snyder went out of the room.

Dad cleared his throat and said, "Sarah, you wanna let me and the boy have a couple moments alone."

"Yeah sure. You take care honey. The doctors are working real hard." Mom left the room. When the door shut behind her with that silent death-like clunk, my heart started to race. There was a silence as Dad fumbled with his hat.

He finally said, "Look, I think we need to talk."

"I'm sorry about the truck," I replied.

"This ain't about the truck. It's about us. You and I used to be close."

"Yeah."

"Yeah. This week's been hell. So, why's nothin' I do good enough for you?"

"I think it's the other way around."

"You're my boy. I've been proud a' you since the day you were born. You're a good son, but I think you're embarrassed by your old man. Maybe you can't respect someone who lives his life as a farmer. I can't be some famous sprinter and I know you think I'm just a hick, but I'm your ole' man. I work hard so you'll be able to have more. I've been tryin' to smooth things over, but you don't seem to wanna go nowhere."

"I know. I saw the way you tackled that guy."

"Yeah, beat the shit outta that asshole." Dad grinned and laughed as he scratched his messy hair.

I tried not to laugh too much because it hurt. I replied, "Yeah, I saw." My smile faded away as I tried to tell him what it really was.

He said, "So it's that. That's what your Mom said. Look, Chad, I was an idiot then. I did some stupid things and that night I was way outta line. I never touched booze again, never. You're Mom and I worked hard to fix things with us. She's let go, but you're still holdin' on and I don't know what to say to . . ."

"Dad, you never said anything to me." I broke down. With death looking me in the eye I couldn't hold anything together. Every dam I'd built busted and the water rushed down my cheeks. "I should've stopped you. You don't know how bad you were. You threw things around the house and you, you hit Mom real bad. I should've stopped you. I stood on the stairs and saw it. When I tried to knock you down, you just threw me out of the way. I failed. After you went roaring out of the house, Mom was in a heap on the floor her eyes were all bruised and she was sobbing like I'd never heard before. I failed." Dad was looking at the ground now. There were tears in his eyes.

He said, "I don't wanna hear you sayin' you failed. You had nothin' to do with it. There ain't no one to be blamed but me. Chad, I wish to God I could make that night go away, but I can't. You never should've seen stuff like that. When I saw your Mom the next morning I nearly died. I didn't remember all that happened, but her face couldn't lie. I've loved your Mother with my whole heart for a long time and seeing what I did woke me up real good. I've never touched it since, ever, and I never will, never for nothin'."

"You destroyed who you were for me, and then you never talked to me about it. Why?"

"I didn't know how to explain any of it to you. I'd set such a bad example. I hoped it'd go away."

"I hated you. I wanted to be anything but you."

"All I can ask is that you forgive me. That's what Mom did."

"You never asked me!"

"I'm askin' now! I want my boy back." Dad was struggling to hold back the tears. I could see without a doubt how much he cared. My Dad, with the heart of stone, needed real feeling. Seeing that and hearing him finally ask for my forgiveness let out a lot of the reservoir of hurt I'd been keeping to myself. With it gone, I found that deep down at the bottom was that little kid that still loved his Dad. He was tarnished and damaged, but he was there.

I replied, "I forgive you." Dad patted my shoulder and then bent down and gave me a hug.

"I know it's gonna take some time, but we've got a start."

"I just hope I have some."

"Don't you think like that. You made it through a whole lotta shit already. This is all you got left. You hang in there."

"I'll do my best. So, what do you think of Jasmine?"

"Her folks got lots a cash. You must a done some talkin' about me because she won't say a thing to me. You probably told her I hate black people like the KKK."

"Yeah, well you do, Dad."

"I've got a lot a reasons, too. I hate that guy on your poster and your rap music because you love that shit more than me. I'm hope'n that will change. But I don't walk around with no cape on burnin' crosses on people's yards."

"That doesn't mean you're not racist."

"It sure the hell does. Jasmine and her family ain't like some of the trash I've met. I worry what they think of us."

"I know Jasmine is open-minded and I'm sure her parents are as well. You don't think you would have a problem if Jasmine and I were dating?"

"I told you, I ain't about hate. As long as they're good hard working people I don't have a problem. Y'know, you needs to know a few things about me. When I was in construction I worked with a lot of lazy niggers. I'm sorry if you don't like the word, but that's what they were – ungrateful wastes of space. They didn't work and they didn't stand for nothin'. That got them on my bad side, but I know there's lots of lazy people and they ain't all black." I was thinking, yeah right, but I didn't say anything. Dad continued, "But, I never told you why I quit my construction job. Well, I was up for promotion to foreman."

"Yeah, I remember you telling Mom about it. Then, the next thing I know you quit."

"I'd worked for that place for ten years. Fifteen, if you included the summers I worked when I was in still in high school. I thought my promotion was a lock. I had the experience and the seniority, plus I was a damn hard worker, but they gave it to this black guy. My boss told me straight out that I was the best man for the job, but he said the company needed to improve its image. He encouraged me to hang in there; the next promotion was mine. I wasn't working for that bullshit. I didn't slave for fifteen years to get pushed under the rug by some bullshit image idea. It just so happens that the black guy they hired was one of them niggers that wouldn't know a hard days work if it kicked him in the ass. I'd always thought about farmin' so I decided it was time to be workin' for myself."

There was a lot more to this than I realized. I asked, "Why didn't you tell me?"

"Because you were a kid. You didn't need to be hearin' all the shit in the world just yet. Y'know, it's not right, a lot of the way the real world is, but when you're a kid you're beyond that. I wasn't going to ruin that for you. Besides, I was embarrassed. It made things a lot harder for us."

"I understand a lot better now. Still, the nigger thing has got to go."

"I'm not saying they all are. Jasmine and her family don't seem like that kind, but they've got to prove they're worth my respect."

"That's racism, Dad."

"No, that's what I've learned. That's why I didn't tell you why I quit, 'cause maybe you won't. Unfortunately that's how I am, but I ain't said I won't change my mind. That's racism." At least he was open to giving them a chance. That was more than I thought he'd do. I was too tired to press him further. I wasn't worried, though. Jasmine wouldn't have any trouble impressing him and neither would her Dad, so I felt good. I started coughing again and the pain really gripped me. I was the big problem right now.

Dad asked, "You all right?"

I got myself under control and said, "Yeah, I guess." I looked him in the eyes and said, "I'm not doing so well." He nodded his head. "I really need to see Jasmine."

"They won't let her in. She wants to, but they won't."

"Damn."

"I'll tell you what. I think I'll be able to convince 'em to make an exception.

"Try not to get arrested."

"Don't worry about a thing. She'll get in."

"Thanks, Dad." He leaned down and we hugged.

Dad turned and walked out. That was the most emotion we'd shared in four years. I felt like I had my Dad back. I started coughing again. About ten minutes later the door slowly opened and Jasmine looked in. Our eyes met. I could see her looking at all of the medical stuff around me. She was trying not to cry but she started to anyways.

I said, "Don't be afraid. It's still me in here."

"I'm so sorry. When I got down to the main office I told the guy what happened. He said there were some suspicious people that had stopped by earlier in the morning. We called the police, but we had to wait until the FBI got there. They didn't want anyone going up until they got there. I wanted to go so bad. When we turned the corner and I could see them around you I nearly died. They took so long to get there." She was crying a lot now. It really hurt me to see how upset she was. She was still standing by the door.

I replied, "I knew what I was doing. I knew you'd get help. You can come closer." She smiled a little and slowly walked closer to my bed. My voice was getting raspier. I fixed my eyes on hers. "There was no way I'd tell 'em where you were. Never. I'm not afraid of dyin' as long as you made it. And you did." The tears were welling in my eyes. I tried to smile. "We did it."

"Don't talk like that. Damn it, I hate to see you this way."

"Believe me I hate to be this way."

"What does this mean?" She made the sign I had prayed she'd seen when Jinnah was dragging me away.

"What does it mean to you?"

"I asked a lot of people before I found someone who knows Indian sign language. It means two things: friend or to love. Indians view them as the same so they have the same sign."

"It means love to me. What does it mean to you?"

"I was hoping it meant love. Did you mean it?"

"Yes."

"You weren't like out of your mind or something?"

"I meant it for the past three days, but I was too afraid to say it." She smiled and touched my hand. I added, "I didn't think someone like you would go for someone like me."

"I was afraid you wouldn't be able to love an African American."

I laughed and she laughed a little. "Hey it's just a year round tan if you ask me. So, you were feeling the same way?"

"Yeah, why's that so crazy?"

I smiled and shook my head. The memory of her standing in her white panties that first night flashed through my mind. "Because you are really really hot, like just wow. And you're smart and tough and just perfect. Too perfect for a klutz like me."

She smiled. "You're more than you say you are. Those nights we slept together were amazing."

"Amazing, I wanted to tell you how I felt but, I . . ."

"Me too." She paused looking at the ground before she lifted her eyes and said, "I love you, Chad. You're the nicest guy I've ever met."

"Wow, you really love me. Me?"

"Yeah, plus you've got a cute butt." I could feel my cheeks getting red.

I said, "I need to confess something. Look, the first night, when you were wringing out your pants, I sneaked a look and I looked at just the right time. You were standing there in your y'know pan, I mean underwear, whatever. It was just a peek, but I feel real bad."

She replied with that cocky little attitude I'd come to love, "What! You better'a not been disappointed!"

"Oh no, no definitely not in that way." She laughed and got a mischievous smile on her face.

"I was watching to see if you peeked."

"You were?"

"Yeah, I didn't see you do it."

"And why were you watching?"

"Because I peeked while you were undressed." That mischievous smile became even bigger. It blew me away.

"You what!" I said and then started coughing once again.

"Are you OK?"

"Yeah, this coughing really kills me."

"You're not mad are you?"

"Mad? No way! I don't even know what to say."

"Yeah, you looked cute in your boxers." I couldn't help but smile.

I said, "You looked like a supermodel. Those little white p. . .underwear, y'know, just glowed on you. It was like seeing a swimsuit model right there before my eyes." She smiled. The smile meant everything for me. It was the seal of truth on everything she said. I started coughing once again. I said, "Things don't look good for me do they?"

"You're going to get better. I'm not going to fall in love and not be able to enjoy it."

I smiled. "I can agree to that."

"I can't believe those assholes beat you up this bad."

"Azi sure got his kicks in."

"Chad, that FBI agent?"

"Agent Snyder."

"Yeah, whatever. He said you helped them out with the name of the last guy and where he was headed, Mexico. I don't exactly remember the name, but I know it's not what you said."

"It's Syed Jinnah."

"That's it."

"I'd be dead if Jinnah hadn't saved me. I didn't get away. I didn't make some trail. He did that and I lied. Jinnah's not a terrorist."

"He sure seemed like one."

"You saw the surface like I did, only a reflection of what we wanted to see. When I was alone with Jinnah I went underwater to discover a whole new world I never knew existed."

"Wow, what did he say to change your mind?"

"It wasn't what he said. Once I got passed myself, it was just who he was." She shook her head in understanding.

She replied, "I guess I better get going."

"Jasmine, "Y'think we might be able, if you'd like, ahh maybe."

"Maybe what?"

"Maybe kiss. I've been dreaming about if for awhile." She looked me in the eyes and bent down real close to my face. She rubbed her hand through my hair and closed her eyes. I closed mine and we kissed. There wasn't a drug in that hospital that could numb my body like that kiss.

She said, "You promise me you'll get better."

"I promise."

"I gotta go. Your Dad threatened to get a 12 gauge out of his truck if the doctors didn't let me in here."

"It's a big gun."

"Then they might've gotten security by now."

"That's good ole' Dad. We fixed things up."

"That's good."

"He's cool with you and you're family. He's got his issues, but he thinks you're good people."

"All you need to do is get better."

"I know." She turned and started to go. Something in me told me I didn't want her to go. I had that sixth sense feeling that made my blood go icy cold. As she reached the door the thought of that death like clunk made me very scared. I called to her, "Jasmine," tears started to pour into my eyes, "I'm real scared." She started to cry a little as she rushed back to me. She knelt down and rubbed her hands across my cheeks wiping the tears away.

"You are going to get better."

"I really wish you could stay."

"I don't want to go, but they've got rules back here."

I nodded my head and said, "Yeah, and we're breakin' 'em all ready."

"Take this." She pulled off a ring from her finger. It wasn't fancy but it was just a cool little ring. She added, "It's my favorite. You can keep it until you can give it back to me."

"Thanks."

She replied, "I love you."

I smiled and shook my head. It was still hard to believe it was true. "I love you too." She smiled and left the room. I rested for the rest of the day.

I spent the next week in and out of the operating room. My parents basically lived at the hospital and they kept Jasmine informed. Mom really liked her a lot, and Dad was OK. Things were great with Dad and I. However, things were not great with me. I felt weaker and weaker every day. I knew it wasn't just me because Mom had a hard time keeping herself from crying every time she saw me. Dad said my story was in the paper. People were calling me a hero. That made me laugh. What happened to me was the biggest story of luck, and I fell in love to top it off.

I remember looking at those white walls one day, holding on to that ring and wishing for something to cheer me up. How that plain empty color made me feel death creeping around me. To get my mind off dying, I started thinking about that night when I peeked. I remembered how amazing she looked, except she wasn't there to smile at me anymore. I remember drifting off dreaming about that first night we had together. The way she smiled. The way her eyes looked. The way her body glowed like polished bronze against the firelight. I remembered my dream about running through the fields together and holding her in my arms – to hold her in my arms and that smile to seal the truth. I started redreaming my dreams and my experiences with Jasmine, the ballroom, the snake, building our debris shelter, the first night we slept together. I imagined myself giving Jasmine the Koh-I-Nur and riding elephant warriors into battle. She would sit on the peacock throne and we would make our own rules. Make our own rules. I never saw the white of the walls again.

Epilogue

Posthumously

I splashed through another reflection I thought I believed. I spiraled down into an acid bath that seared me of myself, only I didn't want the cleaning. At that moment, I lived only in you. If I could, I would be angry and my heart would scream to be with Jasmine, but you're the only one who can feel. Only you can be frustrated, angry, sad, or laugh, or cry.

Was my life unfulfilled? Certainly in years,

but . . . Some people live eighty years without living. It was wild for me during my time, my lifetime. I made my mark, maybe small and brief, but it is my undistinguishable mark. I wanted to be many things and go many places. I didn't get to be married, or go to the prom, or go to college, and so many other things. But deep in my soul what I wanted more than anything was the one thing I found. I'll never know what I missed, but I can't forget what I had in that one moment, my moment.

I never believed a girl would fall in love with all my quirks. I hoped if I cared about her so deeply and protected her like she'd never experienced before, I'd get a chance to be a part of someone else. Jasmine was my life and in that way my life was fulfilled. My mark will live in her as long as she lives, and even longer in you, I hope.

As for heaven, I can't explain the after life. They're many interpretation, just like life. But I do know, just as I was about to live a real dream, I got the dream I always thought I wanted – I'm living in my dreams. I guess I found what I wanted, right?

You're probably wondering what it's like now, being a dream. Am I in Heaven? What is it like? Not like being a kite. Am I in hell? How does it feel? Not like it's real. What about this Purgatory thing? Then there's Karma or Allah? Funny that they should rime. Funny that God and Allah are one of the same kind. I can't explain away the mystery for you, nor can I tell you everything will be fine. Heaven should be the most wondrous time? Right? But, if there's just one drop of fire that pulses through my soul, I ask you this: How could heaven be anything but hell?

Dreams want reality
Reality wants dreams
Life desires death
Death desires life
Life finds death . . .
Death finds new life

I will never give up the only flower to bloom in my life.

Make your own rules!

Since I wrote the book, I might as well write my own bio. So, let's see here. I want this to sound good. Nathaniel Troutman is a graduate of Elizabethtown College where he first began to explore his creativity. He has written numerous short stories and is working on his second novel (at least some days he's working on it). He is also pursuing acting and has produced two independent short films with several incredibly (not) famous friends. After turning down Yale, Harvard, and Columbia for graduate work (I might be making this up at this point) he decided what he really wanted to do was give his parents heart attacks', move to NYC, and write and act. OK, the third person thing isn't working for me.

My dream is to live a creative life. My career is the pursuit of that dream, through writing, acting, and whatever other forms that takes. I act, I write, and therefore I wait. Wait for acceptance, wait for rejection, wait for direction, and naturally, wait on tables. It has taken a great deal of hard work to get to this page, an experience I only hope to build on. I hope you enjoyed *Chocolate Milk*.

N2T@juno.com